LOVE BY PROXY

Praise for Dena Blake

Next Exit Home

"I enjoy Dena Blake's writing, and I enjoyed this book a lot...I especially liked this book because the two single mums who have become mums for very different reasons/experiences are strong women. Proving they are super capable to solo parent and raise rockstar kids. There is something very sexy about a single mum grabbing parenthood by the horns and making it work. I really enjoyed that aspect!...Great small-town romance that packs a punch in the enemies to lovers trope! I'll definitely be rereading this one again soon."—*Les Rêveur*

Kiss Me Every Day

"This book was SUCH a fun read!!...This was such a fun, interesting book to read and I thoroughly enjoyed it; the characters were super easy to like, the romance was super cute and I loved seeing each little thing that Wynn changed every day!"—*Sasha & Amber Read*

"Such a fun and an exciting book filled with so much love! This book is just packed with fun and memorable moments I was thinking about for days after reading it. This is one hundred per cent my new favourite Dena Blake book. The pace of the book was excellent, and I felt I was along for the fantastic ride."—*Les Rêveur*

"The sweetest moment in the book is when the titular phrase is uttered...This well written book is an interesting read because of the whole premise of getting repeated opportunities to right wrongs."—*Best Lesfic Reviews*

"Wynn's journey of self-discovery is wonderful to witness. She develops compassion, love and finds happiness. Her character development is phenomenal…If you're looking for a stunning romance book with a female/female romance, then this is definitely the one for you. I highly recommend."—*Literatureaesthetic*

Perfect Timing

"The chemistry between Lynn and Maggie is fantastic…the writing is totally engrossing."—*Best Lesfic Reviews*

"This book is the kind of book you sit down to on a Sunday morning with a cup of tea and the sun shining in your bedroom only to realise at 5 pm you've not left your bed because it was too good to stop reading."—*Les Rêveur*

"The relationship between Lynn and Maggie developed at a organic pace. I loved all the flirting going on between Maggie and Lynn. I love a good flirty conversation!…I haven't read this author before but I look forward to trying more of her titles."—*Marcia Hull, Librarian (Ponca City Library, Oklahoma)*

Racing Hearts

"I particularly liked Drew with her sexy rough exterior and soft heart…Sex scenes are definitely getting hotter and I think this might be the hottest by Dena Blake to date."—*Les Rêveur*

Just One Moment

"One of the things I liked is that the story is set after the glorious days of falling in love, after the time when everything is exciting. It shows how sometimes, trying to make life better really makes it more complicated…It's also, and mainly, a reminder of how important communication is between partners, and that as solid as trust seems between two lovers, misunderstandings happen very easily."—*Jude in the Stars*

"Blake does angst particularly well and she's wrung every possible ounce out of this one…I found myself getting sucked right into the story—I do love a good bit of angst and enjoy the copious amounts of drama on occasion."—C-Spot Reviews

Friends Without Benefits

"This is the book when the Friends to Lovers trope doesn't work out. When you tell your best friend you are in love with her and she doesn't return your feelings. This book is real life and I think I loved it more for that."—*Les Rêveur*

A Country Girl's Heart

"Dena Blake just goes from strength to strength."—*Les Rêveur*

"Literally couldn't put this book down, and can't give enough praise for how good this was!!! One of my favourite reads, and I highly recommend to anyone who loves a fantastically clever, intriguing, and exciting romance."—*LESBIreviewed*

Unchained Memories

"There is a lot of angst and the book covers some difficult topics but it does that well. The writing is gripping and the plot flows."—*Melina Bickard, Librarian, Waterloo Library (UK)*

"This story had me cycling between lovely romantic scenes to white-knuckle gripping, on the edge of the seat (or in my case, the bed) scenarios. This story had me rooting for a sequel and I can certainly place my stamp of approval on this novel as a must read book."—*Lesbian Review*

"The pace and character development was perfect for such an involved story line, I couldn't help but turn each page. This book has so many wonderful plot twists that you will be in suspense with every chapter that follows."—*Les Rêveur*

Where the Light Glows

"From first-time author Dena Blake, *Where the Light Glows* is a sure winner."—*A Bookworm's Loft*

"[T]he vivid descriptions of the Pacific Northwest will make readers hungry for food and travel. The chemistry between Mel and Izzy is palpable."—*RT Book Reviews*

"I'm still shocked this was Dena Blake's first novel...It was fantastic...It was written extremely well and more than once I wondered if this was a true account of someone close to the author because it was really raw and realistic. It seemed to flow very naturally and I am truly surprised that this is the authors first novel as it reads like a seasoned writer."—*Les Rêveur*

By the Author

Where the Light Glows

Unchained Memories

A Country Girl's Heart

Racing Hearts

Friends Without Benefits

Just One Moment

Perfect Timing

Kiss Me Every Day

Next Exit Home

Love By Proxy

Visit us at www.boldstrokesbooks.com

LOVE BY PROXY

by

Dena Blake

2021

LOVE BY PROXY

ISBN 13: 978-1-63555-973-6

This Trade Paperback Original Is Published By
Bold Strokes Books, Inc.
P.O. Box 249
Valley Falls, NY 12185

First Edition: November 2021

CREDITS
EDITOR: SHELLEY THRASHER
PRODUCTION DESIGN: STACIA SEAMAN
COVER DESIGN BY JEANINE HENNING

Acknowledgments

Most of us have someone in our lives who is always there to cheer us on and support us in our endeavors. Some of us meet that person right away and others don't meet them until life is well on its way. Sometimes we take that person for granted, never realizing our perfect match has been right in front of us all along. Take a look around, see who's there, and embrace them. Family is who and what you make it.

Everyone at Bold Strokes Books takes such great care of my work, and they deserve the ultimate thanks for doing so. Rad and Sandy, thanks for all the online readings and bookathons. Those have been instrumental in keeping us all going during the past year. Thanks to Shelley Thrasher, my editor extraordinaire, for catching the words I use a million times and for continually teaching me how to be a better writer.

To my writing friends, thanks for being there, checking in, and keeping my spirits up. I hope I did the same for you.

To Kate—my other half—my person. That becomes truer with each and every day we spend together. Wes and Haley—you are by far my best accomplishments in life.

Thanks to all you readers out there. 2020 was a tough year for all of us, but you showed up, and you read! Your support means the world to me.

For everyone who is still searching for your person.
Don't lose hope.

CHAPTER ONE

Sophie reached for her coffee and realized the cup was empty. Twisting from side to side as she stood, she tried to work the kink from her aching back—too long in the chair. She straightened her elastic-waisted asymmetrical skirt but didn't bother to tuck in her blouse before she crossed the room. After filling her cup with the last of the pot, she flipped the switch and turned off the coffeemaker. She looked over her shoulder at Tess, who was staring into the screen of her laptop at JB Marketing. Dark circles had begun to surface beneath her eyes. Hers probably looked similar. Too much screen time. She and Tess had been working hard all day getting this pitch together for the new client's clothing store. Everything they sold was made of soft, natural materials, a sort of retro bohemian style, with "kindness matters" a huge part of their style.

"You know what this means?" Sophie held up the pot. "Time for you to go home."

"I know." Tess relaxed into her chair and stretched her arms above her head. "I'm exhausted, but I can't wait to pitch this to Boho Clothes."

Sophie smiled at her excitement as she walked to her desk and flopped into her chair. "You gonna wear some of their stuff?"

"Of course. My closet's full of it." Tess stood and twirled, and her knee-length, flowing skirt flew out and flattened like a saucer.

Sophie couldn't help but watch. Tess had killer legs. "I really like that long blue skirt you have."

"The pleated one?" Tess grinned as though she'd never received a compliment before.

Sophie nodded. "It fits you perfectly. Can you match it with something colorful?"

"Absolutely." Tess packed up her laptop and stood by the edge of her desk. "Aren't you coming?"

She glanced up. "No." She stood. "I have to finish this. You go home and get some rest." She walked with Tess to the door of the office. "Big day tomorrow."

"For both of us. Don't stay too late. Okay?" Tess raised her eyebrows.

"I won't. I promise." Sophie would stay too late, as usual, but she still needed to finish a few details in their backup proposal. Tess had developed the perfect pitch—the one that Joy, their boss, wouldn't want them to give. She wished Joy would focus more on quality than on cost.

Tess pointed to the deadbolt. "And lock this door behind me."

"I will." She watched Tess walk to the elevator and waved when she got on before closing the door and locking it. The agency was located in a safe part of downtown Orlando, Florida, but she was always more careful when she was alone in the office.

She went back to their shared space, flopped into her chair, and looked at what she and Tess had created together. It was over budget, but she had to admit Tess had done a fantastic job on this one. Not that she didn't always give it her best, but this proposal fit the store perfectly. It seemed to pay that Tess's shopping habits gave her intimate knowledge of the clothing and clientele, which was one reason two of their newest clients, Gabrielle and Charlotte, were coming in for the pitch.

Within this proposal they'd planned to hit several social-media platforms hard with pop-up lead ads and clickable links, and follow up with five-second local spots during mid-range TV shows. Airtime was expensive, but Tess's idea would get Gabrielle and Charlotte a lot of attention if they approved it. Tess and Sophie wanted to encourage customers to browse the website and sign up for more information via email or text message. If they could get the customer to the website, the likelihood of them scrolling through the merchandise would go up.

But first they had to get past Joy to let the idea fly. Sophie would finish mocking up the other lackluster proposal to present just in case. From previous experience with Joy, that would be the one she'd make them present first because it was cheaper and within the client's budget. Sophie wasn't crazy about it, but it would do if Gabrielle and Charlotte chose to go that way.

She glanced out the window at the buildings across the way. Streetlights set them all aglow, the various shades of brick presenting a fascinating, geometrical pattern. She checked the time on her phone, nine thirty, and then hit the button in her contacts for Squisito, an upcoming Italian restaurant nearby with chic modern vibes, pizza, and selected Italian specialties. It also contained a buzzing bar stocked with an array of craft beers and cocktails. More is better seemed to be the direction the bar business was taking these days.

She couldn't get enough of their wood-fired oven pizza loaded with vegetables. It was a super-food all on its own, a concept Sophie had brought to the attention of owner, Bridget, when she'd offered to assist with the restaurant's marketing plan. Once Sophie and Tess had become involved in their advertising, Squisito's business skyrocketed. So much so that they'd expanded into the vacant space next door to fill the need of the community. Seemed everyone loved pizza, and making it unique and healthy was a plus. Everyone in the office frequented the restaurant often, both for dine-in and take-out. Sophie called in for delivery occasionally when she was working late.

"Hi. This is Sophie Swanson. I'd like to put in an order for delivery."

"Hey, Sophie. You want the usual?"

"Yes. Please." She rarely veered from the thin-crust veggie supremo.

"I'll put it in. Should be at your door in about twenty minutes."

"Can you ask Bridget to deliver that order for me? I have some paperwork for her to sign. She knows how to get into the building and where the office is located." She didn't have to ask if she was there. Bridget was always there.

"I'll let her know."

She'd reviewed Tess's first choice for the presentation again and had to agree it fit the spirit of Boho Clothes perfectly. But between location, filming, and music, it came in way over budget. When Joy had seen the production cost alone, she'd flipped, and it would only get more expensive. Joy was the boss and decided what to present, and her opposition had been clear, even if it was the better plan. She still held out hope to present it and let the client decide.

A knock on the door brought Sophie out of her thoughts. Her dinner delivery had arrived right on time. She stretched as she stood, then went to the front door of the office and glanced through the window beside the door to ensure it was, indeed, her delivery. Bridget stood across the hallway leaning against the wall. Dressed in jeans and a loose, black, long-sleeved T-shirt, she had her long, dark hair draped across her shoulder on one side. One sneaker-clad foot was pressed up against the wall behind her, and a bag of food hung from her fingers like she'd been waiting there for ages. Bridget was a sexy temptation Sophie found hard to resist.

She unlocked the door and opened it. "Hey, there. I'm glad you were available to deliver tonight."

"I'm always available for you." Bridget crossed the hall and touched her hip with her hand as she passed by her, entering the office. "You hadn't ordered in a while. I thought maybe your tastes had changed."

She laughed. "No. Just haven't had time to feed my hunger lately." She took the bag from Bridget and set it on the reception desk before she grabbed Bridget's face and kissed her. "You still taste good."

"Likewise." Bridget reached around and grabbed her ass. "Feel pretty good too."

"You're such a sweet-talker." She took Bridget's hand and led her into the conference room.

"I've never been in this room." Bridget glanced around. "Couch, TV, table. All the comforts of home."

"Yeah. This will be better for what I have planned. My desk is pretty covered right now."

Bridget grinned as she turned around slowly. "You come here often, beautiful?"

"Not often enough." She pressed her mouth to Bridget's and indulged in the awakening of her senses. It had been far too long since she'd invited Bridget back to play.

Bridget moved her across the floor to the couch, all the while engaging her mouth. Hands slipped under her blouse, quickly raced around to her back, and unfastened her bra. She felt her breasts tumble out freely, only to be caught by strong, warm hands. In most sexual encounters Sophie was the aggressor—the giver, but with Bridget, Sophie became the receiver. It felt wonderful to let someone please her once in a while.

She quickly worked the buttons to give Bridget more access. Soon her skirt and panties were on the floor, and she was in Bridget's lap with Bridget's fingers working spectacular magic between her legs. As she came closer to climax she pressed her chest into Bridget's face, and she took her nipples into her mouth, one and then the other, until finally focusing on one that sent shooting jolts of pleasure to thoroughly ignite the fire stoking below. With one hand behind Bridget's neck and the other holding the back of the couch, she hung on as she crashed into the orgasm.

"That was quick."

"I've been thinking about you all day." Not true, but at least the last hour. "I was ready when you walked in." She kissed her softly before she stood, gathered her clothes, and began dressing. "I'll grab the bag, and we can have dinner in here."

Bridget stood and moved toward the conference-room door. "I gotta get back. The restaurant is pretty busy tonight."

"You're not going to stay for dinner?" Bridget had explained to her long ago that she didn't receive pleasure from women she didn't have a deep connection with, and Sophie had made it clear that she wasn't in the market for that kind of connection. The physical attraction between them had been apparent from the start, but that's where their connection ended. Bridget was ready and willing to fulfill Sophie's needs, and she was damn good at it, but Sophie also looked forward to Bridget's conversation and company on these nights, in addition to the sex.

"Sorry. I can't." Bridget strolled through the office to the door, flipped the deadbolt, then turned and smiled before she kissed her softly. "Next time."

"Promise?" Sophie was disappointed—more than she'd expected.

"I promise." Bridget smiled. She seemed pleased that Sophie wanted more than just sex from her. "Dark-chocolate mousse is the dessert special tonight. I added it to your order. Eat it first." She pulled open the door and left.

Sophie gripped the door, leaned against it for balance as she watched Bridget walk to the elevator, then locked the door and leaned up against it again. Bridget had never given her an in-depth explanation of why she couldn't or wouldn't receive gratification casually, but Sophie got the feeling she had a valid emotional reason. Would there ever be a day when she called for a delivery and Bridget wouldn't deliver—when Bridget found that deep connection with someone? Sophie would be disappointed, but happy for Bridget when that day came.

The vision of the older, more sophisticated woman who broke Sophie's heart flashed in her mind—the reason she wasn't able to become deeply involved with anyone. She'd been so young and naive when she'd met her, she'd gone all in on the relationship without realizing the feelings were one-sided. She'd never expected to be pushed aside and treated like a minor detail in someone's life like she'd been. Sophie had learned a painful lesson from that experience, and she was careful not to do the same to the women she became involved with—while also never letting her feelings go that deep again. Would there ever be a time when she became more involved with someone than just for sex? She shook her head. She doubted it. Relationships took effort and nurturing—two things she hadn't been able to master over the past twenty-five years, thanks to one severely broken heart.

She went to the reception desk and took out the dessert. Then she fished around in the bag for a spoon before she took the top off the plastic container and dipped a huge bite into her mouth. She swirled the rich creaminess of the chocolate around with her tongue. She would forgive Bridget for leaving this time, but only because of this.

Once finished with the mousse, she gathered up her laptop and placed it into her bag just in case a spectacular idea hit her, and she needed to make more changes when she got home. She glanced at her cell phone and saw several missed calls from Tess. She immediately hit the call-back button and put it on speaker.

The phone rang four times before Tess answered, which was odd. "Hey, gorgeous." Her usual response.

"What's up? I saw you called a couple of times while I was in the conference room setting up for tomorrow."

"Nothing. Just checking to make sure you didn't stay there all night. Are you about done, or do you want me to bring you dinner?"

"I ordered pizza, and I'm getting out of here now." Background noise filled the speaker. It sounded like she was in traffic. "Where are you?"

"Nowhere. Just watching TV."

It sounded much more realistic than TV, but Tess didn't have any reason to lie to her. "You're not already on your way here, are you?"

"Uh-uh. No. I'm actually getting ready to turn this show off and slide into bed. You need to get home and do the same."

"On my way as soon as I hang up."

"Be careful, please."

"I always am. See you bright and early in the morning." She hung up, grabbed the pizza and the rest of her stuff, and headed for the door. She was going to rest well tonight, thanks to Bridget.

CHAPTER TWO

Tess straightened her high-waisted, pleated, navy skirt and applied anti-static spray before she checked the buttons of her powder-blue, floral, Peter-Pan-collared blouse. She glanced at her shoes as well to make sure she hadn't mismatched her navy flats this morning. She purposely kept a spare pair of shoes in her office now because dressing in the dark was hazardous to her wardrobe. She'd made the mistake of going into a pitch without checking her wardrobe before and had been embarrassed on occasion to learn a button had been unfastened, her skirt was clinging to her legs, her shoes were mismatched, or something else had gone awry.

She was nervous this morning for some reason. Pitching a client had never bothered her before. Why was it happening today? Maybe it was because she loved this clothing store so much—did most of her shopping there. Maybe it was because her boss, Joy, had been giving her so much push-back lately on *everything*. She hadn't taken this job to be forced into doing things someone else's way. She'd taken it because Sophie had promised her that she'd have creative carte blanche. She did for a while, but soon after she'd been hired, Joy had bought out her partner in the firm and had immediately implemented her penny-pinching methods. Those won out over creativity. She hadn't signed up to use Joy's mediocre ideas instead of her own.

"Okay. So, let's go with idea B." Joy glanced around the room and landed her gaze on her. "Will that work for you, Tess?"

"I like idea A better." And she did. Especially for this clothing line, and these clients. Sisters Gabrielle and Charlotte were young and trendy. She'd gotten that from their first meeting at their store. She'd also brought them in. She shopped at Boho Clothes often and, after meeting them, had mentioned she could help them out with advertising.

"But that's not going to work with the client's budget, and we're not a public-service company doing pro bono work here. We all need to get paid." Joy looked so smug with her platinum-blond hair pulled back and fastened into a bun and wearing her Ralph Lauren pencil skirt and matching jacket. She never changed her look—wore anything else—anything softer. She probably hit the designer sale at Macy's every year and had an outfit in every color.

"Right." Tess blew out a breath.

"So. We're good?" Joy raised her eyebrows.

She nodded and headed back to her office. They were in no way good. Idea B was shit, but even though this was Tess's client, it wasn't her decision to make. As usual. She really needed to find another company to work for or another profession altogether. Being a graphic designer at a small marketing firm had never been her dream job. She'd been well on her way doing freelance work, when her choices to do what she wanted had all washed away with the hurricane that took her house near the coast years ago. She'd had to find a way to make ends meet somehow. If it hadn't been for Sophie bringing her in here, at JB Marketing, she might have ended up working somewhere even less appealing.

It wasn't like she was a snob. She'd waited tables when she was in college, but that was miserable on her feet, and she didn't intend to move backward. Taking a tiny step forward into this stop on the road to another opportunity seemed to be the better option. Tess had never thought she'd be micromanaged at this stage in her career, or she would've seriously considered other opportunities. She loved words—working with them—manipulating them. Poetry was once her goal, and she still dabbled in it, using her vintage forties typewriter to capture her thoughts on weekends. She loved the way the words looked in vintage typeface.

She could never get Joy to see her vision or anything else from the design aspect. To Joy it was always about the budget. Most times the minimal amount of dollars they had to work with didn't coalesce with the product or business they were trying to promote. Multiple times clients went somewhere else to find what fit their needs.

"So we're going with what we discussed, right?" Sophie raised her eyebrows as she set her folder on the desk.

"Right." It was a shitty idea, and she didn't know if she could, but she would try—for Sophie.

"I don't know if Joy will let us get by with another rogue presentation…but if idea B doesn't gel with Charlotte, because we know she's the one that calls the shots, I think idea A will blow her out of the water." Sophie tugged her lips into a soft smile before she reached into the desk drawer, took out a lint roller, and ran it up and down her navy slacks. As she bent, her champagne, silk blouse fell open, giving Tess a view of her breasts.

She relaxed just a bit. It was good to know she had Sophie's support. "Your button came loose again." She reached into the drawer and took out a safety pin. "You really need to let me fix that for you."

"You're not my tailor." Sophie dropped the lint roller into the drawer and swiped the safety pin from her.

"Do you have a tailor?"

"No. But I'll find one."

"And you're going to spend twenty bucks to have someone cinch the buttonhole tighter? Just give it to me, and I'll do it." It was an easy fix, and she already had all the sewing tools.

"Fine. But you have to do it by hand. I don't want it getting snagged with that old sewing machine of yours." She spun and moved toward the door. "I need to go to the ladies' room in case this goes long."

"I ruin one lousy pair of pants, and you never let me forget it. It's an antique, and I've had it fixed since then."

"They were expensive, and I really liked them." Sophie glanced over her shoulder. "Wait for me?"

"Of course." It was heartwarming the way Sophie used the word *us* when she spoke about issues with Joy, when she knew it was only Tess that Joy had issues with. Sophie was a true team player to the end—at least with Tess she was. That was a sign of their years-long friendship. Tess and Sophie were each other's person—their ride or die. They loved each other through thick and thin. Nothing had ever come between them—not even relationships with other women. Sure, Sophie dated some women Tess couldn't stand. Like the barista who corrected her on how to make coffee and insisted on the kind she should drink, or the philosophy professor who was ridiculously pretentious, always quoting famous people to make others feel stupid. Thankfully, Sophie grew tired of them too, but she would never stand in the way of Sophie's happiness—ever.

"You ready?" Sophie peeked in the door.

"As ready as I'll ever be." She headed to it.

Sophie blocked her path. "Listen. I know this isn't the way you want to go with this one, but let's get through today, and maybe we can change it later down the road." She raised her eyebrows and smiled. "Can you get on board with that?"

"Getting on board a sinking ship isn't the smartest decision."

"Tess." Her name whooshed out of Sophie's mouth with a soft sigh.

"Okay. I'll be good, but if they ask about another plan, I can't guarantee my silence."

"That's fair. Just let me handle that if it happens." Sophie turned, and they headed to the conference room.

Heat rushed Tess's face as she entered and flashed back to the night before when she'd come back to bring Sophie dinner. The image of half-naked Sophie mid-climax on the couch pressed up against a faceless woman was nothing less than fabulous and impossible to erase.

"Are you okay?" Sophie's voice was soft—nothing near the raw intensity she'd heard the night before.

Tess shook the sexy vocals from her mind. "Yes. Why?"

"You look flushed." Sophie felt Tess's forehead.

"Just nervous." Tess sucked in a deep breath and continued into the room.

"Hello, Gabrielle. Charlotte." Tess dipped her head and waved from the front of the room, while Sophie went to each one of them separately, extended her hand, and shook theirs.

"It's good to see you again." Sophie motioned them to the best seats at the table.

"Same." Gabrielle lifted an eyebrow and smiled at Sophie. "We're excited to see what you've created for us." She took her seat but almost missed it entirely because she was still watching Sophie as she moved around the table.

Sophie sat at the end, ready to hit start on the presentation loaded on the laptop in front of her. She'd set it up to project onto the large fifty-inch TV hanging on the wall.

They went through the presentation they'd created with women of all ages wearing different pieces of the clothing lines Gabrielle and Charlotte's store carried. Tess watched them as they watched the presentation. Not a smile in the room besides Joy's. She glanced at Sophie, who seemed to have noticed too. They were in trouble.

After they finished the presentation, Gabrielle cleared her throat and looked at her notes. "I'm not sure this fits the demographic we're trying to hit." She lifted the top page of her notepad and let it drop. "Can we do something more upbeat—maybe with more trendy music?" She handed the pad to Charlotte.

Gabrielle had hit the nail on the head. It wasn't even close to what Tess had envisioned. Plus, music was a huge part of any advertisement. It had to grab the potential customer's attention. Joy had axed everything Tess had planned. "Well, we—"

"We can certainly change the music," Sophie said.

"And the actors? Can we make them a little younger?" Gabrielle's face was as still as stone.

Charlotte flipped the pad closed and handed it back to Gabrielle "This is very different from what we discussed, Tess, and honestly, I don't like this theme at all."

"Wait." She opened her pad folio, took out a sketch pad, and laid it in front of the clients. "I have another idea?" She didn't dare look at Joy. She was doing exactly what she shouldn't—showing them her original ideas, not the ones Joy had altered.

Gabrielle smiled widely and handed the sketch to Charlotte. "This is much fresher. Tell me how you'd present it."

She took in a deep breath to calm her nerves and glanced at Sophie, who nodded. This was her moment, and she didn't want to blow it. "I consider your clothing little nuggets of joy in my life because every time I bring home a new item, it brings me happiness. So much so that I want to share it."

"That's absolutely true." Sophie smiled widely. "She actually summons me to a watch party."

Charlotte lifted her eyebrows and tilted her head, silently asking for more information.

"Sophie is required to come to my house and watch me mix and match the new items I've brought home with all the other clothing I have." She spun as though she were in a fashion show, and the bottom of her pleated skirt flew out. "We can create a spot where you have several friends meeting at home within a huge walk-in closet—where they're picking out pieces of clothing and trying them on together." She widened her eyes with excitement. "Or even at the store—maybe just them—sneaking in after hours in low lighting. When the lights come on, the excitement begins. It would be like a wonderland of fashion." She grinned. "Like the pure-imagination candy scene in *Willy Wonka and The Chocolate Factory*, only with clothing and accessories."

Sophie chimed in. "Yes. Even using *that* song sung by a woman with a faster pace. And adding an intro with a celesta, like in 'Dance of the Sugar Plum Fairy' from *The Nutcracker Suite*, will make it even more magical."

Tess glanced around the room waiting for the shoe to drop. Gabrielle and her sister weren't speaking, only staring at the sketch on the pad and then at each other.

Then Gabrielle broke into a smile. "I love that idea. Do you have something for that mocked up? Can you show us?"

Tess seemed to have dazzled them this time. She hadn't expected that. "I absolutely do and can." She rushed to the spot where Sophie was sitting, grabbed the computer, and clicked a few buttons. She brought up the plan A presentation she'd created and let it run. She'd already had the song recorded by one of their usual artists exactly the way she'd wanted it sung with the right tempo.

Once it was finished, the room was silent until Joy stepped forward. "I think the idea we presented earlier will bring in a wider clientele."

"I don't agree." Gabrielle picked up the first page from Tess's sketch pad, then looked at Tess and Sophie. "Do either of you?"

"I think the one you have there—the one we just viewed—will work better." Tess knew Joy was pissed, but they were going to lose the client otherwise.

"I can guarantee no one knows your clothing line better than Tess." Sophie jumped in. "How about we revise this, come up with some new numbers, and meet again at the beginning of next week."

Joy's eyes narrowed. "But—"

Charlotte held up her hand. "Play it again, please." Magical music filled the room as the sisters watched the clip intently. When it was over, and after several moments of silence, Charlotte finally spoke. "I know this might cost us a little more, but we're willing to pay more for quality like this." Apparently, she *was* the one who handled the store's money. Just as they'd thought.

Tess had to forcibly prevent herself from squealing and jumping for joy.

"You know that means you'll probably have to work through the weekend." Joy growled into Tess's ear. She was clearly pissed.

They wouldn't because Tess had already done most of the work. She'd gone all in on this one.

"But we're willing to do it to make Gabrielle and Charlotte happy." Sophie turned around, pulled her eyebrows together, and whispered to Joy, "This is what *they* want, and Charlotte just said they're willing to pay for it."

"Absolutely." Joy plastered on a smile that wasn't the least bit genuine.

"Can I keep this?" Gabrielle held up Tess's design sketch as she gathered her pad folio from in front of them.

"Of course." She smiled. "Let me make a quick copy of it.

That's only a preliminary mock-up." She'd made some changes to the hard copy that would need to be transferred to the digital design.

"I really like it, Tess. You're very talented." Gabrielle handed it back to her. "I can't wait to see the final."

A chill ran through Tess as she rushed down the hall to the copy machine. The client really wanted *her* idea, and Joy couldn't do a thing about it now.

When she came back into the room, everyone was standing, Sophie and Gabrielle detached from the rest of the group. She could tell right away from their interaction that they weren't talking business. Her stomach twisted. Hopefully Sophie wasn't going to mess this up by getting involved with the client.

Joy caught her eye and waved her over. She avoided Joy and went straight to Sophie and Gabrielle. "Here you go." She refused to listen to any of Joy's complaints right now.

"Thank you." Gabrielle glanced at the sketch and then back at Sophie. "I was just telling Sophie that I admire how well you two work together. You really complement each other. If I didn't know better, I'd think you were a couple."

"Oh, no." Tess shook her head. "We're not."

"Sophie has just explained that to me." Gabrielle veered her gaze to Sophie and then back to her. "Being lifelong friends seems to work even better for you two."

She noticed the card in Sophie's hand as she slipped it into her pocket. It had a number written on the back. Gabrielle's personal contact information, for sure.

She'd gotten the vibe from Gabrielle when shopping at Boho Clothing that there might be some interest, but that was clearly a gay vibe only. She was interested in Sophie, of course. There wasn't anything about Sophie not to be interested in. She was a catch for anyone who could manage it.

Gabrielle glanced at Charlotte as she appeared in the doorway. She'd stepped out to take a phone call. "We need to get going." She glanced back at Tess and held up the sketch. "This is exactly what we want." She veered her gaze back to Sophie and smiled. "Hopefully, we'll talk soon." She headed across the room and said her goodbyes to Joy, who had gone straight to Charlotte when she'd reappeared.

"You're not going to call her, are you?"

"No. I would never mess this one up for you." Sophie grinned. "You knocked it out of the park today."

"I did, didn't I?" She let the fine feeling of accomplishment fill her, and it was wonderful.

"Yeah, you did." Sophie gave her a shoulder bump.

Sophie was proud of her, and that made the feeling even better.

CHAPTER THREE

Still jazzed from this morning's success, Tess sat at her desk and stared at her computer screen, had been like that for hours. She'd been filled with satisfaction until she'd received her new assignment. Joy wanted another cookie-cutter proposal for the next client, and she hated that. When she'd joined the team here at JB Marketing, she'd thought she'd have more creative control. It had taken her five years to figure out she didn't have much at all. With each and every proposal Sophie would convince her she'd have more control on the next project. That never happened and was never *going* to happen.

"You working on the next one?" Sophie dropped the files she was carrying onto the desk across the room and then plugged her laptop into the docking station.

"Trying." She continued to stare at the project template she'd pulled up. It consisted of several sections, including project background, deliverables, and time frame. She typed multiple question marks in each area, but no matter what she tried to envision, her mind was blank. She was still focused on how her last proposal had been hijacked this morning. Thankfully, she'd been able to steal control back.

"Sounds like your fingers are working their magic." Sophie crossed the office and rounded Tess's desk. "I was way off. You've got a lot of unknowns there." She laughed.

"Did Gabrielle ask you out?" She couldn't resist asking.

Sophie nodded. "To discuss the campaign over dinner."

"Of course she did." She slapped her laptop closed and stood.

"I'm heading out." She slid the device into her bag, along with a few notes about the project she'd jotted down during their last meeting. They shared an office because they were a team, and that's what teams do. Sometimes Sophie was too much for her, and she had to have her space.

"I told her I was busy." Sophie went back to her desk.

"You did?" Tess didn't know why that surprised her.

"Of course. I would never discuss business without you, and that's all it would be." She smiled as she nodded. "You want to grab some dinner?"

"No. I don't think so. I'm not hungry." She just wanted to slide into bed and sleep for the next few days. Anything would be better than working in this idea prison.

"That doesn't seem quite fair. I turned down a very nice dinner invitation this morning." Sophie closed her laptop and slipped it into her bag. "I would love your company."

She squinted her eyes and tilted her head. "Would you?"

"Of course." Sophie glanced down at the desktop and shuffled a few folders around. "There's no one I would rather spend time with." Sophie didn't react with any real feelings. She never did. "We can just have drinks and some appetizers. Fried cheese, mushrooms, egg rolls. Spinach dip and chips. You know, the stuff that adds inches to our hips in a matter of minutes." She slid her hands down her lovely ones and then clasped them together in front of her. "What do you say? We can celebrate our success today."

"Boneless wings?" Maybe drinks and fried foods was exactly what she needed.

Sophie nodded. "Absolutely."

"Okay. Only one drink."

"Yes!" Sophie grinned and gathered up her things.

"You two finished for the day?" Joy appeared in the doorway to the office. "Going out for drinks?" She raised her eyebrows.

"After that presentation, I'm beat." Sophie slid her bag over her shoulder. "I'm going home to take a long bath and let the muscles in my neck relax." She kneaded her neck with her fingers. Sophie always put on a great act.

"Me too. Sounds like a great idea." She rounded her desk and brushed past Joy, who didn't budge to let her through. She didn't want to have any more interaction with Joy than she had to this afternoon.

"You two taking that bath together?" Joy's voice was filled with sarcasm, as always.

"Ooh. Wouldn't that be lovely?" Sophie's voice was just above a whisper. "You'll rub my neck, won't you, Tess?"

"Yes, but I get the bath pillow." She giggled as she glanced over her shoulder to find Sophie right behind her. Sophie gave her a sly wink, and they headed out the front of the office.

They each went to their separate cars. Sophie's BMW 650i convertible was flashy just like Sophie, and Tess's Toyota Camry was affordable. Sophie had bought the BMW used and fully loaded—the only way she could afford such a fancy car.

❖

They entered the almost empty bar, which was usually packed. It was still early. Only a little after four, but today had been a day of all days. A definite excuse to hit the bar. Tess went straight to their usual table—farthest from the front, on the wall, and closest to the corner of the long, aged-wood bar. Several antique shoe-making tools hung neatly above the table. It wasn't the trendiest place in town, with just a bar top and a number of half-moon tables lining the wall, but Tess loved it here. The place reminded her of simpler days, when time seemed to go much slower.

They didn't need to look at the drink menu. They'd been here enough times to know exactly what they wanted. Sophie waved at the bartender, and he immediately came over to take their order.

"Afternoon, ladies." He wiped the table quickly with a bar towel. "What can I make for you today?"

Sophie spoke up immediately. "I'll have an old-fashioned, and she'll have a sidecar."

She was fine with Sophie ordering her drink. Even though they weren't a couple, it made her feel pampered—loved, even.

The bartender went back to the bar and began preparing their drinks. It seemed like only a moment or two before he was setting them on the table in front of them, along with a basket of pretzels.

"Sorry about today. I'm sure we'll get Joy's wrath tomorrow when she actually realize just how much it's going to cost up front."

"No worries at all. I thoroughly enjoyed it. In fact, I almost lost my shit when you put your hand up and gave her the silent shut-the-fuck-up." Sophie sipped her old-fashioned. "I thought her eyes were going to pop out of her head."

Tess glanced up at the tiled ceiling. "I'm not sure I want to do this for the rest of my life, Soph."

"Do what?"

"Work for Joy—work for *any* marketing company."

"What else would you do?"

"Write poetry—illustrate children's books—paint. Anything but what I'm doing now." She sipped her drink. "I want to get back to my roots."

"I thought you liked graphic design. What exactly do you mean by roots?"

"I do, but I thought things would be so much different before I went to college—before I joined the working class."

"Like…"

"For instance, look at the craftsmanship in this place." She touched the pattern on the wall. "You just can't capture this kind of skill with a computer."

"Sure you can. You do it all the time."

"Maybe so, but then Joy tries to change it. How can someone with the name Joy suck so much enjoyment out of something?"

Sophie laughed. "Come on. She always comes around."

"Eventually." She sighed. "Maybe I'm just tired of the battle."

"So why don't I take on the battle from now on, and you stay in your creative bubble?"

"That doesn't seem quite fair." It's what Tess needed, but it wasn't at all equitable.

"I don't mind. Someday I'll need you to do something for me." Sophie took another drink.

"So, I'll owe you?" She tilted her head.

"You already owe me plenty." Sophie grinned. "Doesn't that come with our friendship?"

"Friends don't owe friends. They're always willing to help."

"Ah. So, that's what we're calling it now." Sophie held up her glass. "I'm always glad to *help* you, and I'm sure you're always willing to *help* me."

"Exactly." She clinked her glass against Sophie's before she drained her drink. That one seemed to have gone fast. "Let's order some fried foods to help soak up this alcohol before we get sloshed."

Sophie waved at the bartender, who immediately came their way. "Another round of drinks, please."

"Anything else?"

"Yes, please." Sophie glanced up from the food menu. "We'll have some boneless wings, sauce on the side, some fried cheese bites, and the sampler."

"And…" Tess raised her eyebrows at Sophie.

"And some fried green beans just to keep it healthy."

He smiled. "I'll get that order in right away."

Sophie tugged at his neatly rolled sleeve before he turned to go. "And several sides of ranch dressing."

He nodded and went back to the bar.

Sophie giggled, the drink suddenly hitting her. "Think he knows we're tipsy?"

Sophie winked. "Possibly." She reached across the table and took Tess's hand. "It's going to be okay, Tess. I'll take care of Joy. She's just a micromanager with a little bit of money who doesn't have any idea how to add creativity to advertising."

She sucked in a deep breath. "I know you will." She always did, and she was grateful for that. "You're right. She totally sucks at it. I still wonder how she got into this field to begin with."

"Probably thought it was easy." Sophie crunched on a pretzel.

"She's lucky to have us."

Sophie hit the table lightly with her fist. "Damn right she is."

She giggled as the bartender placed their second round of drinks in front of them. "Your food should be ready soon."

"We need it sooner than soon. I'm starving." Tess grinned at the bartender.

"I'll see what I can do."

"You certainly get demanding when you drink." Sophie pushed the pretzels her way. "Have some of these."

She widened her eyes. "I wasn't rude, was I?"

Sophie laughed. "You and that cute face of yours could never be rude."

"Good. Cause I like this place and would hate to be thrown out for being an asshat." She reached for her drink.

Sophie put her hand on her wrist—stopped her from picking up the glass and scrunched her eyebrows together. "Let's wait and have some food first. 'K?"

"Okay." She released the drink, grabbed a pretzel, and popped it into her mouth. It was amazing how well Sophie knew her. She always took care of her.

❖

Tess glanced up when the waiter delivered the bill in the usual aged hardback book. They'd been so entranced in conversation that she hadn't noticed how busy the bar had become.

Sophie held up the book. "Did you ask for this?"

She nodded. "I did."

"Come on. Stay for one more drink." Sophie didn't seem drunk at all, considering the number of drinks she'd had.

Tess glanced at her watch. She'd switched to water when she'd finished drink number two, which was hours ago, after they'd plowed through the appetizers. "It's almost ten, and I need to get some rest if you expect me to perform tomorrow." She took her bag from the hook under the table. "I'm not a genius like you. This creative brain needs downtime to function properly." She reached for the bill and opened the hardback book to glance at all the customer writings inside. Most were just silly one-liners, but sometimes she found something meaningful. One in particular caught her eye. It read, *You must dig deep within your soul to find the true happiness you deserve.* Words were never truer for Tess. She'd been trying to do just that, but perhaps she hadn't been digging deep enough. She squinted to see the handle written under the quote but couldn't make out the letters after the ampersand.

Sophie took the book from her. "What's so interesting this time?" She ran her finger through the writings until she came upon the one Tess had been looking at. "Maybe you should contact this woman." She took out her phone and turned on the flashlight. "At blairsyrose."

"Absolutely not. I will not meet the love of my life through a late-night drunken scribble in a bar-tab book." She took some cash from her wallet and tossed it on the table.

"You act as though you've done it before."

"I have. It was a huge mistake. It's not a good idea to contact someone because of a simple mindless jot they made at the end of an alcohol-fueled evening."

"You never told me that."

"Why would I? It's embarrassing."

"What if they wrote it at the beginning of the night?"

"It's the *bill* book." She tilted her head and widened her eyes.

"I see your point." Sophie pushed Tess's money back to her and then dug into her purse and pulled out a wad of cash. "Tonight's on me. You can get it the next time."

"You never let me pay."

"My idea. My treat."

"It's always your idea."

"Hmph. So it is. Besides, you switched to water hours ago. Didn't think I noticed, did you? You need to drink more." Sophie winked as she stood and put on her suit jacket. "Dinner next time. You can pay then." A button popped open. Apparently, she'd removed the safety pin before leaving work. "Whoops." She fumbled to fasten it before she slid her hands down her hips to smooth her pants.

A jolt hit Tess right in her midsection, and she had to look away. "Deal."

Drunk Sophie was ridiculously sexy, even to Tess. That was a fact she couldn't deny. It was sober Sophie that didn't play well with women, the reason she'd never maintained a lasting relationship.

"At the swankiest restaurant in town." Sophie swayed into her. "I've paid for a lot of appetizers."

Tess grinned. "It would be my pleasure." She looped her arm in Sophie's "I'll take you home."

"I'm fine."

"No. I'm fine. *You're* drunk." She held Sophie's arm firmly. "I'll drive you."

"Okay." Sophie stopped resisting, wrapped her arm around her shoulder, and let Tess lead her to the parking lot.

CHAPTER FOUR

S ophie opened her eyes and, as they adjusted to the darkness, she tried to figure out exactly where she was. In the passenger side of an empty car.

The door pulled open, and there stood Tess staring down at her. "Did you enjoy your little nap?"

She swung her legs out of the car. "I'm sorry. I don't know what happened."

Tess chuckled that sweet soft chuckle of hers. "It's okay. We've had a long day."

"What day is it? Tuesday?"

"We're way past Tuesday." Tess glanced at her watch. "Technically, it's almost Friday."

"Shit." She'd lost a few days somewhere. The week had gone super-fast. Must have been the amount of prep required for the day's presentation.

Tess helped her out of the car, and the door swung closed behind them. Tess wrapped her arm around her waist to walk her to the door. The woman was a saint of a friend—always had been.

Once the door was unlocked and she was inside, Tess turned to go.

"You want to stay for another drink?" She wasn't ready to end the night. The nap had revived her.

"No. And you should go to bed." Tess opened the door. "I'll swing by and get you in the morning. We'll pick up your car at lunch." She poked her head through the crack in the door as she pulled it behind her. "Good night." She smiled before she closed the door.

Alone again. She went into the bedroom and changed into a T-shirt and pajama pants—the DC Comics themed pair she loved. They were broken in just the right amount to be soft and stretchy. She headed back into the kitchen, took a highball glass from the shelf, reached into the freezer for a couple of ice cubes, and dropped them into it. Then she stole a piece of cheese from the refrigerator before she poured herself a bit of bourbon and splashed it with water. She wasn't tired, and her buzz had faded to a low hum. She wouldn't be able to sleep. Alcohol had become an enemy to sleep since she'd turned forty.

She dug deep into her purse and searched for her phone. She hoped she hadn't left it at the bar. She felt the smooth, rectangular shape, snatched it from the bottom, and held her thumb on the home button. The screen lit up in the faded light of her living room. She hit the photo button and stretched the image with her fingers. @blairsyrose was going to get a viewing tonight.

She went looking for her laptop. It wasn't in the usual place on the dining-room table. She searched the room. It was in her car. She quickly typed a text message to Tess.

Where is my laptop?

Go to bed.

Someone will break into my car and steal it.

That's the way to think positive.

Fuck. I need to get it.

It's by the table in the entryway. Now go to bed!

Yes, ma'am.

She rushed to the entryway. Her bag was right where Tess had left it on floor by the table. She snatched the laptop out of the bag, went to the living room, and flopped on the couch with her legs outstretched onto the coffee table and her laptop settled on her legs.

The first pinned post on @blairsyrose's page said, *If you're here on my page, it isn't by accident*. Totally true. She read through a few more posts. All various quotes from different noted sources. At least she wasn't plagiarizing anyone. She swigged her drink, stood, and went to the kitchen for another slice of cheese and a splash more bourbon. She put the bottle back on the shelf. No more of that tonight or she'd feel like shit in the morning. Was probably going to feel that way anyway.

She stared at the computer screen as she paced in front of the couch. She'd never communicated with anyone online who was outside of her friend circle. Watching *Catfish* on TV had scared her out of that. What if she created another account? One that didn't include any of her personal details? She shook her head. Then *she* would be the catfish. Maybe that was exactly what she needed to do to protect herself.

Ten minutes later, she was all set with her new account labeled The Perfect Pitch. Her new identity had been established with multiple really old pictures she'd taken around Orlando—none with her as the focus point—and definitely no selfies, which her other account was filled with. She hadn't lied really. She'd given herself the same profession, same interests, just a generic label and semi-blurred profile picture. The hat and sunglasses were hard to see past. Now for her first message to @blairsyrose.

I'm not here by accident...

A response came back immediately with the pinned quote—an automatic response. That wasn't promising.

Another message came right after it. *How did you find me?*

Another canned response? Maybe. She typed, *The bill book at The Speak Easy.*

Are you drunk? Nope. This one was live.

Why would you think that?

It's after midnight, and you found me at a bar.

She smiled. *Buzzed, not drunk.* The best way to be.

Why did you contact me?

She really didn't know why, other than she was alone. *I don't really know why.*

Lonely?

She thought about it for a minute. Was she lonely? She'd wanted Tess to stay. Did that make her lonely? *Maybe a little.*

It's okay to be lonely sometimes. We all need company now and then...even online.

You probably have lots of people contacting you. I'm sure you're never lonely.

You'd be surprised. What's your name? Or should I just call you lonely?

No. Don't call me that, because I'm not. Call me Sophie. She hit send before she'd thought that through and cursed herself for not being more careful.

Sophie...that's a pretty name. Are you named after someone?

My grandmother. What shall I call you?

Seems we have something in common already. My middle name, Rose, was my grandmother's name, but you can call me Blair.

She wondered if that was actually true. *It's a pleasure to meet you, Blair.*

The pleasure is all mine, Sophie.

Her vision clouded as she drifted off to sleep. The message beep woke her.

You still there?

She glanced at the time on her computer. It was close to two now. She had to be up and ready in six hours. Tess was picking her up. *I have to go. Need to get some sleep before work.*

Okay. Sweet dreams.

She quickly typed, *Can we chat again tomorrow night?* then hesitated before sending the message. Catfish rushed through her mind, but she truly wanted to find a connection with someone. She closed her eyes, took in a breath, and hit send.

The response didn't come right away. Her gut sank, and she stood and paced the living room. She was being stupid to think anyone could form a connection with someone online at all, let alone in only a few hours. Her computer beeped, and her heart raced as she dropped to the couch and read the message.

I would love that, but I have a full weekend. Work related. Can we try for Sunday? Possibly later in the evening.

Her stomach vaulted into somersaults. *What time?*

Let's say around nine?

Nine on Sunday works for me.

Au revoir.

Good night. She slapped her laptop closed and held it to her chest. At least that gave her some time to prepare. How was she going to continue conversing with this woman and not sound stupid?

CHAPTER FIVE

The obnoxious horn honking in Sophie's head became louder as she cleared the fog from her mind. She opened one eye, then the other, then snapped them both closed again. The room was ridiculously bright. She really needed to get some blackout curtains. Either that or stop drinking. She rolled over onto her side and hit the snooze button on her phone before she pulled the blanket over her head. Blackout curtains it would be.

Nine minutes later the alarm jolted her from her sleep once again. She hit the snooze several more times before she finally rolled out of bed and slogged to the bathroom to turn on the shower. The image she saw in the mirror startled her. Matted blond hair and bloodshot eyes with smudged mascara surrounding them—forty, or forty-five to be accurate, wasn't looking any better on her. Especially since she'd stayed up most of the night. She blotted her makeup-remover bottle with a cotton pad and wiped the blackness from her eyes. A shower would have to work the rest of the magic.

She tugged off her T-shirt and let her panties drop to the floor along with it before she stepped into the hot, streaming water. She felt light-headed. She cooled the water and braced herself against the wall. When was she going to learn not to drink so much? With every year she aged, alcohol affected her more. She let the warm water stream across her head and face before she turned and let it massage her shoulders. She soaped up and rinsed quickly before she tugged at the towel slung over the top of the rail, dried, and got out. She didn't have a lot of time this morning.

She stared into her reflection in the mirror. The circles under her eyes were still dark. The shower hadn't helped much other than to wake her up and perhaps blanket the smell of the alcohol still lingering in her pores. Her attention went immediately to the one gray hair above her forehead sparkling in the bathroom light. She snapped up the tweezers on the basin and plucked it out. She'd always loved the natural blond color of her hair, only adding highlights during the summer and lowlights during the winter. That didn't seem to be covering all the gray any longer. She was going to have to take a new tack with the traitors emerging from her scalp. It would have to do for now. She blotted the excess water from her hair before she tossed the towel back over the shower rail.

She took her robe from the peg behind the door and slipped it on, then rushed to the kitchen and chugged half of a sports drink before she poured herself a mug of coffee. How in the world she'd remembered to load the coffeemaker and set the timer last night amazed her. Autopilot must have kicked in. The alarm on her phone rang, the third of many she'd set for this morning. She needed to get moving. Tess would be here soon to pick her up. She filled two travel mugs with coffee and then popped a pod into her espresso machine and let that stream into one mug, then did the same for the next. After that she added a spoonful of her vitality concoction—the only thing that kept her going these days—into each one.

She stopped in the living room as she passed the couch. She really didn't have time this morning, but she backtracked, sat, and opened her laptop. The messenger application had a notification. She clicked on the icon, and the message stream from Blair opened.

A new message had been posted that simply said, *Have a wonderful day, love. I'm looking forward to Sunday night.*

She quickly typed *me too,* then erased it and typed, *Last night was...*

"Shit. What was it exactly?" She flopped back into the couch. "It was only a conversation, dummy." But it seemed more like an awakening of some sort—definitely a conversation that wouldn't let her sleep. All she could think about was what Blair's voice would sound like—what the words she'd written would sound like *in that voice*. How her lips would move as the words came through them. How Blair's lips would feel against her own. "Fuck."

She leaned forward, punched the delete button repeatedly, then typed, *I'm looking forward to it as well.*

It wasn't original but would have to do for now. She didn't have the time or energy to think of something witty this early. The way Blair had affected her last night was entrancing. Even though she was dead tired, and a wee bit drunk, getting to sleep had been extremely difficult after their communication.

"Blair Rose." She said it slowly. If that was her real name, it was beautiful.

The fourth alarm for the morning shrilled from the bedroom. She slapped her laptop closed and ran to get dressed. She had only thirty minutes until Tess would be at her doorstep—bright and cheerful as always, ready to be her chauffeur to work. Tess was such a good friend.

She'd just finished her makeup when the doorbell rang and she heard the door open.

"I'm here, Sunshine." Tess's voice sang through the house.

Sophie smiled. Tess was always in a great mood in the morning, even after late nights. Sophie had no idea how she managed it. "I'll be right out."

Tess appeared in the doorway to the bathroom dressed in a white, flower-patterned sundress. A bright-yellow sweater covered her shoulders. "You look kinda fabulous for someone with a hangover."

"Aren't you the sweetest." She'd thrown on a pair of khaki slacks and a bright-coral blouse and then used every conceivable remedy for this one, but still Tess was lying. She couldn't hide the dark circles under her eyes. "I did something last night." She rushed past Tess into the living room and gathered her bag.

Tess followed her. "I know. I was with you. You hit on the hot, curvy server again."

She opened the front door and allowed Tess to go out in front of her, then locked the door behind them. "No. Not that. After I got home."

"Please tell me you found a magnificent new masturbation technique that put you right to sleep," Tess said over her shoulder as she walked. "I need you to run interference with Joy today. I'm pretty sure she'll still be pissed off at me." She continued to the driver's side of the car.

Sophie rushed to the passenger side and pulled open the door. "Fuck Joy." She tossed her bag into the back seat. "She's never going to get rid of you. She needs you." She slid into the car.

Tess started the car and it hummed. "So, what did you do after you got home?" She put it into gear and started backing out of the driveway.

"I contacted Blair."

"Who's Blair? Do I know her?" Tess scrunched her eyebrows as she looked over her shoulder to see behind the car.

She'd forgotten Tess wasn't aware she went by just Blair. "@blairsyrose."

Tess hit the brakes hard, and she lurched against the seat. "Are you kidding me?"

She took in a deep breath to settle her stomach. "Nope. I couldn't sleep, so I poured myself another drink and took the plunge into online flirting."

"She flirted with you?" Tess continued backing out of the driveway, looking both ways before hitting the street.

"Technically, no. But we did start a dialogue. We're going to talk more Sunday night."

"You *talked* to her?"

"Yes. I mean, no. We messaged back and forth." *Au revoir* flashed through her mind in the sexy, imaginary voice she'd created for Blair. How could she keep up in a conversation with someone who seemed so eloquent? Especially for more than a couple of hours with no dinner activity and outside interaction. This was going to be a challenge if she chose to continue interacting with Blair online. "She called me 'love.'"

"Love?" Tess stared at her for a moment before letting her eyes veer back to the road. "Are you sure she used the term *love*?"

"Yes. I'm sure. I read it again this morning. She also didn't say good night. She said au revoir. Do you think she's from France?"

"Maybe, but Blair isn't a traditional French name, and lots of people say au revoir just to sound fancy. If *she is* from France, be prepared for the fact that she could possibly still live there."

"Well, that's not promising."

"Could've been here on vacation. One of the perils of online dating." Tess shrugged. "Put it on your list of things to ask her."

"Oh, yeah. Last night you said you've dated someone online, right?" Something new that Sophie had learned and wondered why Tess hadn't told her about it.

"I wouldn't call it dating. It was only a few conversations that fizzled out quickly." Tess shivered like she'd eaten a sour lemon. "So what do you want to discuss with Blair?"

"I don't know. I've never had deep conversations with anyone I've dated. We never get that far. It's usually dinner, a few drinks, and then sex."

"How do you know where anything's going with anyone if you don't ever have deep conversations?"

"By the third date, if we get that far, I know where it's going."

"Are you serious? By the third date I barely know a woman. You can't possibly have spent more than a total of nine hours with them by that time. Fifteen at the most."

Sophie stared out onto the road and grinned.

"Oh. I forgot." Tess popped herself on the forehead with her palm. "You jump right in on the first date." She hit the turn signal and merged into traffic. "Still, counting the hours of the actual date and possibly a couple of active hours during sex it can't be more than six hours a night. So eighteen hours?"

She pointed upward.

"Eight?"

She rolled her lips in. "More like twelve."

"Wow. Really? You have sex for six hours?" Tess stared at

her with her mouth agape. A car honked, and she pulled the wheel, veering back into their own lane.

"There might be a little dozing here and there, but yes. I like sex, so I spend a lot of *date* time there."

"Wow." Tess reached for Sophie's travel mug. "What do you put in that coffee?"

She laughed. "Collagen peptides to start, and a shot of espresso."

Tess took a sip of her coffee. "Tastes just like mine."

"I loaded yours up this morning too." She grinned like she'd just pulled off the perfect prank. "To give you extra energy today." Tess hadn't been willing to try it on her own.

"I already have plenty of energy." Tess handed the mug back to her. "So, maybe you should slow it down a bit. Get to know the woman before you have sex."

"Sometimes that's difficult. I'm usually not the only one tearing the clothes off."

"Okay. So, what about this woman, Blair, that you've met online? Can you take that slow?"

"You know I'm not good with words."

"That's a bunch of hooey. You're great with words when you want to be."

"Only with people I know."

"So, act like you're old friends." Tess said it like it was a no-brainer.

"I can't with her. She's well versed—sophisticated." Sophie took in a breath. "I'm afraid my immature witty banter won't go over well." She'd already built Blair up way more than she should have.

"Okay. So then, what?" Tess pulled into the parking lot in front of the boutique-style office building where they worked and slid the car into park.

Sophie didn't know how she was going to handle it, and then the idea hit her. "Hey. What if you help me write her?"

"Oh no. You're not dragging me into this." Tess opened the car door and got out.

Sophie rushed to get out as well. "Come on. Please? You said I should take it slower." She retrieved her bag from the back seat. "You can make sure that happens."

"They need to be *your* words, and *your* feelings, not mine." Tess hit the button on her key fob, and the car chirped.

"How about my feelings and *our* words?" She scrunched her eyebrows. "Pretty please? Can I come over tonight? I wouldn't ask if I didn't need your help."

Tess stopped walking for a minute and blew out a breath. "Fine. I'll fix dinner and help you get started, but you're going to have to take over when it gets intimate."

She widened her eyes. "You think it'll get intimate?"

Tess continued to the entrance to the modern, window-paned, building. "Plenty of people have formed lasting relationships after meeting online."

"Whoa." She yanked open the door to the private lobby entrance of JB Marketing and let Tess enter before her and head up the stairs. "Let's not get ahead of ourselves here. She seems nice and all, but that doesn't mean I'm going to put a ring on her finger." Probably never would. Something about being tied to one person for the rest of her life scared her.

"Good, because I won't let you until I approve her."

Tess laughed, and she couldn't help but join in. She had a way of making everything seem right in the world.

As they entered the office Sophie found Joy waiting for her. She'd thought she was going to get through yesterday's presentation without backlash, but that wasn't the case. The short-fused Molotov cocktail combination between Tess and Joy had been easily ignited, as usual.

"Hey." Joy trailed her closely. "We need to talk."

She knew that was coming. "Got it." Instead of following Tess into their shared office, she veered her path into Joy's office. She didn't want Tess to be part of this.

"Yesterday was uncomfortable at best." Joy tossed her pad-folio onto the desk. "You know Tess blew it again."

"No. She didn't. She just made you a whole lot of money." If

Tess hadn't showed Gabrielle and Charlotte her original plan, they would've gone somewhere else, and all the money they'd spent on prep work would've been lost. "And what do you mean *again*? You should be thanking her for showing the client plan A." She should've let Tess give Joy a dose of kiss-my-ass, which she totally deserved.

"She doesn't listen—goes rogue with ideas I've already shot down. Yesterday was a perfect example."

It seemed that Joy had stewed heavily on Tess's performance last night. Sophie leaned against the desk and crossed her arms. "But they loved it."

"And it's going to cost us more money to produce."

"So what? They're willing to pay for it, and if the campaign makes more money in the long run, aren't we in better shape?" She gripped the edge of the desk. "It'll bring in other clients, instead of us searching for them all over town." JB hadn't had any walk-in clients in quite a long time, which left a lot of soliciting up to them all.

"I want to bring in another partner to work with you—someone better suited for your style."

"Absolutely not." She wouldn't work with anyone else. "Tess knows my style, and she gets how I think. She's a creative genius. No one else at this firm works as well together as we do. Remember the last time you tried to split us? We all failed." And they had. Neither of them had produced anything worth pitching at all. Not many others in Sophie's profession could live up to her standards. Probably because Tess had set the bar so high. "Tell you what. If you bring in someone new, I'll be happy to mentor them as a compromise." She really didn't want to, she didn't have enough time in the day to do her own work, but if it got Joy off her ass as well as Tess's, she would help someone else.

"The next pitch is going to be done my way." Joy planted her hands on her hips.

"Aren't they all done your way?" She shrugged. "I mean, when was the last time you let us go into that room without changing part of our presentation?"

"That's my job."

She shook her head. "No. Your job is to make sure we're successful." She pushed off the desk. "So far you haven't made a single one of our pitches better. You've only tied our hands on resources." It irked Sophie that Joy was only concerned with the money. Pleasing the customer always came second.

"All the campaigns have done well for the customer."

"But they could've done a whole lot better." If Joy would let them handle things the way they wanted, the firm would have clients lined up for representation.

"When you start putting money into the business, you can start dictating the directions we move in." Joy rounded her desk and flopped into her chair. "Until then, what I say goes."

She clenched her fists as she spun and left the office. There was absolutely no reasoning with Joy.

CHAPTER SIX

W as that about me?" Tess's forehead crinkled, and her face took on an expression like that of a lost child, filled with innocence and need. It always did that when she was worried.

"No. Joy's just being her usual bitch self." She sat at her desk, removed her laptop, and clicked it into the docking station. "She wants me to mentor one of the newbies."

"Where does that leave me?"

"Right where you are. I agreed to do it, but not at the expense of breaking up our team." She glanced up. "I would never do that."

Tess smiled. "I'd understand if you think you'd have more success with someone else."

Sophie stood and put her hands on her hips. "Where is that coming from?"

"Yesterday." Tess looked at her computer screen briefly. "Maybe I should've left it alone, let Joy convince them the cheaper plan would work."

"Did it sound like the client thought it would work—or even wanted it?"

"No, but—"

"They loved your plan. Right?"

Tess nodded. "They seemed to."

"Then you did the right thing. Fuck Joy and her budget." She pressed her fingers to her forehead. She hadn't avoided the headache part of the hangover after all. "If we'd settled for plan B and it didn't work, you wouldn't have been able to set foot in Boho Clothes again. We can't have that. You look too cute in their clothes."

"True. I can't live without shopping there." Tess smiled as she reached into her desk, took out a bottle of ibuprofen before she got a bottle of water from the mini-fridge, and handed them to her.

"Thanks." She popped a couple of pills into her mouth and washed them down. Tess knew her better than anyone else ever could. She wouldn't dump her just because Joy didn't like the way she operated. She would never do that to her best friend.

The room was silent except for the light, soothing piano music Tess had playing from her portable speakers. Sophie wasn't having much luck working, her mind still captured by the beautiful voice she'd imagined from last night. Not even Joy could ruin that. Blair hadn't sent many messages, but the ones she *had* sent were intriguing. She seemed well-educated, and her words were eloquent and to the point. Nothing simple about her, though. How was she going to continue an online dalliance with this woman, let alone an in-person encounter, if she had to keep up with her in conversation?

She typed out a couple of simple flirty phrases, then glanced across the room at Tess, who seemed engrossed in her work. Good. No chance of her coming her way and seeing what she was working on. She read them back to herself in her head.

Aside from being sexy, what do you do for a living?

Lame.

Are you a magician? Because when I talk to you, you make everyone else disappear.

Nope.

Are you a camera? Because I look at you and smile!

Ugh. She let out a huge sigh. She hadn't even seen her yet. She was going to have to up her game if she was ever going to be able to talk to Blair on her level. She'd already put her on a pedestal, and she didn't even know her.

"Everything okay over there?" Tess looked over her monitor at her. "You need some help?"

"I'm fine. I just need more water."

Tess started to get up.

"I'll get it. You keep doing what you're doing." She crossed the room to the mini-fridge and plucked out a bottle. "You want one?"

Tess smiled. "Sure. Want to look at this new design while you're up?"

She walked behind Tess's desk and handed her the water. She'd fleshed out the details of the presentation she'd given the client yesterday, which was perfect. "Have I told you lately how talented you are?"

"Yes." Tess grinned and relaxed into her chair. "But tell me again."

"You, my dear, are the most talented woman I know. You never cease to amaze me with your creativity." She rubbed Tess's shoulder. "I don't think I would survive here without you."

"Aw, that's sweet. But we know who has the brains in this duo." Tess smiled up at her.

Sophie's stomach fluttered, and she enjoyed the sensation. It felt good to be appreciated. "You like my catchy gimmicks and phrases, but you're the one who makes them shine."

Tess covered Sophie's hand with her own and sighed. "We do make a great team."

"Absolutely." She gave Tess's hand a squeeze before she headed back to her desk. "We're never going to let Joy break us up." She sat and stared at the page of ridiculous lines she'd written to use on Blair. She highlighted all of them and hit the delete key. Witty banter wouldn't carry her with this one.

Not too much later she heard Tess's stomach let out a loud growl. It felt like she'd typed a million horrible, cheesy lines and had been staring at her computer screen for hours.

"I'm starving." Tess widened her eyes and laughed.

Sophie stood and stretched. "Ready for lunch?"

"Yes." Tess popped out of her chair and went to the mini-fridge, where she took out a large, brown paper bag. "I packed us lunch. Thought maybe we could go to the park and eat—get some sunshine." She crossed the room. "Might make your head feel better."

She grabbed her bag from her drawer. "I'm up for anything that will make this hammer vacate my skull."

Once they reached the park, Sophie took the blanket and the bag Tess had packed from the back seat and followed her to their usual spot near a huge oak tree. Tess always wanted sun and shade. She was a little quirky that way. She never wanted to spend too much time in either, and this spot provided a little of both.

"Is here okay?" Tess asked, as though it wasn't where they always ended up.

"It's perfect." She handed Tess the blanket and waited for her to spread it on the grass. She set the bag of food in the middle before she lay down on the sunny side and let the sunshine wash across her face. The heat felt good on her throbbing head.

"Why do you want to stay there? At JB?" Tess's voice was soft and curious.

"I don't necessarily want to stay *there*. You know I need to have a safety net before I leave anywhere." She'd been banking money into her savings for years, hoping to someday have her own marketing company, but the startup costs were high. She could probably count on some clients following her, but the majority would stay with Joy until they realized she had no idea what she was doing. She had to have enough money to sustain them until that happened.

"I have boiled eggs, salad, and cucumber sandwiches. Thought you might need something lighter than we ate last night."

She rolled to her side, took one of the boiled eggs, added some salt and pepper that Tess had brought, and bit into it. Tess was right about that. Fried foods wrecked her system now that she'd aged. Even if forty was the new thirty, her body didn't seem to acknowledge that fact.

She took a swig of water before she finished the egg and snagged one of the small sandwiches Tess had prepared. "These are awesome."

"You say that every time you eat them."

"Because they are. Just like you." She watched Tess draw a beautiful sketch of a bird pecking at the seeds on the tips of the blades of grass. "I feel bad that your talent is wasted in your job. Why don't you paint or write on the side more?"

"It takes inspiration for both." She set the pad aside and took a bite of her sandwich, chewed, and swallowed. "Haven't had a lot of that lately."

"Well, someday you're going to have to get back out into the world and find someone who inspires you." She grinned. "Maybe even have a date or two."

"Possibly." Tess took a rolled-up towel from her bag and set it behind them. "How about you take a short nap while I draw a few more sketches?"

Subject change—Tess's way of avoiding anything that had to do with meeting someone new. She guessed Tess just wasn't ready for all the work it took to get to know someone. Honestly, Sophie hadn't been sure she was herself until last night. Something within her had definitely changed.

Sophie closed her eyes. A nap would certainly help her dragging ass today. It seemed like only a few minutes before she heard Tess's voice come through the fog in her head.

"Wake up, sleepyhead." Tess was gathering up the containers and placing them back into the bag. "We should go if you want to pick up your car on the way back."

❖

Sophie scanned the parking lot as Tess pulled up next to her BMW. It was hard to tell which vehicles belonged to people frequenting the bar and which belonged to people who worked in the buildings surrounding it. She slid out of the passenger seat.

"I'll wait until you get into your car and follow you back."

"No need. I have to go inside for a minute. I can't find my credit card. I might have left it here last night." She closed the car door before Tess could protest. She knew very well that her card hadn't come out of her wallet last night. She'd paid in cash.

She waved at Tess as she backed out and then checked Twitter for the passcode to the penthouse club. She didn't know if the bartender would have any information on Blair, but it was worth a shot.

The elevator ride was the same as always, slow and noisy, but the club looked different in the light of day. The skylight was open, and the sun lit the bar with little help from the lamps on the wall above the tables. A few people sat scattered at the bar drinking, and a couple at a table was finishing a lunch of cocktails and what looked like wings. Just the thought made her stomach squirm.

She stood at the end of the bar and waited for the bartender to appear. He seemed to be missing in action for the moment. When he came through the entrance from the back room, she caught his eye, and he smiled and immediately came her way. Not the same bartender as the night before. Much taller, with a shadow of a beard covering chiseled features.

"What can I get you?"

His long, lush lashes mesmerized her. Why were some men blessed with such gorgeous lashes when she had to thicken hers daily with mascara? "Nothing to drink, thanks. I was wondering if I can ask you a few questions about something written in one of the bill books."

"Ask away."

She glanced at the stack of different-sized books in the corner behind the bar. "May I look really quick to find the one I'm curious about?"

He took the stack from the corner and set them in front of her. "Knock yourself out. I'll be back in a minute." He headed to the other end and refilled a customer's beer from the tap.

She flipped through several books until she found the right one just in time for the bartender to come her way again.

"Find it?"

"Yes." She turned the book to him and pointed to the quote from @blairsyrose. "Do you know who this person might be?"

He flattened his lips, then sucked in a hiss through his teeth. "It's hard to say. A number of people write in those. Could be anyone."

She flipped through a few more books and found several other writings from @blairsyrose. "She's written in more than one. Are you sure you might not have a clue?"

"Sorry. I honestly don't pay much attention to those." He took another huge stack of books from beneath the bar and set them in front of her. "You're welcome to look through them to see if you can find out more."

It made sense they would use a lot of books, change them out over time, but she hadn't realized just how many. Disappointment clenched her stomach as the sliver of hope she'd had of finding Blair in the flesh disappeared. She would skim through as many as she could, but she really didn't have time. If she didn't get back to the office soon, Tess would come looking for her, or worse yet, she and Joy would get into it again while she was gone.

The bartender appeared again. "I found one more." He handed the book to her. "You done with these?" He picked up the small stack closest to him. She nodded, and he put them back in the corner behind the bar.

She flipped open the one he'd handed her. Not a lot written in this particular book, one of the newer ones, she suspected. She flipped to the title page, which seemed to still remain in some but not others, and found a message. Her stomach dipped as she read it.

Happiness is meant to be shared—find it—let it seize you.
@Blairsyrose.

The ink looked new. There was an imprint and a bit of ink-bleed of the writing on the opposite page. She glanced around the bar wondering when this had been written—wondering if Blair had been there today—possibly sitting in this very same spot. Heat rushed over her. What a stroke of déjà-vu that would be. She shook her head at herself. She was getting way too wrapped up in someone she barely knew. She slipped the book into her bag and stacked the remaining books into one pile, then pushed them across the bar.

The bartender came her way again. "Find what you were looking for?"

"Not really, but thank you for letting me search." She stood and gave the bar one last once-over.

"Maybe you can come back tonight and look some more." He took the last stack of books and put it behind the counter. "There are more in the back. We rotate them out."

"Maybe." Probably not. She snatched a five-dollar bill from her wallet and set it on the counter before she left. She slung her bag over her shoulder and palmed the outline of the book through the leather. She'd found something, but it seemed any information about Blair would have to come from the woman herself.

When she reached her car, her phone pinged. She fished it out of her purse and looked at the screen. Tess had sent a text message.

You okay?

Yeah. Just did some investigating while I was there.

Any luck?

Not much, but something. I'll show you when I get back to the office. She hit send and typed another message. *Can you really help me with this tonight?*

Of course.

You're the best.

I know. Tess punctuated it with a shy smiley face.

She dropped her phone into her purse, took out the book, and slid her hand across the fabric binding. She could barely read the title, *Emily Dickinson Selected Poems.* She assumed the club picked up their books at a used bookstore. Who in the world would get rid of this one? She flipped it open and to read the message again.

Happiness is meant to be shared—find it—let it seize you.

Maybe she should stop overthinking and let herself be seized.

That was ridiculous. She shook her head, tossed the book back into her bag, and fired up the engine. Happiness had never seized her, not on even one day in her life. She doubted it would ever happen unless she forced it.

CHAPTER SEVEN

Tess snagged a cart from the usual area at the entrance of the grocery store and then went straight to the produce department—her usual first stop. She tended to shop daily to ensure her food was fresh and that she didn't waste. More than one time in the past she'd bought for the week and ended up throwing something out because her plans had changed, and she hadn't gotten around to cooking. She bagged a few onions and a head of garlic before she strolled to the mushrooms and individually chose the freshest ones. A pot of mushroom soup sounded good tonight. It seemed like forever since she'd had it. She never made it for just herself, so Sophie's company was the perfect excuse to indulge.

"Hey." The familiar voice of Brandy, the produce manager, startled her. She seemed to work every day.

"Hi." She continued picking through the mushrooms. "Do you ever take a day off?"

"On occasion. What's on the menu tonight?"

"Mushroom soup."

"I have a fresher batch in the cooler. I can bring some out if you'd like." Brandy hooked her thumb over her shoulder toward the back of the store.

She spun the bag hanging from her hand and tied a loose knot in the top. "Thanks for the offer, but these will be okay."

"You have quite a few there. Expecting company for dinner?"

She nodded. "A friend's coming over."

"Lucky girl."

She smiled at the compliment. "That would be her call to make."

"Beautiful and modest." Brandy smiled as she took the bag from her and placed it in her basket. "Maybe someday I can convince you to make soup for me?"

"Possibly. If you ever take a night off."

"I'd take every night off for you."

"That's sweet of you to say. Wouldn't they miss you here?" She tried to suppress the heat in her cheeks.

"They'd make do." Brandy put her hand on the cart. "So how about it?"

"Are you asking me to make you dinner?"

"No." Brandy's cheeks reddened as she shook her head. "I'll buy dinner if you'll agree to go out with me." Brandy had asked her out at least once a week for the longest time, but she just wasn't ready to venture into the dating pool yet. People who got over bad breakups quickly amazed her.

"Listen, Brandy. I'm really flattered, but I—"

"I get it. You don't find me attractive." Brandy raked her fingers through her short, dark hair.

"No." Her stomach dropped at the thought of hurting Brandy's feelings. "That's not it at all." She couldn't help but assess Brandy's strong biceps peeking from underneath her black, short-sleeved T-shirt. She was tall, strong, and powerful—not at all unappealing. In fact, she'd stolen glances at Brandy more than once while she shopped, but she just wasn't there yet. "I'm not dating *anyone* right now. I'm just not ready yet."

"Your ex must've done something pretty awful." Brandy was fishing, but she wasn't prepared to tell her about Lindsay. Not right now, here in the produce section of the grocery store. She'd bail mid-story—never make it to the checkout counter.

"Let's just say it was a breakup I don't want to repeat and leave it at that."

"Will you let me know when you *are* ready to start dating?"

"You'll be the first one I call."

"Okay, then." Brandy smiled and released the cart. "I'll see you tomorrow, then."

"Yes. You probably will." Relieved that Brandy seemed to accept her reasons for rejecting her offer, she pushed the cart farther down the aisle and quickly turned the corner.

She hoped that had satisfied Brandy for the time being and she didn't ask her out again next week. She hadn't lied—she wasn't ready to date anyone new—but she wasn't sure Brandy would be the first woman she'd go out with when she was. Forcing something new with someone waiting in the wings didn't feel right. What if she didn't live up to Brandy's expectations? She'd rather just leave it up to fate. She had to give Brandy credit, though. She was certainly persistent.

When Tess pulled up in her driveway, her neighbor, Janet, was out front tending to her hydrangeas. Although technically not friends, as in let's hang out together daily, they'd become fairly friendly over the years. Janet was a sweet woman who shared her beautiful backyard pool with Tess whenever she felt the need for a swim. That usually included a nice glass of wine as well. With blond hair and dark, tanned skin, she wasn't as old as she looked, maybe in her mid-fifties. The Florida sun had given her a more weathered look than she deserved. Dressed in deck shoes, capri pants, and a blue-and-white polo shirt, Janet looked as though she was ready to go sailing any minute, even though they were hours from the shore on either coast. She got out of her car and walked to the edge of the driveway.

"Your flowers sure are beautiful this year. You have the greenest thumb of anyone I know."

"All it takes is a little attention."

She glanced at the dried-up shrubs in her own yard. "Guess I've been neglecting mine."

"You work too much." Janet frowned. "I bet if you spent as much time on your social life, you'd find someone to help you make your yard beautiful."

"Or I can just hire a gardener." She grinned. That would be a whole lot safer than a new relationship at this point. "It's good to see you, Janet."

"You too." Janet gave her a wave.

Tess turned and went back to her car, retrieved her groceries, and went inside the house. She dropped the groceries onto the counter, then went to the bedroom to change out of her work clothes. She chose a pair of black leggings, white slip-on Chucks, and a comfortable pink terry crew-neck tunic for the evening ahead before she went back to the kitchen and began to work on dinner prep.

After taking a package of sliced cheddar cheese from the refrigerator, she placed several slices neatly on a plate before adding a variety of olives, covering it with plastic wrap, and sliding it back into the refrigerator. She grabbed the cutting board from the end of the counter, where it leaned against the pantry cabinet, and then took the mushrooms, onions, and garlic from the grocery bags. She chopped the onions and placed them in the pot with butter and olive oil. Then she chopped the garlic and washed and sliced the entire bag of mushrooms she'd picked out. A few thoughts popped into her head about what Sophie could write to Blair, so she flipped the burner on low and stopped what she was doing to put them on paper.

Tess sat at her antique typewriter and plucked out a few lines. In a matter of minutes, she created a style guide, including keywords and several harmless sweet lines Sophie could use with her new paramour. She hadn't been seated long when the doorbell rang. She didn't have to answer the door, because she knew it was Sophie and that she would let herself in. She usually gave her a warning with the bell, which Tess had told her wasn't necessary any longer. Sophie had said that, although it would be entertaining, she didn't want to catch her dancing around the house naked again. That had been a thoroughly embarrassing moment for Tess, but Sophie had seemed quite amused when it had happened.

"Honey. I'm home," Sophie's voice rang through the house as she entered. "Something smells wonderful. And I'm not saying that just because I'm starving."

She smiled. "How long has it been since you've had a home-cooked meal?"

"Haven't had one since the last time you cooked for me. I've been living on takeout and salads."

"Well. You'll have to come over more often, so I can pamper you a bit more."

"You don't have to ask me twice. I'll be here anytime you say the word." Sophie plucked a slice of raw mushroom from the board and glanced over Tess's shoulder. "Maybe more since you're going to help me." She talked as she chewed. "You'll probably be sick of me sooner than you think."

"Sick of you? Never." Tess pulled the page from the typewriter and handed it to Sophie, then went to the kitchen, finished chopping a couple cloves of garlic, and dropped them into a pan with onions that were already sautéing in butter.

"You make cooking look so easy." Sophie glanced at what she had typed.

"It isn't always, but this soup is extremely easy and quick." She took the mushrooms from the counter and dropped them into the pan with the onions and garlic. The aroma was just as fabulous as she remembered.

"So that's it? Just those few ingredients turn into this fantastic bowl of warm, creamy soup?" Sophie put the piece of paper on the counter before she opened the bottle of white wine she'd brought and poured them each a glass.

"That's it."

"What do we do while we wait?" Sophie handed a glass to Tess.

"We drink wine and make garlic bread." She held up her glass and clinked it against Sophie's and took a sip. "Have you thought about what you want to say to Blair?" She set her glass on the counter before she sliced the loaf of French bread down the center, cutting it in half. "Do you think that's her real name?"

Sophie shrugged. "She said Rose was her grandmother's name."

"Out of the blue?" She rubbed a clove of garlic across each half of the bread before she spread butter over it and wrapped it with foil.

"Not exactly. I told her I was named after my grandmother."

"Oh." She wondered if the woman was just saying things she thought Sophie wanted to hear to gain her trust.

"Someday, I'm going to convince you that everyone in the world isn't out to get you."

"Not sure that will ever happen." She heated the oven and slid the loaf onto the rack.

"You can't let one bad relationship turn you against the whole world or every woman in it. Lindsay wasn't your perfect match, or you'd still be with her."

"I'm not against every woman." She leaned against the counter. "I've had one or two relationships since."

"I wouldn't call those relationships, and they left because you didn't trust them."

"Trust must be earned."

"Do you trust me?"

"You're probably the only woman I trust."

Sophie grinned and held her glass up. "Another victory for me."

She wiped her hands on the dish towel, then picked up her glass of wine from the counter and took a big gulp. "Just don't let whatshername get in the way of that. Okay?" She set her glass on the counter, opened the refrigerator, and took out the small plate of cheese and mixed olives she'd prepared earlier.

"Ooh, cheese."

The excitement in Sophie's voice made her laugh.

"It takes so little to please you." She removed the plastic wrap from the plate.

Sophie immediately took a piece, ripped it in half, and popped it into her mouth. "It really does."

"Brandy was at the grocery store again today."

"Damn. Does that girl work every day?"

"Right?"

"She ask you out again?" Sophie ate the other half and washed it down with a sip of wine.

She nodded as she slipped an olive into her mouth and chewed. "She's relentless."

"Did you say yes this time?"

She frowned. "You know I'm not ready for that yet."

"Jesus, Tess. It's been almost a year since you broke up with Lindsay. If you wait much longer, you're going to be a virgin again."

"We both know that's a bunch of hooey."

"Is it?" She snagged another bite of cheese. "Do you even remember how to make love to a woman?"

"That's something I'll never forget. It's instinctual." She winked, then laughed at herself. Nothing had come that easy with her ex—one of the reasons they were no longer together.

"Uh...okay." Sophie laughed along with her. "You still have the vibrator I gave you, don't you?"

She looked at the ceiling. "Yes." Sophie was the only one she could share so freely with.

"You haven't forgotten what it feels like, right?"

"No. I know what it feels like." She blew out a breath. "Just not quite the same without another woman, though."

"When's the last time you've had something between your legs besides a vibrator?"

"Last night." She gave Sophie a toothy grin.

Sophie raised an eyebrow. "A pillow doesn't count."

She chuckled under her breath. "You know me too well." She wasn't sure if that was good or bad.

"Sounds like you have an opportunity just waiting to happen. Get back out there. Call Brandy. Let her fuck you into oblivion."

"That sounds *so* romantic."

"Sorry." Sophie rolled her eyes. "Let her pleasure you until you see stars shooting from behind your eyelids." She grinned. "Better?"

"Not really." The words tumbled out of her mouth with a chuckle.

Sophie went to the stove and lifted the top off the pot. "Is this ready yet?" She grabbed a spoon from the drawer and took a taste. "Oh my gosh. This is delicious."

"Get away from there." Tess shooed her away from the stove and took a couple of bowls from the cupboard. "Grab the bread from the oven."

Sophie took the bread out barehanded and dropped it onto the counter. "Fuck."

"Did I mention it would be hot? Since it was in the oven and all?" Tess took a clean towel from the drawer and handed it to her. "Can you slice it and put it in there?" She pointed at the basket on the counter.

Sophie opened the foil, sliced it, hissing in between touches, and dumped the bread into the cloth-lined basket on the counter. She draped the towel over the basket to keep it warm.

Tess shook her head. "I gave you the towel to protect your hands, silly."

"Those instructions would've been more helpful a few minutes ago." Sophie took the bread to the table, along with the cheese tray, and then came back to get the bottle of wine and their glasses.

Tess met Sophie at the table with the bowls of soup. She had to admit, it did smell wonderful.

Sophie slurped a spoonful into her mouth. "This is delicious."

"Yeah?"

"Yeah. I need you to make this for me more often." She swirled her spoon in the soup. "Add this to my list of favorite meals."

"So, do you think Blair will cook you your favorite meals?"

Sophie pulled her eyebrows together. "Why would she? That's your job."

Tess laughed. "I guess it is." It seemed she was in no danger of being replaced. At least not right away. That made her feel a whole lot better about helping Sophie find her words.

CHAPTER EIGHT

The weekend had gone by faster than Sophie expected. She'd spent several evenings this week and most of the day today with Tess, after their usual Sunday brunch date, so they could discuss her responses to Blair. Tess had fixed her dinner again tonight, and she'd barely made it home from Tess's house before nine. Tess was still uncomfortable with the idea of writing for her but had understood Sophie's predicament more when she'd read Tess a couple of lines she'd written. Tess had laughed at her phrase: *I was feeling a little off today—but you've turned me on again.* She'd made her promise not to use it on any woman—ever. By the end of the day, Tess had made her promise not to use *any* of her cheesy lines.

She rushed to her laptop and signed in to her messenger account to see if Blair had sent anything. Nothing yet. She took the laptop with her into the bedroom and set it on the bed while she changed her clothes. She draped a stray pair of leggings over the integrated camera to make sure it was hidden. Even though she had a slider to cover it, she always worried about it. Once she had put on her sweatpants and T-shirt, she tossed the leggings into the hamper, which was overflowing. She really did need to do some laundry and housework, but she hated both. After sliding into bed, she glanced around the room and had second thoughts. Communicating in bed was a bad idea. She didn't want to rush this one. No good would come of it if she forgot her promise to Tess and the banter got racy.

Her computer chimed, and she rushed into the living room with her laptop as she read the message from Blair.

Something unexpected has come up, and I won't be able to chat tonight.

Her stomach sank, and she dropped onto the couch to respond. *I hope everything is okay.*

Yes. All is good. It's work-related.

What do you do? Maybe I can help.

The odds of her knowing anything specific about Blair's profession were slim, but she was good at improvising.

The dot above Blair's name went gray. Sophie guessed she didn't have time to explain—or just didn't want to. She was surprised at how disappointed she was and a tad pissed at the quick conversation exit, but it was probably for the best that Blair wasn't able to chat tonight. She had no idea what she was going to say anyway. She and Tess hadn't really gotten around to talking about that earlier. They'd mostly laughed at her cheesy lines and how well they worked on some women. They'd had fun with each other more than anything else. She needed the kind of relationship like she had with Tess—free and easy, with no pressure to be anyone but their true selves. Only with the addition of sex—lots of sex.

❖

Multiple chimes from Sophie's phone brought her out of her sleep. Still in a bit of a daze, she wasn't sure where the noise was coming from until another burst of consecutive chimes rang from her phone. She'd forgotten that she'd set her social-media messenger notifications to push just in case Blair got loose from work last night and wanted to chat. She picked up her phone and glanced at the time at the top of the screen. *Three a.m. Ugh.* A little presumptuous to message at this time of the morning. She set the phone back on the nightstand. She was still a little pissed about the rushed blowoff Blair had given her last night. Another cluster of chimes sounded. She stared at the ceiling, trying to ignore the urge to respond before she gave in and grabbed her phone. She hit the home button and clicked on her instant-messenger app. A string of message appeared.

Good morning.

You awake?
I can't sleep.
Sorry about last night.
It couldn't be helped.
Helloooo.
You there?
I really am sorry.

Blair was doing a lot of apologizing for someone who didn't care. Sophie flopped back onto her pillow and responded. *I'm here. A little sleepy, but here.*

I'm sorry. I know it's early, but I felt bad about exiting our chat so quickly last night.

Yeah. I wasn't thrilled about it either. She quickly erased that and wrote. *It's okay.*

But was it really okay? And what exactly was this early morning messaging about? It had better not be a booty call. She shook her head at herself. It wasn't like she hadn't done that to someone else before. She had, but *never* over instant messaging.

No, it isn't. I hadn't planned to be away long, but after I finished my work, a friend needed help.

I hope your friend is okay.

She is, but I can't really talk about it. Can we start over again tonight?

Helping a female friend late at night seemed personal. She wasn't sure what she was getting herself into here—wasn't sure if she wanted to continue the communication. Blair had cut her off last night, and she wasn't used to being treated like that. Even she didn't do that to other women. Maybe Blair was a catfish indeed.

Please? I promise to do better.

Against all of her instincts she typed back, *Okay. Going back to sleep now.*

Then Sophie turned off her phone and dropped it onto the nightstand. She was done with Blair for now and would need to do some serious thinking about her next steps, if any, with her.

CHAPTER NINE

Tess repeated the sentence. Still no response. "Hey. What's going on with you?" Again, no response. Well, this was getting annoying. She went to the coffee pot on the table near the door, poured a cup, and walked to Sophie's desk. "Did you have a late night?"

Sophie looked up at her in a daze. "What?"

She handed her the coffee. "You seem distracted. Were you up late messaging with Blair?" She knew they were supposed to connect.

Sophie let out a slow breath and flopped back in her chair. "Nope. She blew me off."

"Oh. That's not good. Why?"

"Said she had work stuff." Sophie raked her fingers through her shoulder-length, blond hair.

"What does she do?"

"I don't know" Sophie shrugged. "She signed off without answering last night. Kinda left me hanging."

"Maybe she's a doctor and it was an emergency."

Sophie let out a quick breath and rolled her eyes. "If she's a doctor, I doubt she'd be leaving random messages in bar-tab books."

"Yeah." She scrunched her nose. "You're probably right." She went back to her desk. "But you never know."

"She messaged me early this morning."

Tess peeked over her monitor at her. "How early?"

"Three-ish."

Tess let her mouth drop open.

"I know what you're thinking, and that didn't happen."

"No one messages at three in the morning unless it's an emergency of one kind or another, and you don't know her well enough for a call for help." Tess was pissed as she sped across the office again.

"She wanted to apologize."

"No. Absolutely not. You send flowers or message later, at a decent hour."

"She can't send me flowers. She doesn't know where I live, and it's partly my fault. I turned on the notifications for my messenger app. That's what woke me up."

"Did you change it back?"

Sophie shook her head. "No, but after I accepted her apology, I turned my phone off and went back to sleep."

She picked up Sophie's phone and handed it to her. "I suggest you turn them off unless you don't mind her waking you during the wee hours of the morning again."

"Can you fix it? Those settings always confuse me."

Tess punched in the passcode and opened the notification settings. She turned off the sound alert but left the banner alert on. "There." She handed the phone back to Sophie. "Now you can see the notifications, but they won't make noise."

"Thanks." Sophie dropped her phone to the desk. "God knows I need the rest to get rid of the dark circles under my eyes." She laughed.

"Stop. You look beautiful, as always." Total truth, Tess thought as she went back to her desk. "So are you messaging with her tonight?"

"That's where we left it."

"Okay. I'll plan on dinner alone then." She sank into her chair. She tried to hide her disappointment and seem upbeat about the whole Blair thing, but she was going to really miss her evenings with Sophie. They probably spent more time together than was healthy for either of them. Sometimes it prevented her from going out with anyone else, including Brandy from the grocery store, which was fine for now. In truth, she didn't have any desire to get back into dating since her breakup with Lindsay.

❖

Tess decided to have lunch alone today. She was normally a trusting soul and believed most people, took them for what they told her. Something in the back of her mind told her she shouldn't trust Blair. As she weaved through traffic on the fifteen-minute drive to the bar, she hit the number for it in her contacts. She went there often and knew the key to getting inside. She listened to the message as it came through the car speakers. "Welcome to The Speak Easy. Leave a message letting us know how many shoes you'll be dropping off and at what time." The club's unique way of taking reservations.

She glanced at the car clock. "Just one. I'll be there at twelve thirty."

She'd gotten away for lunch later than usual, but the drive was always shorter during the day than in rush-hour traffic. Street parking was packed from the office buildings surrounding it, as usual. She wondered how many were actually there for the bar alone.

She found a parking spot, went inside the building, and caught an elevator right as the doors were closing. The doors jerked open again, and the two people there stared at her as though she'd added ten minutes onto their ride up.

The elevator stopped only once, and the two annoyed riders exited quickly. She guessed they were making it back to work from their lunch hour with no time to spare.

No one would ever expect a secret bar in one of the oldest buildings in Orlando, especially housed in an old shoe-repair shop, kept almost exactly like it was back in the 1800s. She especially liked coming here on Halloween. They always ran a silent vampire movie in the outside breezeway with classic eerie music playing in the background.

After providing the password to the doorman, she stepped inside, surprised at how busy it was for this time of day. Did people regularly go drinking at lunch? She went straight to the bar and took a seat. The bartender was nowhere to be found. Maybe restocking from the back. Soon a tall man with dark hair pulled back into a ponytail came from the rear, wiping his hands with a towel like he'd just washed them. He glanced over his shoulder and flattened his lips like he was irritated. Must be having back-office issues.

"What can I get you?"

"Some fried cheese to go."

"Something to drink while you wait?"

"A glass of rosé?" She hated to sit at a bar and not order anything to drink.

The bartender took a bottle of rosé from the glass-doored refrigerator and poured her a glass. "I'll get that to-go order put in."

She glanced around the bar as she sipped her wine. When she'd dropped off Sophie to get her car last week, Sophie had said she needed to pick up her credit card. But she had paid in cash. She remembered because she'd made a fuss about paying. She guessed Sophie didn't think Tess would remember that detail. Unless Sophie didn't remember. She was pretty drunk. Maybe she couldn't find it and was trying to retrace her steps. It wouldn't be the first time.

Sooner than expected, the bartender came from the back and set her order on the counter. "Another glass of wine?"

She looked at her glass, surprised to see that she'd almost finished it. "No. Thank you." She reached into the box and snagged a piece of cheese. She'd need to eat something as soon as possible to absorb the alcohol, or she'd be taking a cab back to work.

"Can I get you anything else?"

She swallowed and grabbed another piece from the box. "Maybe. My friend and I were in here one night last week. There was a message in one of these tab books." She held it up before she slipped a couple of twenties into it and pushed it across the bar. "She signed the message with @blairsyrose. Does that sound familiar to you?"

"I can't say that it does. All kinds of people write in these books."

"Do you know anyone named Blair? A regular maybe?"

"Sorry. I don't, but if you want to leave me your number, I'll ask around."

"That would be awesome." She pulled a business card from her bag and wrote her cell number on the back.

He read the front and then the back. "She a friend of yours or something?"

"A friend of a friend actually. Just trying to get in touch." She slid off the barstool and took the to-go box from the counter. "I'd appreciate you letting me know if you find out anything."

"Now that I have your number, maybe you and I could have coffee or something."

"Sorry, but I'm—"

He put up his hand. "No need to explain. Just thought I'd give it a shot." He hung on to her card and went to the other end of the bar.

She was flattered but hadn't expected that at all. The trip hadn't been fruitful except for a small boost to her ego from the wrong sex. When she glanced over her shoulder, she saw the bartender hand her card to someone in the back room. She had a bad feeling that her number might end up in one of the bill books.

CHAPTER TEN

S ophie had rushed home and changed into her yoga pants and a T-shirt. The day had never gone slower, and work had been as stressful as usual—a Monday from hell. She had no idea how she was going to solve the rift between Tess and Joy. That had slowly become wider, like the San Andreas Fault as it was rocked by each new earthquake. Sophie heard her computer beep, rushed to it, and opened her social-media messenger. A message from Blair appeared.

Hey, love. Won't be able to chat again tonight. Work beckons.

Her disappointment hit her square in the chest. She was really looking forward to unwinding with Blair. She typed in a quick response. *I've been thinking about you all day.*

And I you. You seem to monopolize my thoughts lately. Sigh.

Then talk to me.

I wish I could tonight, but this can't be avoided.

Maybe later then?

She hated to beg—actually had never begged any woman to talk to her before.

There was no response from Blair, and the chat icon went gray. Her disappointment quickly morphed into anger. What the hell was going on with this woman? Maybe she wasn't as interested as she seemed.

She picked up her phone and hit the FaceTime button for Tess. She needed her help with managing her irritation, or this whole thing with Blair was going to crash and burn prematurely.

"Well, hello there, gorgeous. I wasn't expecting a call from you tonight." Tess's infectious smile immediately wiped out her anger. She always seemed so happy to talk to her. "I thought you were courting Blair tonight."

She frowned as she thought of Blair's quick exit. "I need your help with that. Can you come over?"

"Nope. Already in my jammies. Not going out tonight." Once Tess had moved into jammie mode, she rarely left the house. Sometimes that extended for entire weekends.

"Then can I come over there?" Asking was just a formality. Tess wouldn't refuse her.

"Only if you bring ice cream," Tess sang through the phone.

"Done. I'll be there in twenty." She rushed into her bedroom and plucked an outfit from her closet, along with a pair of shoes for the morning in case she stayed later than expected and ended up sleeping over.

She loved the fact that Tess lived close and she could go by anytime. She sometimes wondered why they didn't live together— share the same house, just not the same bed. That always came back to their different dating lifestyles. Blair needed her space to bring women home when she wanted, and Tess needed her serenity. She also worried that Tess might be appalled by the number of women she dated. So, it was a no-go on the living-together situation. Besides, Tess had a spare bedroom, and she'd made it clear that Sophie could use it anytime, which she did.

She drove through The Point, a local, privately owned restaurant and creamery. As usual, after seeing the juicy burgers and fries on the menu, she couldn't resist ordering them. She'd been eating a lot of greens for lunch lately, so she felt okay with it. She also got the usual double scoop of strawberry ice cream in a cup for herself and a hot-fudge sundae with two cherries for Tess to put in the freezer for later. As soon as Tess got a whiff of the burger, she'd want half, and Sophie would gladly split it with her to save herself from a stomach explosion during the night. The fries she might fight Tess for.

She pulled into Tess's driveway and gathered up the food from the front seat of her car. She left the clothes she'd brought lying on the back seat. She'd get them later or in the morning if she decided to stay the night. After letting herself into the house, she unpacked the food and placed the ice cream in the freezer.

Tess appeared in the kitchen like the stealthiest of ninjas and peeked over her shoulder. "You got a burger?" She sounded like a child who'd just had her Halloween candy taken away.

Sophie smiled as she nodded. "Split it with me?"

Tess groaned. "If I must." She took a knife from the block and handed it to her.

Next, Sophie took two small plates from the cabinet and divided the fries between them, snagging a couple as she plated them. They were always mouthwateringly hot and crispy right out of the bag. Tess didn't always eat the fries, but Sophie had gotten the family size just in case. She wouldn't deprive her of such a treat.

They sat adjacent to each other at the kitchen table, which had an extended view of the TV. It looked like Tess had been watching one of the late-night shows, but it was too early for that. She avoided the news like the plague—felt it was too depressing for such a soft soul to deal with daily. If something was going on in the world Tess needed to be aware of, Sophie kept her informed.

Tess stared at the screen as she ate silently, which was unusual. "Is this a special?"

"Last night's show. I recorded it."

"Who's on?" It had to be someone interesting, or Tess would've turned it off when she got there.

"Emily Blunt."

She grinned. "Setting those sights pretty high, aren't you?"

Tess didn't veer her eyes as Emily appeared on the screen. "Isn't she gorgeous?"

"I can't disagree with you there. You know she's married, right? And straight." She took a bite of her burger and enjoyed the deliciousness of it.

Tess raised an eyebrow. "Stop crushing my dreams."

She dropped her burger to the plate and pressed a napkin to her lips. "I had no idea you were so serious about her. Let's move to the UK and devise a plan to make her yours." She raised her eyebrows.

"Or better yet, New York. I think she has a home there, and that's three thousand miles closer."

Tess laughed so hard her food threatened to tumble from her mouth. She covered it and scrambled for her napkin. "I'm too late again, as usual."

"To be fair, I think you were involved with someone else when she got married. So you can't blame her for moving on."

"True."

"That doesn't mean you can't adore her from afar."

Tess narrowed her eyes. "And wait in the shadows until her marriage crumbles into dust and she's free again."

"I don't see that happening, but you can still dream." She stood and took their empty plates to the dishwasher and loaded them, then retrieved their ice cream from the freezer.

Tess followed her and grabbed a couple of spoons from the kitchen drawer. "So what's going on with Blair?"

"Nothing. Absolutely nothing." She handed Tess her sundae and continued to the couch.

Tess trailed her closely. "Explain that to me."

"I feel like I've done something wrong. She keeps canceling on me, and it's irritating as fuck." She flopped onto the couch and spooned a chunk of ice cream into her mouth.

Tess flopped down next to her, and the cushion dipped, moving her closer. "Or maybe she has a job with deadlines." She bumped her with her shoulder. "You know, like we do?"

"Could be." She swirled her spoon in her ice cream. "But when I asked her about her job last night, she flat-out ignored me."

"Ignored you, how?"

"No response, and then she immediately went offline."

"Hmm." Tess spooned a bit of fudge into her mouth and seemed to contemplate her next words before she swallowed. "I wonder what that's about."

"I don't know, but it's very frustrating." She looked up at the ceiling. "I can't do this on my own. I need your help. I'm not sure I have enough patience for it."

"It takes time to form relationships. It's not always sunshine and roses." Tess plucked the cherry from the top of her sundae, then pulled it from its stem with her teeth.

"Probably why I've never stayed in one."

"Let me ask you something. Do you remember the first time you fell in love?"

Her stomach clenched. "Yes." She did, and the pain of the breakup still stung after all these years.

"Think about all the things you know now that you didn't know then."

"That's a huge list." She'd been so young and inexperienced.

"Right? What would you do differently?"

"Everything." She wouldn't get involved with someone so much older than herself, which was funny because she dated much younger women all the time.

"I'm sure there are some things you'd want to keep the same." Tess reached over and touched her hand lightly. "Like your first time with her or your first kiss."

A jolt shot through her as she thought of it. "Yes. Those were good. Awkward, but good."

"Okay. Now think about how you felt. Give me some words to describe it."

"It was weird. I never thought it would happen the way it did."

"That's all you remember?"

"You asked for reality. We were outside and it was cold. I was pressed up against a building. It was a make-out session with lots of hand movement in all the wrong places." She shrugged. "It was exciting and awkward at the same time. I can't really change the circumstances to romanticize it."

Tess giggled. "I guess not."

"I suppose yours was better?"

"My first kiss was with you. Remember that night we were watching TV in your apartment?"

"Right." She blew the word out. "You hadn't kissed anyone before and wanted to know what it was like." She remembered the awkwardness of kissing her. Tess was young for her age and curious—an explosive combination. Sophie had kissed her but couldn't be the one to give her more experience on that, or they'd never have remained friends. "It was a good kiss, right?"

"Yeah." She let out a quick breath. "I caught your cold and was sick for a week after."

She couldn't hold her laugh. "I totally forgot about that." She nudged her with her shoulder. "I gave you the full girlfriend experience."

"You sure did. I had to cancel my date for the weekend because of it."

"Oh my gosh. I forgot that's why you wanted to practice." She grinned. "I'm sorry. I ruined your date."

"No, you're not."

"You're right. I hated that girl. She would've broken your heart."

"Yeah. I heard she hooked up with someone else that very night we were supposed to go out, and I never heard from her again."

"So your first kiss was pretty good then, right?"

"Sure. Aside from the fever and congestion—*and* all the extra homework I had to do from missing my classes."

"You survived—got your degree. Didn't you?" They'd met in college. Tess started right out of high school, and Sophie had gone back after realizing she needed an education to succeed in her career. "Next time I promise to do your homework for you." She leaned forward and puckered her lips.

"Not happening. You're just going to drop me for your online paramour."

"Ha! You know me too well." She cupped her hands under her boobs. "Someone's got to give this basket of goodies some attention, right?"

"Oh my God. You're terrible." Tess's cheeks reddened.

"All I know is if I don't get my muffin buttered soon, my vagina is going to shrivel up."

Tess laughed—a huge unfiltered laugh—and Sophie couldn't help the grin that spread across her face.

"We'll make sure Blair is interested in your basket of goodies—and your muffin."

"You're my favoritest, bestest friend ever." She pulled her into a hug and squeezed her tightly.

"I know. Who else would let me practice kissing with them?" She held up her finger. "But you have to promise me you won't use any of those ridiculous terms for your body parts when you flirt with Blair, or this whole thing is off."

"Aw." She frowned the fakest frown she could make. "You take all the fun out of it."

"Save it for when she's totally in love with you and won't dump you because of it."

She grinned. "Deal."

"What's on your list to ask her?"

"Where she grew up. Where she lives now. Where she works?"

Tess wrote them down on a pad she picked up from the table. "I'm adding does she have a big family and is she close with them? That will tell you a lot about her, and people you'll have to contend with in the future if this works out. Also, has she been in many relationships, and when did her last one end."

"And if she asks me the same, I'm going to say *never* because I don't do relationships well."

Tess smiled and drew a line through that one. "So, maybe we leave the relationship questions out for now. Until you think it might be serious. Okay?"

She nodded. "Okay."

Sophie honestly didn't know what she'd do without Tess. She'd been in her life for so long, she knew everything about her and accepted her for who she was. She couldn't say that about many people, including her own family. Tess was her family.

Chapter Eleven

Tess had barely had time to make it home and change her clothes when she heard Sophie come through the door of her house and chant, "Honey, I'm home." They'd taken a break last night, since Tuesday was her soak-in-the-tub, self-care night, but had planned to have dinner and then continue working on some phrases she could use for Blair tonight.

"Be right there." She sighed at her reflection. *Not getting any better than this.* She twisted her hair into a messy bun and fastened it with a clip before she hung up her dress and met her in the kitchen. "Did you bring me flowers?"

"I brought you something better. Chinese food." Sophie gave her a goofy grin. Still dressed in her navy slacks and light-blue, button-down shirt, she was as breathtaking as always. Even after a long day at work.

"You're such a romantic."

Sophie laughed as she took the multiple boxes of food from the bags. "I got all your favorites."

"Did you bring several people to help eat it as well? This will last for days." She went to the cabinet, took out a couple of plates, and then stopped to grab a handful of spoons from the drawer as she carried them to the table.

"The way this is going, I think I'll be here a lot this week. If not, you'll gain a few pounds eating it without me."

"Just what I need."

"Come on. You're gorgeous, and you know it."

"Sigh. I wish someone besides you would notice that."

"Are you kidding? You get noticed more than anyone I know." Sophie opened the refrigerator and plucked a half-full bottle of white wine from the door. Then she crossed the kitchen to retrieve the glasses from the cabinet.

"By whom?"

"Brandy, for one. Are you ever going to give that poor girl a chance?"

"She is sweet, but she just doesn't do it for me." She spooned out a small helping from each box onto their plates. "Don't get me wrong. She's attractive, has a beautiful smile—seems to be the perfect butch. There's just no spark."

Sophie laughed as she carried the wine and glasses to the table and split what was left in the bottle between them. "Well, you haven't let her get close enough to ignite anything yet, have you?"

"Trust me. I can tell." She wrangled a bite of lo mein noodles with her chopsticks. "Besides. Look who's talking. Miss Noncommittal."

"Hey. At least I'm trying, aren't I?"

"With some crazy catfish you might never see."

"One must have faith, grasshopper."

"Yeah. Well, so far she hasn't inspired much of that in me." She spooned more cashew chicken onto her plate. "She'd better stop blowing you off, or she and I are going to have words." It was already mid-week, and Sophie had told her that Blair hadn't been in contact since Monday night. She seemed to be busy more often than she was free.

"Aw. I love it when you get protective." Sophie grinned as she took a bite of broccoli beef. "Don't worry. She gets one more chance, and that's it."

"You've been more tolerant with her than you have with anyone." She took another bite of her food, chewed, and swallowed. "I think she intrigues you."

"Maybe." Sophie took a sip of wine. "I think it's mostly curiosity now. I want to match the words with a face."

"What if she's not attractive or looks like the bride of Frankenstein?"

Sophie raised an eyebrow. "That would be a dream come true. Elsa Lanchester is gorgeous."

"Bad example, but you know what I mean. She might not be beautiful on the outside."

"You know I'm not that superficial." Sophie dated all types of women. Many were beautiful, but some not so much.

"That's true. I hope you haven't built Blair up so high in your imagination that she can't possibly compare."

"Considering our last few communications, she's not even close to anything like that."

"Good." She finished the last of her food. "Did you get fortune cookies?"

"Just a few." Sophie dumped a bag of cookies onto the table. "Guess they thought we were having a party." She reached for a random cookie.

Tess put her hand on Sophie's. "You know the rules. You have to choose the one facing you."

"Which one is that again? They all look like they're facing me."

She pointed to one closer to Sophie. "The one where the two pointed ends, not the rounded part, is facing you. And don't rip it. If you do that, your fortune won't come true."

"Yes, dear." Sophie cracked open the fortune cookie and laughed before she read it aloud. "You will soon find a new relationship."

Tess raised an eyebrow. "Well, it's not wrong."

"Total BS." Sophie pushed the pile of the cookies toward her. "Let's see what yours says."

She plucked one that was pointing toward her from the center of the pile and broke it open. "Love is around the corner."

Sophie chuckled. "Brandy's around a corner, *somewhere*."

She tossed it onto the table. "You're right. Total BS." She grabbed Sophie's bag and slipped the fortune into her wallet. "You have to keep the fortune, or it won't come true."

Sophie swiped Tess's fortune from the table and pinned it to the refrigerator with a magnet. "That goes for you too."

As Tess cleared the table, Sophie began gathering all the containers of leftover food and placing them in the refrigerator. "Do you ever get tired of me…I mean coming over all the time—feeding me?"

"Technically you fed me tonight." She slid the plates into the dishwasher.

"I know I bought it, but we always end up here at your house."

"I don't mind going over to your house, if that's what you're getting at."

"No. Not getting at that at all. My house is a complete mess right now."

"Don't you have a cleaning service?"

Sophie shrugged. "I do, but she stopped showing up, and they never sent anyone else."

Tess flipped the dishwasher closed and put her hand on her hip. "You slept with her, didn't you?"

"Possibly, but it's not like I treated her badly. I told her from the start I didn't want to commit."

"I know there's more to it than that. Tell me."

"Fine. She showed up one morning before my night-before left." Sophie scrunched her eyebrows together. "In my defense, she gave me no notice, and it wasn't her usual cleaning day."

"Someday, you're going to have to stop juggling women like they're interchangeable."

"Not until I find the right one." Sophie's phone chimed. "Maybe that's her now." She snatched her phone from the table and read the message. "Blair wants me to FaceTime with her." Her eyes widened. The terror in Sophie's face was clear.

Panic rushed through Tess. She was worried for Sophie and the outcome of this situation, but she nodded anyway. "Go ahead."

"No. I can't."

"Why not?"

"It's too early. I haven't even talked to her on the phone. Plus, I'm at *your* house."

"She won't know that, and after all the blow-offs, don't you want to make sure she's a real woman?"

"What if she doesn't find me attractive?"

"Where's that coming from? You're beautiful." She'd never once heard Sophie's confidence falter.

"Not as beautiful as I used to be." Sophie dropped onto the couch and dropped her phone onto the coffee table. "It doesn't matter anyway. My phone is almost dead."

"Stop that right now. You're the most gorgeous woman I've ever known—and I've met some real stunners."

"You're just saying that because you're my best friend and you love me." Sophie stared up at her, and Tess couldn't recall a time when she'd seen her so insecure.

"I do love you, but you're still beautiful, inside and out. So much so that I wonder why someone hasn't snatched you up already."

Sophie veered her gaze back to her phone. "That's my fault. I guess I wasn't ready to be snatched until now."

That was news Tess hadn't expected. It was clear she had to encourage Sophie to talk to Blair, even though she wasn't sure that was the right move. "So, you haven't spoken to Blair on the phone yet?"

"No." Sophie scrunched her eyebrows as she spoke. "I can't even get her to communicate with me in writing. Besides, do you think I can carry on a conversation without inserting flirty banter and sexual innuendo?"

Tess smiled. Sophie clearly knew her limitations. She was relieved to hear that Sophie hadn't been talking to her. But she still worried that Blair wasn't who she said she was. Everything was still pretty vague. Decision time—Tess grabbed her phone from the counter, turned off the caller ID, and handed it to Sophie. "You can't look at me while you're talking to her." This way she'd at least have Blair's phone number so she could give her a piece of her mind if she continued to string Sophie along.

"What did you do? Did you set it to record or something?"

"No. That would be invasive. I turned off my caller ID so she wouldn't have my number instead of yours." She might like vintage things, but that didn't mean she wasn't tech savvy.

"Oh. Gotcha. I'll get her number." Sophie's fingers worked the keys on her phone. After a minute or two it chimed again.

She pulled the club chair adjacent to the couch to where it was on the other side of the coffee table facing Sophie. Then she went back to the kitchen and took a pad and pen from one of the drawers before she flopped into the chair.

"Ready?"

"As I'll ever be." Tess relaxed into the chair. "Remember. Don't look at me when you're talking. I'll hold the pad right above the phone. Try to be nonchalant about it when you read it."

Sophie typed in the number and hit the FaceTime button.

It rang only once and then, "Good evening." A low, throaty voice came through the speaker.

"Hi. I wasn't expecting your voice to be so...low." And ridiculously sexy.

"And I wasn't expecting yours to be so sweet." Blair laughed. "I'm teasing. You have a lovely voice."

"I don't know about that." She glanced at Tess, and she nodded. "But thank you."

"It's great to actually hear your voice. It fits perfectly with your words. I'm glad you called."

"Same." The reflexive term came out of Sophie's mouth.

Tess pulled her eyebrows together, wrote something on the pad, and held it up.

"I mean, it's really good to hear yours as well, after imagining it for so long."

It really wasn't very long, but whatever. Sophie had added the last part herself.

"Are you watching TV? You seem distracted."

"Can you hold on for just a minute?" Sophie paused the call. "She knows something weird is going on here."

"Tell her you're watching the sunset."

She nodded and took the call off hold. "No. I'm actually looking at the sky. There's a wonderful sunset this evening."

"Oh. Let me go look."

Tess rushed around to Sophie's side, just out of view, to see if she could catch a glimpse of Blair while she was moving about. She saw several decorations on the wall, including hanging verse canvases she recognized, in the background as Blair walked to the window. She wondered where in her home she'd been talking from before. The sun's glow on her face was perfect. Blair wasn't a catfish at all. She was absolutely beautiful. Long, auburn hair flowed across her shoulders, a petite nose, full lips, and—Blair turned back toward the screen, and Tess stumbled backward. Gorgeous sea-green eyes.

"Has anyone ever told you how beautiful you are?" Sophie seemed to be finding her own voice.

She gave her a thumbs-up, but Sophie didn't look at it. She remained focused on the screen, clearly mesmerized by the woman she was communicating with.

"Yes, but it's nice to hear it from you." Blair's voice was soft and smooth.

Tess cringed. Not the modest or self-deprecating response she'd hoped to hear.

"You have beautiful eyes. Almost the color of copper in the sunlight."

Blair was right about that. Tess glanced at Sophie's eyes and took in the light, flaky, starburst nuances of them, along with the bold brown outline surrounding them. She hadn't noticed that before. They were indeed beautiful.

"I want to see them—I want to see you in person."

Absolutely not. Tess shook her head and waved wildly at Sophie.

"I'm pretty busy at work right now."

"We could meet for coffee." Suddenly Blair sounded a bit desperate.

"Or a drink at The Speak Easy?"

Tess narrowed her eyes and wrote NO in huge letters and held it up. Too many drinks with Sophie would only lead to sex. And this wasn't about sex.

"Coffee would be better." Blair didn't seem to like the idea of meeting at a bar either.

Tess held up the pad and mouthed an emphatic NO above the phone at her again.

Sophie glanced up and then back at the screen. "I'll need to check my schedule."

"I get the feeling you don't trust me." Blair frowned.

"Why would you say that?"

"Well, you're hesitant about meeting me, and your number is blocked."

"Oh." Sophie glanced at Tess above the phone.

She scribbled quickly on the pad and held it up.

Sophie read what she had written, then focused on the screen again. "This is my work phone, and I'm not lying. I'm extremely busy with a project at work. I spend any free time I have right now eating, sleeping, or messaging with you."

She could see Blair smile. She seemed to be satisfied with Sophie's answer. She wrote something new and held the note up above the phone.

"I don't want to be worried about time when we meet." Sophie closed her eyes momentarily before she continued. "I want it to be endless."

Tess sighed at the addition. Sophie really was a romantic at heart. She set the pad on the table and remained on standby while Sophie continued her conversation with Blair.

CHAPTER TWELVE

Here we go again. Sophie thumbed through a client file and listened as Tess and Joy battled over creative control. Work would be so much easier if Joy would just let Tess do her job the way it was meant to be done. As it was now, Joy would take the micromanager-of-the-year award easily.

"You have no idea how much money I've put into this company—how strapped I am because of it." Joy was practically shrieking now.

"Then you're going to get what you pay for, and that isn't much." Tess countered, her voice level slipping into a higher pitch.

Others in the office were gathering at the door to watch the showdown. Not that it was new or anything, but when it happened, it was always a blowout.

"It is what it is." Joy's voice lowered as she noticed the crowd.

"You're going to lose every single client we have if you keep that attitude."

"I'm not going to continue this battle with you. If you don't like it"—Joy raised her hand and pointed to the door, but didn't look at anyone besides Tess—"you're welcome to find employment elsewhere."

"Are you firing me?" Tess's eyes widened as her hands went to her hips.

"Not yet, but if you can't get a handle on your budget, I'll have to reconsider."

"Maybe I should reconsider." Tess moved closer, coming at Joy hot. "I don't even—"

"Stop." Sophie dropped the file onto the desk as she bolted from her seat and stepped between them. "Go home, Tess. I'll come over later and we'll rework this."

"Fine." Tess ripped open her drawer, tugged her purse from it, and rushed out the door, scattering everyone as she moved through it.

Sophie followed Tess to the office door and closed it. "Don't you think that was a little harsh?"

"That wasn't even close to what I wanted to say."

"You need to lighten up on her. She can't work under this pressure. Her creativity sucks under stress."

"Why are you always protecting her, even though she's completely capable of a standing up for herself?"

"She's my partner. She'd do the same for me."

"I know she would, and that's a problem. You need to step back and look at the situation. Tess doesn't seem to be a good fit here."

"She's a rock star at what she does. You can't deny that. You just don't like her methods. If you'd only trust her, you'd be making a whole lot more money." When it came right down to it, money was where it lived with Joy.

"Maybe so. We seem to disagree on most everything, but you're letting your personal feelings for Tess cloud your judgment. I honestly don't think she even wants to work in marketing. At least not this piece of it."

"That's bullshit, and you know it. She loves her job. If you'd stop making it so difficult for her, she'd be fine."

"Correction. She loves working with *you*." Joy shook her head. "She's in love with you, and you take advantage of that fact."

"That's absurd. Tess could never be in love with me." And if she was, Sophie would never take advantage of it.

Joy let out a short laugh. "That's a thought you might want to reconsider. When's the last time Tess dated—spent any time with anyone other than you?"

It had been a while. She crinkled her nose. "That's just because we've been working so much." Plus, Tess had been helping her communicate with Blair. They'd been together almost every night this week.

"Is it? It's not like she hasn't had people ask. I've heard her on the phone declining offers. The only time she goes out at all is with you."

"We have fun together. We're just friends." They were, weren't they? She *had* been monopolizing a lot of Tess's time lately.

Joy raised her eyebrows. "If you say so, but it sounds like the feeling's mutual."

"Just let her alone, Joy. She needs this job."

"I want her to take the next week off." Joy held up a hand. "Don't worry. She'll still get paid. You can work this next one up alone." Joy spun and walked to the door. "I'll call her this evening and let her know."

"No. I'll tell her." Sophie gathered up her laptop and rushed out the door. Some of what Joy said made sense. It couldn't be true, though. If Tess was in love with her, why would she be helping her romance another woman? Why would Tess spend every moment of her free time helping her get closer to Blair? Why would she stay in a job she hated? Would Tess do that just to be close to her? Would *she* do that just to remain close to Tess? She groaned as the sinking feeling hit her stomach. Yes. She would. She would be miserable without Tess. Was that what love was? True, she enjoyed Tess's company more than anyone else's. But she'd never thought of Tess in a romantic sense…before now.

When she drove out of the parking lot, she immediately hit the speed dial for Tess and weaved through traffic as it rang through her car speakers.

"If Joy cuts corners on this one, I don't know what I'm going to do." Tess was still pissed.

Sophie immediately wanted to go to Tess to calm her down, but Joy's words about the relationship between them rang in her head. "Why don't we take a break tonight? Start fresh in the morning." She would wait until later to tell her that Joy wanted her to take a few days off.

"I'm all in for that." Tess blew a breath into the phone. "We can grab some dinner and then catch a movie or something."

"I think I'll just go home."

"Oh. All right." The disappointment in Tess's voice was clear. "I can just work on some things for you to say to Blair."

Again, why would Tess be helping her with Blair? Maybe what Joy had said was completely wrong. She shook it off. She wasn't going to let Joy ruin her friendship with Tess. "No. On second thought, let's take a break from that too. Your idea to grab a quick dinner and then see a late movie is just what we need tonight."

"I haven't been to the movies in forever." Tess's voice immediately lightened. She was always so easy to please. "What sounds good to you?"

"You pick."

"There's that romantic comedy playing that I've been wanting to see."

Not Sophie's first choice. She was more into suspense than romantic comedies. "Okay. Sure. Where for dinner?"

"Your turn. I chose the movie."

"Italian sounds wonderful, but it has to somewhere I can get something light, or I'll be asleep halfway through the movie."

"If you're tired, we can just order in and watch something on TV."

"Nope. Not that I don't love your decor, but we need a change of scenery. How about The Tavern?"

"Ohh." She widened her eyes. "That's one of my favorites, but it's kind of pricey."

"No worries. My treat." It was a fast-casual restaurant, and they'd be able to get in and out within an hour. "If you'll check the movie times, I'll make a reservation and pick you up in an hour." She needed to go home and change.

"Sounds great. I'll see you then."

She ended the call and then held down the home button on her phone and told Siri to call The Tavern. Once she'd made the reservation, she veered into the closest Starbucks to get a cup of coffee. It was going to be a late night.

CHAPTER THIRTEEN

The movie was getting close to the happily-ever-after part when Tess felt Sophie lean into her shoulder. She was asleep, as usual. Sophie rarely made it to the end of a movie in a theater, even when it was one she'd picked out, unless it was an afternoon matinee, which they took in on occasion, ditching work under the guise of doing research. They spent a fair amount of time working offsite without telling Joy where they were to avoid her unwanted input.

She shifted closer to let Sophie rest her head on her shoulder and then enjoyed the end of the movie with soft, breathy snores whispering in her ear. For romantic comedies, she always imagined herself in the place of one of the characters. Tonight she imagined Sophie as the other, which was new. Her heart warmed as she watched the couple reunite and share a final passionate kiss before going back to their lives hand in hand.

Completely satisfied with the future promise that came at the ending of the movie, she took a deep breath as the credits rolled. Would she and Sophie ever get through all their struggles in life to finally find their happily-ever-afters? Would they have that together, or would they each still be searching for something that didn't exist outside of what they already had? Would exploring anything between them destroy their friendship that had withstood all of life's struggles?

She admitted that the thought had entered her mind before, and she'd always tossed it out easily, aware of Sophie's fear of commitment. This time it was becoming more of a challenge to dismiss. During the past few days, while helping Sophie with her new paramour, she was seeing a whole new person—one that seemed to be ready to settle into a permanent relationship. Would it be selfish if she stopped Sophie from meeting Blair?

Sophie began to stir as other people stood and moved through the aisles to leave. "I'm sorry. I fell asleep." Sophie pulled her eyebrows together as she stared up at her. The regret in her eyes clear. "Was it good?"

Tess nodded. "No worries." She kissed her forehead. The movie wasn't even the best part of the night. "Come on. Let's get you home and into bed."

On more than one occasion they ended up in one car, leaving from one another's house. And it was the same tonight. Tess would take Sophie home with her, and she would stay over in her very own bedroom Tess had created just for her.

❖

Tess couldn't sleep. Every time she closed her eyes, she and Sophie appeared behind her lids in bold, vivid color, living the happy ending of the movie they'd seen tonight. She was deep into rethinking the story when she heard a noise in the hallway. She slipped her feet into her slippers, took her robe from the bottom of the bed, put it on, and headed into the hallway.

The darkened figure she saw standing in front of her door startled her. *Sophie.* "Hey. What are you doing up?"

"I don't know. My eyes just popped open, and now I can't get back to sleep. Maybe I should head home."

She wasn't dressed to leave. She seemed as though she was waiting for Tess outside her bedroom door. That was silly. Why would she be doing that? She shook the thought from her head. "How about we have some tea? Maybe that will help you relax."

"As long as it's caffeine-free. I think the coffee I had earlier is doing a number on me."

"I bought chamomile." She tied her robe as she headed into the kitchen. "It's commonly regarded as somewhat of a sleep inducer."

With everything in such an uproar at work, she'd been having a bit of insomnia herself lately.

While she grabbed the box of tea bags from the pantry, Sophie took the electric tea kettle to the sink and filled it with water, then set it back on its base and pressed the heating button. Tess retrieved a couple of mugs from the cabinet and dropped a tea bag into each one. Sophie carried them to the table and waited for her to bring the kettle. While she was waiting for the water to boil, Tess found a box of ginger cookies and took them to the table.

"My favorite." Sophie gave her a huge smile.

"I know." Tess warmed. It felt good to make Sophie happy.

It seemed like it was taking forever for the water to boil, but then the lever flipped, indicating the water was hot. Tess grabbed the kettle, took a seat at the table adjacent to Sophie, and poured the steaming water into each cup. She let the bag steep for a couple of minutes before she blew on her tea and took a sip. Sophie did the same, and they sat in awkward silence. This was weird, because silence had never felt awkward between them before.

"So, why were you up?" Sophie took a bite of cookie and washed it down with another drink of her tea.

"I kept thinking about the ending of the movie." She blew on her tea before she took a sip, letting the warmth fill her mouth.

"The part where they kissed?"

"You saw that? I thought you were asleep."

"I was." Sophie hesitated and sipped her tea. "They always kiss at the end."

"Not always, but most of the time. Do you ever think we'll find someone like that?"

"You probably will." Sophie tilted her head. "Me? I doubt it."

"Why do you think that?"

"I'm too old and set in my ways." Sophie plucked another cookie from the package, broke it, and popped a piece into her mouth.

As she reached over and snagged a piece of the cookie, she noticed Sophie staring at her. She glanced down to see that her robe had come open and her cleavage was making a grand appearance from her silk camisole. She heated all over, her neck and chest probably red as a raspberry right now. Sophie had sneaked glances of her boobs before, and it had never affected her this way. She wasn't sure why it was happening now. She picked up her cup and placed it strategically in front of her. Sophie immediately shifted her eyes to her own cup, picked it up, and took a sip, while looking anywhere but at Tess. It was evidently affecting Sophie differently as well.

"Do you want to come to bed with me?"

Sophie's eyes snapped back to hers. "What?"

"I mean, come to bed to talk more." What the hell was she saying? "Or just sleep." Suddenly she was very nervous.

"No." Sophie stood abruptly, took her cup to the dishwasher, and loaded it. "I'm going to head home and take a shower."

"It's two o'clock in the morning." She crossed the room and loaded her cup in the dishwasher as well. "You can do that here—in the morning."

"I might as well go now." She yawned. "I'll need fresh clothes."

"You have clothes in the closet of your room." It was technically the guest room, but Sophie was the only one who ever used it.

"I do?" Sophie scrunched her eyebrows together and then headed down the hallway.

"You've left a few things here, now and then." She followed her into the bedroom. "I washed and hung them. You practically have a whole wardrobe here now."

She took out a pale-green button-down. "I've been wondering where this was." She took out a long-sleeved, scoop-neck navy cotton shirt and held it up. "This one too."

"There are a couple pairs of pants too." She plucked them from the bottom rung. "I ironed them."

"Tess…you really didn't have to do that. I don't even iron my clothes." Sophie laughed and examined the crease of the pant legs. "It's perfect."

"I know. I can tell." She grinned. "I probably should've given them back a while ago, but I keep forgetting and figured you'd need them again on the occasion you were too tired to drive. Like tonight."

"Some girl's going to hit the jackpot with you, Tess."

"Well, I don't know about that, but I *do* have a few tricks up my sleeve to keep a woman happy." Her cheeks heated as Sophie stared at her. It seemed they were having a moment.

Sophie cleared her throat. "The exact words a woman wants to hear before she gets into bed." She grinned and winked as she took the pants from her and hung them back in the closet, along with the shirts.

"Yes. I'm sure they are." She spun and crossed the hall to her room. "Get some sleep. I'll see you in the morning." Like that was even possible now after that little exchange. Tomorrow was going to be a bitch of a day.

CHAPTER FOURTEEN

Sophie sat on Tess's couch and stared blankly at her laptop screen. She'd had to drink a gallon of coffee at work today just to keep herself focused. Thank God it was Friday and she'd have the weekend to recover. She absolutely hadn't been able to sleep last night with the scent of Tess filling her head. The pillowcases, the sheets, even the T-shirt she'd borrowed to sleep in were everything Tess. Being there had completely aroused her like never before. She hadn't really slept through the end of the movie. She'd dozed on Tess's shoulder but had woken after just a few moments. She'd felt so comfortable she hadn't wanted to move, but she couldn't tell Tess that. She might get the wrong idea…or maybe it was the right idea.

According to Joy, Tess's feelings were obvious. She'd never considered Tess as a sexual partner before yesterday, and now she couldn't stop thinking about it. Every part of her had tingled as she'd thought about the possibilities of lying in bed next to Tess last night, pressing up against her soft curves, and doing so much more. It had been enlightening but also excruciating. It had taken all her willpower to say no to her invitation to come to bed and talk more—not take advantage of the situation. More than talk would've taken place if she'd gone to Tess's bed. The throb between her legs had made that clear. She couldn't do that. Not with Tess. That might literally break their friendship in two.

She had to get Tess out of her thoughts somehow. With Blair— she would shake what Joy said from her head and focus solely on

Blair from now on. She didn't know why she'd let Joy get to her in the first place. She was rarely right about anything.

Joy had taken the day off, so work today had been uneventful, calm even, but she hadn't had the opportunity today to tell Tess that Joy wanted her out of the office next week. She'd promised herself she would tell her tonight. She settled into the couch and took in a deep breath. "So, hey." She glanced at Tess and then back at her computer. "Joy wants you to take next week off."

"What? Then what are we going to do about this next client?" Tess sank onto the couch next to her. "She wants you to do it alone. Doesn't she?"

"Yes, but I wouldn't do that to you. We'll still work on it together." She smiled softly. "You both need a little space. I'll just come over after I get done at the office, and we'll deal with it."

"It's okay. You can do it without me if you want."

"No. I don't want that. We're in this together. I need you, Tess." She took Tess's hand and squeezed.

Tess immediately released it and went into the kitchen to pour them a couple of glasses of wine.

"I made a list of words you said that I should and shouldn't use in conversations with Blair." She was still uncomfortable with her ability to communicate appropriately with Blair, and Tess was great at keeping her words on the classy side. Her computer chimed, and a message from Blair popped up. Just two words.

Call me.

"She's messaging me now."

"What'd she say?" Tess's voice echoed from the kitchen.

"She wants to talk on the phone again."

"FaceTime?"

"She didn't say that. What should I do?"

"Call her."

A shiver ran through her. The last call had been stressful enough. "Really?"

"Really. You can have a simple conversation with her. Can't you?" Tess sat down next to her and handed her a glass of wine. "I was worried last time, but you did great."

"I don't know. What if I get tongue-tied and mess it up?" She took a drink of wine.

"I have never seen you once mess anything up with a woman."

"Fine." She took in a deep breath to settle herself. Her heart was racing like a Ferrari at the Grand Prix. She found Blair's number in her phone, which she'd added to her contacts after their FaceTime call. She hit the call button and put it on speaker.

Blair answered immediately, "Hello, beautiful." Her familiar, low, sultry voice came through the speaker.

"Hello." That was all Sophie could muster. She didn't know why.

"So, I'm curious. Tell me about what you do." Blair jumped right into conversation.

"I sway people's opinions about products." Total truth. When it came right down to it, that's what marketing entailed.

"Oh, really?" Another sexy nuance of Blair's voice rang through.

She imagined what that sexy voice would sound like in the throes of sex. Tess snapped her out of that thought when she bumped her on the shoulder and pointed to the pad of paper.

"That's a fancy way of saying I'm in marketing."

"No need to be fancy with me." Blair let out a throaty laugh that totally went with her voice, and it hit Sophie right in her midsection. A good sign.

Tess scribbled more words, and she read them, shook her head, and mouthed no.

Tess wrote yes in all caps.

Sophie rolled her eyes. "Can I admit something to you?"

"Of course."

"I'm usually pretty confident around women, but you make me nervous."

"Really? Why?"

"You just seem so…elegant."

"I'm flattered that you think so, but I'm just me. Nothing fancy. Okay?"

"Okay." That exchange helped her confidence a bit. She took in a breath and smiled at Tess. "Now tell me about what *you* do."

"I'm in the business of making people happy."

"Well, that sounds rewarding." A little ambiguous, but it was something.

"It's *very* rewarding." Blair's voice rose. "Describe to me your ideal weekend. Where would you go? What would you do?"

That was an abrupt subject change. "Are you a travel agent? Trip planner?"

"Just tell me."

She glanced at the pad of paper. Tess had written "avoidance" in all caps, and she agreed but wasn't ready to call Blair on it. "I'd take three days at the Palm Coast Club Resort to do nothing but relax on the beach, maybe play a round of golf, and eat everything on each restaurant menu."

"Well, then why don't you do it?"

"It's an exclusive club. You either have to be a member or have oodles of money to afford the accommodations."

"I bet I know someone who can get us a couple of rooms there for the weekend."

She looked at Tess and let her mouth drop open. "Really?"

"Really?" She heard some motion in the background and wondered what Blair was doing. "I have a friend who handles the events there. I just sent her a message."

"Wow. That would be—just wow." She glanced at Tess, who pointed to the piece of paper where she'd written a response for her. "I mean, that would be wonderful. It would be my pleasure to spend time with you over a weekend, no matter where we spend it."

"Will next weekend work for you?"

"Um…" She scrunched her eyes at Tess as she scribbled large letters on the paper. "Yes. Absolutely." She said it but wasn't sure about her answer. Suddenly she wasn't feeling as confident about meeting Blair as she'd thought. Her first instinct was to say no.

"Wonderful. I'll make all the arrangements and get back to you." There was more sound in the background, almost like someone else was in the room. "I'm sorry. I have to deal with something. We'll talk again tomorrow night, okay?"

"Sure. You have my number."

The line went dead. No sweet sign-off again, just like when they were messaging. "What do you think that was about?"

"I don't know, but you're going on an all-inclusive weekend-getaway next weekend." Tess clapped her hands, ridiculously excited for her.

She stared at the phone screen and then dropped it to the coffee table. "I don't want to go without you."

"Well, that would be a cozy threesome—one too many, and pretty awkward."

"You could stay in my room with me."

"No. I can't. What if you two end up back in your room? Don't you think she would wonder what was up with that?"

All the time she'd spent with Tess over the past week had done nothing but confuse her about what she wanted in life and who she wanted to have it with. But it seemed that Tess hadn't been wondering about those things at all.

"I guess you're right." She picked up her phone and shifted it from hand to hand. "I'm just afraid that once we're face-to-face, I'm going to blow it." She slid the phone onto the table, bolted from the couch, and paced to the kitchen. "She'll see the real me and be disappointed."

"Oh my gosh, Sophie." Tess twisted and stared up at her from the couch. "She's going to fall in love with you immediately. The *real you* is perfect."

"You think so?" She glanced back at Tess to find some emotion in her eyes, anything at all that told her she was jealous or sad. There was nothing like that—only happiness.

Tess stood, crossed the room to her, and held her by the shoulders. "I know so."

"Come with me. Please?"

"I'd be an unnecessary addition to this outing." Tess touched her cheek, and a jolt shot through her. "You'll be fine." She brushed past her, poured them both more wine, and handed a glass to her. "By the time you get back, Blair will be hopelessly in love with you."

"Maybe." She took a gulp. But would *she* be hopelessly in love with Blair? Was that what she really wanted? She set down her half-full glass of wine. "Time for me to go home."

"Are you okay to drive?"

"I'm fine." She grabbed her purse and fished her keys from it.

"Hey, remember. If you're worried about what to say, don't talk to her until tomorrow."

"I won't." She picked up a pad of paper and pen and wrote down her social-media login and password. "Here's my login information in case you want to send her a message for me." She rushed out the door. It was only a weekend, but she was so confused about her feelings that she didn't want to talk to Blair, let alone see her, at this point.

❖

Sophie had just headed into bed after finishing a couple more ideas for work when a message from Blair popped up on her phone. Tess had told her to ignore any other messages she received tonight. She would help her in the morning. She stared at the first line showing in the pop-up.

I can't sleep. Our weekend...

She cleared the message from her home screen before she dropped the phone on her nightstand and changed into a T-shirt, as she usually did for bed. Then she slid under the covers, turned out the light, and stared at the blank ceiling until her eyes adjusted. The ceiling lit up with the light from her phone. She glanced at the screen—another message. *Damn it.* She picked it up, unlocked it, and read the full messages.

I can't sleep. Our weekend getaway plan has me imagining all sorts of things with you.

I need to know if you're imagining them too.

Bubbles appeared on the screen and disappeared again. Blair appeared to have stopped writing. She dropped the phone beside her on the bed. The room lit up again—another message. She picked it up and read it.

Please answer.

She quickly typed. *Sorry. I was in the shower.* Starting off with a lie wasn't good.

That bar of soap was very fortunate to wash such a beautiful body.

She grinned. She could do banter, even if it was a bit formal. *Honestly, it could've used some help in several areas. Too bad you weren't here.*

That can be remedied.

Panic raced through her, and she dropped the phone like a bolt of lightning had come through it. No way was she giving Blair her address. She took in a deep breath to settle herself before she picked it up again.

I'm intrigued.

She laughed at herself. She *had* learned something from Tess. Sweet, beautiful Tess.

Her phone rang, jarring her out of her thoughts. It was Blair. She hit the green button before she could talk herself out of it.

"Hi there." That was her usual response when answering a phone call from someone she knew. Apparently, she was getting more comfortable with Blair.

"Hello, love." Blair's voice was soft and low. "I have something I want to read to you."

"Okay. Sure." Not quite what she expected.

Wild nights—Wild nights!
Were I with thee
Wild nights should be
Our luxury!
Futile—the winds—
To a Heart in port—
Done with the Compass—
Done with the Chart!
Rowing in Eden—
Ah—the Sea!
Might I but moor—tonight—
In thee!

"Emily Dickinson. One of my favorites." Sophie knew a bit of poetry.

"Here's another." Blair's sexy voice filled her head.

At the touch of you,
As if you were an archer with your swift hand at the bow,
The arrows of delight shot through my body.

Blair hesitated, and Sophie finished reciting the poem.

You were spring,
And I the edge of a cliff,
And a shining waterfall rushed over me.

"Witter Bynner." Sophie smiled, thrilled at herself for remembering the poem.

"That's correct. I wasn't aware there was more to that one. You know your classic poetry."

"I work in advertising. Poetry knowledge is a must." She lied. Any and all poetry she knew was because of Tess. So many times Tess reminded her of the beauty in life—how tastefully it could be described.

"That's right. You told me that. Well, I'm still impressed."

Still impressed? Was that some sort of jab at her profession?

"So…that was just a primer."

"Oh? What's next? Something from Sylvia Plath?"

"No. You've shot me speeding way past poetry…what are you wearing?"

Really? That's where we're going now? A girl could get serious whiplash from this sudden shift of gears. "A T-shirt." She rolled her eyes at herself. What was wrong with her? She was usually much more inventive than that, but she hadn't expected this conversation tonight.

"As soon as I slide into bed with you, that comes off."

"It does, does it?"

"Yes. I grab the edges and rake my nails against your sides as I pull it over your head."

Sophie raked her own nails along her sides. "I like that."

"Good. Your cheeks are flush as I kiss you. I pinch your hard nipples, and you moan. Let me hear it."

She pinched her nipple and moaned, but she wasn't feeling it yet. Why was she letting Blair run this show when she was usually in charge?

"I slip my hand between your legs and feel the heat." She laughed—a low, sultry sound. "You're very wet. Can you feel it on your fingers?"

She reached between her legs. Not wet at all. She had to get her mind in the right space for this. She put the phone on speaker and dropped it onto her chest before she closed her eyes and let her imagination loose. The voice on the phone became softer… sweeter…*Tess*. Wetness coated her fingers.

"You feel my breath against you."

"Yes." Tess's gorgeous blue eyes appeared in front of her as she imagined her dark strands of hair trailing down her belly. "I can't wait to run my fingers through your beautiful dark hair."

"Yes, tangle your fingers in it—tug on it. Pull me closer."

"I want you closer   all over me." The scent of Tess's perfume filled her mind.

"I'm right here, love. Right where you want me. My tongue working my magic on you."

"Absolutely." She could see her lips, her mouth, her tongue… Tess tasting every part of her. "I want your tongue inside me."

"Not yet, love. I'm circling your nipples—sucking them hard into my mouth, then trailing my tongue across your belly."

Deep-blue eyes flashed in her head, darkening as desire overtook them. She let out a long, slow moan.

"There you go. Just like that. I'm going to make you beg for me to let you come."

"Yes. Please let me—make me." Tess between her legs was better than anything she'd ever imagined. "I need to come—now."

"Let go—let it happen."

And she did. Shouting into the empty bedroom, she took herself to an orgasm so strong she almost fell off the bed. *Oh my God.* Her heart thudded. What had she done? She'd just had the most fantastic orgasm imagining Tess had given it to her. There had to be some unspoken rule about that, didn't there? She'd almost shouted Tess's name but bit it back and swallowed it hard.

"I can't wait to have you in my bed." Blair's deep voice resonated through the phone.

When reality hit her, she suddenly felt sick. Blair wasn't the woman she wanted to be with *at all*, but she had to finish what they'd started.

She took a deep breath. "Tell me what you want me to do to you."

"I want you to ravish every part of me."

"My fingers are inside you." For some reason she couldn't say tongue. The thought of that made her cringe.

"Deeper."

"Yes—so deep, the friction of my palm is lighting up your clit."

"Oh my God. Yes. More of that."

Blair seemed to like it dirty, so she continued. "I'm going to fuck you hard."

"And bite my nipple hard…please."

Jesus. No nipple biting, ever. Sucking, possibly nipping, yes. But biting, no. Sophie wasn't into pain. Maybe necks or even shoulders, but only if Blair was on her back and Sophie was making her come so hard she couldn't do anything else.

Her mind wandered as a long, loud moan came through the phone. She couldn't help but wonder if Tess liked it dirty. She shook her head. Tess would never go for anything like that. Would she?

"Baby, that was wonderful."

Baby? When did love change to baby? Something wasn't right about Blair. "It was my pleasure." Not really, but hey, it wasn't Blair's fault she'd had a revelation during her own orgasm.

"How did you know exactly what I like?"

"Um…just guessed." She'd had a fair amount of practice at

phone sex and knew the basics of what most women needed to orgasm. Blair seemed to accomplish it quicker than most. "I need to get some sleep. Big day tomorrow."

"Okay. Listen. I have to get a lot of work done over the next few days. I'm not sure when I'll be able to talk again."

Was she actually getting a blowoff after phone sex? *Whatever.* "Me too." She needed some distance from Blair to figure out what was going on with Tess.

"But I want you thinking of me for the rest of the night."

"How can I not?" That wasn't happening. All she could think about was Tess. Her beautiful blue eyes, her gorgeous smile, and every other part of her. *Shit.* "Good night."

"Good night." Blair's voice was softer and somewhat different.

She hoped she hadn't given herself away, made Blair feel used in any way. She herself could handle that feeling, but she didn't like giving it. That wasn't her intent when this booty call began. Tess flashed through her mind again. But it had certainly turned out that way. Oh, boy. This development was going to be a problem.

CHAPTER FIFTEEN

The pasta rustled out of the box as Tess poured the shells into the boiling water. She dropped in some salt and gave it a quick stir before she turned and took a block of cheese from the refrigerator and set it on the counter in front of Sophie. "Can you grate the Parmesan?" She handed Sophie the grater and a small wooden board. "About half a cup will do. Maybe a touch more."

"On it, chef." She began grating the cheese. "It still amazes me how you can cook without measuring a single ingredient."

"When you cook enough there's really no need unless it's something precise like a cheesecake or soufflé. Guessing at measurements for those would be disastrous."

"Those are safe with me because *if* I ever cook, I always measure." Sophie shuffled the rest of the ingredients around on the counter. Tess had set everything out to make sure they were all at room temperature. They blended so much better that way.

"Then I'll leave the cheesecake-making to you." Tess grinned.

"If I keep up this dinner schedule, I'm going to have to cut cheesecake out of my food choices permanently. I'll probably gain ten pounds before I ever meet Blair face-to-face."

"Ahem. Wasn't it you who requested my special mac and cheese tonight?"

Sophie scrunched her nose up and grinned. "You don't have to give me everything I ask for."

"I don't, do I?" She started gathering the ingredients and headed to the refrigerator.

Sophie rushed around her and blocked her path. "But I need this tonight." She grasped the refrigerator-door handle and pretended to go weak. "I might die without it."

Tess couldn't help but laugh at her antics. Sophie had a way of bringing out the best in any situation, and she didn't mind cooking for her. All it took was milk, cream, cheese, breadcrumbs, and broccoli. She'd had all the ingredients in the house because it was one of her go-to comfort-food meals. It was delicious and super cheesy.

"Well, we can't have that." She set the items on the counter and then sliced a glob of butter and dropped it into the red enameled cast-iron Le Creuset Dutch oven Sophie had given her, then flipped on the stove. She'd thought the gift was much too expensive at the time, but she'd used it more than any other pot in the kitchen.

She melted the butter and whisked in the flour until she created a smooth roux before she added the milk and cream. It was possible to make the dish without the cream, but she loved the velvety texture it added. Stirring the mixture constantly to prevent lumps, she brought it to a simmer. Next came the sharp provolone and Parmesan cheeses. She continued whisking the blend until it was melted and smooth.

"Your turn." She transferred the wooden spoon to Sophie before she took a pinch of salt and sprinkled it over the top.

Sophie stirred the cheesy goodness as Tess scooped the shell pasta out of the water and dropped it into the pot, then spooned in a ladle of pasta water.

"Why do you add the water from the pasta, again?"

"It makes it even creamier."

"Like the cheese and cream didn't do that already."

"It can never be creamy enough for me." She handed Sophie the bowl of broccoli crowns she'd cut and washed earlier. "Now toss these in and give it a good stir."

Once it was all mixed together, she handed Sophie the breadcrumbs. "Sprinkle these on top and put it in the oven. Then we're free to drink wine for the next twenty minutes."

"My favorite kind of dinner." Sophie added the breadcrumbs and carried it to the oven.

"Hang on a minute." Tess tossed a sprinkling of Parmesan cheese on top as well. "That will make it crunchier." She opened the oven door, and Sophie slid the dish inside.

"Creamy and crunchy all in one. The perfect balance."

"Right." Tess closed the oven door and threw up her hand for a high-five from Sophie but was pulled into a hug instead.

"Thank you for always being here for me." Sophie held her tightly and didn't release her right away.

Tess wrapped her arms around her—let Sophie's warmth rush through her. It seemed like they'd been like that for several minutes when Sophie broke free and cleared her throat.

"Sorry. I guess this whole Blair thing is getting to me." Sophie took a bottle of chardonnay from the refrigerator and opened it.

Tess brought the glasses to the counter, and Sophie poured the wine into them. "So, what's going on with Blair?"

"I don't really know." She took a sip of wine. "Our conversation was different last night."

"It sounded fine to me."

"We talked again after I got home." She held up her hand. "I know you told me not to, but she kept texting. I couldn't just ignore her."

Tess was dying to know more but didn't want to seem too eager. She took a drink of wine and then swirled the wine in her glass. "This is good." She picked up the bottle and read the label.

"I thought we'd try something new. The lady at the liquor store recommended it."

Tess set the bottle on the counter and veered her gaze to Sophie. "So, what was different?"

"Well, she wasn't nearly as formal as before, for one." Sophie avoided eye contact as she picked up the bottle and topped off their glasses. "She called me 'baby.'"

She raised an eyebrow. "Really? What were you talking about?"

"We started out discussing poetry. She read me a few poems, which, thanks to you, I actually knew."

"Which ones?"

"The first one was 'Wild Nights.'"

"That's a common one." Emily Dickinson was one of Tess's favorites. "What else?"

"'At The Touch of You.'"

"Witter Bynner. Not so common." Blair could've found that on any obscure erotic poetry site. Tess could only imagine what Blair was hoping to accomplish by reading these poems to Sophie. "And that led to—"

Sophie looked her straight in the eye and then veered her gaze to the glass in her hand. "Nothing. It led to nothing at all."

Not the whole truth, she suspected. "So where did *baby* come from?" She checked the oven timer. Almost done.

"I don't know. She just said it, and I was surprised." Sophie drank the rest of her wine and refilled her glass.

Tess got a sinking feeling in her stomach. Sophie was bad at hiding things from her, and she clearly wasn't being truthful. Something had happened between them that she didn't want to reveal. Whether that something was good or bad, she couldn't tell. Sophie was undoubtably rattled about the whole thing.

"So, where does that leave you with her?"

"It leaves me with a few days before the weekend to think about how I feel." The timer chimed, and Sophie hopped up to grab the oven mitts. "I'll get it. You go sit down."

Tess did exactly that and then watched Sophie take the dish from the oven, bring it to the table, and set it on the hot pad Tess had placed in the corner spot between them. She closed the oven before she turned off the kitchen light and came back to the table while Tess connected her phone to the small Bluetooth speaker on the counter behind them.

Tess had already spread a 1950s flower-patterned tablecloth on the table and set out the plates, silverware, and napkins. She'd accented it with a small, vintage mason jar that contained a mix of summer daisies. Meals were eaten with less formality now than they were in earlier times, but Tess liked the magic that a beautiful table setting brought. It wasn't that much extra work, and it made everything perfect. Sophie, on the other hand, was happy with a balance of candlelight and soft music.

Soft jazz filled the small space as Tess dished out a healthy portion of mac and cheese for each of them. It looked perfect, and she couldn't wait to eat. She relaxed into her chair and waited for Sophie to take the seat adjacent to her.

Sophie brought the wine to the table and refilled their glasses. The bottle was getting low. Tess hadn't realized they had drunk that much. She needed to get some food into herself before the effects of it kicked in.

"This looks wonderful." Sophie dug in immediately and let a soft moan come from her throat as she chewed. "You've outdone yourself once again."

"Thank you." She took a bite and swallowed. "It did turn out pretty good."

"It never tastes this good when I order it out." Sophie glanced up from her plate at her. "Maybe it's the company that makes it better."

"It's definitely the company." Tess's cheeks warmed, and she reached for her wine. Not knowing quite what to say next, she felt the awkward discomfort of silence as she ate. The poems Sophie had mentioned earlier ran through her head. They were much more intense than she would've expected so soon. She had to let it go. She really didn't want to know if Sophie had been intimate with Blair. That would mean her instincts were way off, and that was a huge problem she would have to deal with.

Sophie set down her fork and broke the silence between them. "I hope you know how much I appreciate these dinners we have. You and I." She glanced at her plate. "I don't ever want them to stop."

"You never know. Blair might be a fabulous cook."

"I guess that's possible, but still. I don't want these to end even if she is."

"Well, then we won't let them." Tess was always willing to accommodate Sophie for dinner. Maybe she shouldn't be so easy in the future. Maybe someone else should start filling this role she'd created for herself in Sophie's life. Cutting the cord might be the best thing for Sophie—for both of them.

❖

Tess finished drying and putting away the last of the dishes as Sophie drained the sink and wiped down the counter. They always performed well as a team at work and at home. Even after what Sophie had said about their dinners, Tess knew she might be doing it all alone again soon.

Sophie tossed the sponge into the sink and leaned against the counter. "I wrote something last night. Can I read it to you?"

"Absolutely."

Sophie went to the living room, took her laptop from her bag, and set it on the coffee table. Tess sat beside her as Sophie wrestled through her bag, then opened the laptop and took a piece of paper that had been trapped on the keyboard and handed it to her. "Maybe you should just read it."

"Okay." She stared at Sophie's beautiful handwriting and then began to read the words aloud.

On a cloudy day I'm thinking of you.
Suddenly the sun breaks through.
Emotions running deep and strong.
They cannot be suppressed.
Hope thunders in the midst of desire.
Try as I do, not to overwhelm you, my love.
I simply cannot live without you.
My sunshine on a cloudy day.

Her voice faltered as she pressed her hand to her chest and let the beauty of the words sink in. She hadn't realized Sophie had formed such deep feelings for Blair. She settled herself—tried to get her emotions in check before she spoke. "You wrote this?" she asked softly.

Sophie nodded.

"This is beautiful. Straight from your heart."

Sophie nodded again. "Tess, have you ever been in love?"

"I was in a relationship for three years."

"I know, but you weren't truly, deeply in love, were you?"

"I thought I was, but when I look back on it, there were days when I wasn't sure."

"To me being in love means that nothing else matters."

"Other things have to matter, Soph, or you can't live." She laughed. "Who would pay the mortgage on this Cinderella castle?" She lifted her hands in the air.

"Be serious. That's not what I mean." Sophie threaded her fingers, gripped her hands together, and dropped them into her lap. "What I mean is that *other people* don't matter. You might see a beautiful woman—I mean a really beautiful woman, she might even ask you out, but you're not interested because your heart belongs to someone else. All you want to do is be with *them*. No one else."

"You really have developed some strong feelings." Tess was stunned. How could that have happened so quickly?

Sophie nodded and looked out the window. "And I don't know how to tell her."

"Why don't you just do it?"

"What if she doesn't have those kinds of feelings for me?" Sophie stared out the window. "What if she's dating other people?"

"Then she's crazy—and I'll tell her so." It killed her to see Sophie falling in love with someone else, but she would do everything in her power to help her gain happiness. Even if that meant it wasn't with her.

"What if I'm not really sure what this is? What if it's just infatuation? What if I want to experience you—I mean her first."

You? Her stomach jumped. Was that a mistake or just a true slip of the tongue? "Have I ever read you my favorite poem by e.e. cummings?" She stood and reached for a book on her shelf.

"Is it that one that says something like I carry your heart?"

"No. That one's gone way too commercial."

"Then I don't think you have."

Tess opened the book to a bookmarked page and began to read.

your little voice
   Over the wires came leaping
and i felt suddenly
dizzy
   With the jostling and shouting of merry flowers
were skipping high-heeled flames
courtesied before my eyes
     or twinkling over to my side
Looked up with impertinently exquisite faces
floating hands were laid upon me
I was whirled and tossed into delicious dancing
up
Up
with the pale important
    stars and the Humorous
     moon
dear girl
How i was crazy how i cried when i heard
    over time
and tide and death
leaping
Sweetly
  your voice

Sophie stared at her for a moment. "That's just...well, it's just beautiful."

She nodded. "I hope to be able to feel that with someone someday. I hope you do too."

Sophie grinned. "That's a big ask for someone who's been single most of her adult life."

"Don't discount it, Soph. There's someone out there for you. I know it." She took her hand and held it—let Sophie's warmth wash through her and then brushed it off. "That someone could be Blair."

Sophie glanced at their hands and then stared into her eyes. "I might never find that person, Tess."

Whatever was happening between them seemed much deeper

than friendship. So much deeper than she'd ever experienced within any relationship she'd ever had.

"I know you think that, but have faith." She released Sophie's hand and cleared her throat. "Either way, I'll always be here for you." Considering Sophie's fear of commitment, she knew she might be the only person to remain in Sophie's life for the duration. In which way she wasn't sure at this point. Everything seemed to be changing since Sophie had begun communicating with Blair.

"I know you will. I trust you with my life, Tess."

"What if that person—"

The laptop beeped, and Sophie's attention went immediately to it. She pulled up the chat with Blair.

The first words appeared on the screen. *Hey, love.*

Sophie quickly typed back *Hey, there*, with a smiley face punctuating the end.

I know we hadn't planned to talk tonight, but I've been thinking about you all day.

Yeah?

Yeah...sigh...you were fabulous over the phone. I can't wait to try that in person.

Sophie hesitated for a moment and then typed, *Same, but I'm still at the office. Can we chat later?*

I'll be waiting.

Sophie slapped the laptop closed, then turned back to Tess. "Sorry. What were you going to say?"

Tess had to move—now. She stood and raced into the kitchen. Clearly what she'd thought was happening between them wasn't what was happening at all. "What if that person is Blair?"

Sophie followed her. "What if she isn't?"

"Go home and talk to her, Soph." She took Sophie by the shoulders, spun her around, and pushed her to the living room. "You have to give it a try, or you'll never know." She packed up the laptop and handed the bag to Sophie before she went to the door and opened it.

As Sophie crossed the room toward her, Tess couldn't tell if the look in Sophie's eyes was one of surprise or confusion. Whatever it was, Sophie had to figure it out. Tess couldn't do that for her.

"Thanks again for dinner." Sophie stepped out the door into the darkness. "I'll call you tomorrow."

As Tess watched Sophie get into her car, she resisted the urge to call her back inside and spill her emotions out onto the floor in front of her. That would do neither of them any good until Sophie resolved her feelings for Blair. But had she really just sent Sophie home to have another round of phone sex with Blair? She wouldn't intervene now when she wasn't really sure of her own feelings. Was she jealous of what Blair brought out in Sophie—things Tess had never been able to evoke before? It wouldn't be fair to get in the middle—to interrupt what might be happening between Sophie and Blair if she had no idea why these feelings were coming to the surface now.

She sat down at her antique typewriter and began to type.

The time we spend together
is precious and fleeting.
Like a rainbow after a summer shower.
To capture it is impossible,
but the desire is in constant remain.

She ripped the verse from the typewriter wheel and slapped it facedown on the desk. This was a definite problem.

CHAPTER SIXTEEN

B lair had read Sophie several poems, but none so deep and meaningful as the last one Tess had read to her this evening. It seemed it was dear to her heart, and now it would be to Sophie's as well. Why had Tess never shared it with her before? Why did she care what her reasons were? Tess seemed to be changing before her very eyes—or maybe it was she who was changing.

Tess seemed to be born out of her time. She loved everything vintage, antique even. That made her more beautiful in so many ways. She was sweet, unpretentious, and unassuming. Sophie had no idea why someone hadn't already snatched her up and married her. Lindsay, Tess's ex, had never realized or truly appreciated the treasure she had.

She had to get Tess out of her head. She'd told Blair she'd contact her tonight, but she wasn't sure quite how she'd get through it. The more time she spent with Tess, the more interest she lost in Blair.

She reached into her bag, took out her laptop, and turned it on. She also found the book Tess had read the quote from earlier. She'd wanted to remember it, so she'd borrowed the book when Tess wasn't looking. She wouldn't miss it for a night. As she fanned through the pages to locate the poem, several small, folded pages fell out. The paper was hand-picked and special ordered. Tess's usual choice.

She closed her eyes and held the pages under her nose—crisp and delicate like Tess. Her stomach bounced, and she slid the pages back into the book. She held the book, waiting for the feeling to subside. Confusion hit her hard as the battle waged inside as to whether she should read what Tess had typed. Her curiosity won, and she took the pages from the book and unfolded them. The poem had been typed on Tess's antique typewriter. The unique font made it look all the more special.

An orchid hanging from the vine
that has not truly bloomed yet.
For she holds so many feelings inside,
just waiting, hoping for the moment when
she can actually set them free.

A profound woman whose confidence
attracts in an absolute subtle way,
yet she is a fragile creature
whose deepest need beyond anything else
is only to be loved.

A mystifying being that hasn't realized,
and will probably never know,
how utterly fascinating she is
in another's eyes.
A woman who has absolutely no idea
how much richer her life will be
as she grows older,
reaching her fullest beauty,
inside and out.

Who had Tess written these beautiful words for? Was there someone she longed for? She hadn't mentioned anyone lately. Surely this wasn't meant for Lindsay. Nothing about this spoke about that woman. Lindsay was a selfish, narcissistic, toxic partner who took the best of Tess and left nothing for anyone else. She remembered days when she could barely get Tess out of bed because of the emotional damage Lindsay had inflicted.

But somehow, Tess still mourned the loss of the relationship—not the loss of Lindsay, but the comfort that having someone to come home to—the comfort that having a lover provided. She read the verses again. No. This poem was definitely not about Lindsay. She folded the pages and slid them back into the book.

She heard her computer beep. Blair.

Home yet?

She slapped it closed and groaned. She couldn't converse with Blair knowing in her heart that she was falling in love with someone else. She paced the living room. She had to send her some type of message. After all, she'd had phone sex with the woman—even though it hadn't been her she'd been thinking about during it. Blair didn't know that. She flopped down onto the couch, opened her laptop, and typed a quick message.

Not feeling well tonight. Can we push to tomorrow night?

She hit send without reading it back to herself. She heard her phone ring immediately in her bag. She ignored it.

A message came across her screen soon after.

Sure we can "push" to tomorrow. I tried to call. Is something else wrong?

She chided herself for being so curt. This wasn't a business meeting.

No. My phone's dead. I'm sorry. I had a long day and just need to sleep.

Okay then. Not going to lie. I'm disappointed. I took the night off to talk to you, but we'll talk again soon. Feel better, love. Au revoir

Good night she typed back, then slapped her computer closed and stuffed it into her bag. Laying on the guilt wouldn't make her want to talk to Blair more. It actually made her want to put an end to this charade immediately. The quicker the better.

No way was she going to be able to continue with Blair at this point. She rushed to the bedroom, stripped off her clothes, and put on a T-shirt. Heading to the bathroom, she tossed her dirty clothes on top of the already full hamper. After glaring at herself in the mirror, she pumped a small amount of facial wash into her hands and lathered her face. *Aren't you beautiful, love?* She was beginning to detest the term of endearment Blair had given her, and she really didn't deserve it now.

After rinsing and drying her face, she ran a stripe of toothpaste onto her toothbrush and stared at herself as she raked it back and forth across her teeth. She was the most horrible person on the planet. She spit and rinsed, wiped her mouth, and then stared at herself again. But was she really? She hadn't expected or even wanted these feelings she'd developed for Tess. She'd fully planned to continue whatever this was with Blair until tonight, when it had hit her square in the chest. She went into the bedroom, flopped onto the bed, and stared at the ceiling. She was falling in love with Tess.

❖

"Oh my God." Air whooshed from Sophie's lungs when she hit the floor. She literally rolled out of bed as she was reaching for her phone on the nightstand. Nine thirty. She was going to be late for her usual brunch date with Tess. They always went at the same time to the same café. Definitely creatures of habit, and she liked it that way. She bolted up from the floor and sent Tess a quick text.

Overslept. Getting in the shower. I'll be there soon.

She dropped her phone onto the bed before she headed to the bathroom, stripping her T-shirt off along the way. She flipped on the water, then turned to the sink and brushed her teeth before stepping into the shower.

The hot water felt good rushing over her shoulders. She flipped around and let it run across her face. Sleep hadn't come easy last night, and her eyes were going to show it. She'd thought up a hundred scenarios lying in bed on how the situation between her and Tess could play out. Tess could reject her, and things would remain the same. Would she be able to ignore her feelings for Tess? What if everything changed—if her feelings made Tess feel uncomfortable and she ended their friendship? She would never do that, would she?

Tess could also embrace love with her in all its glory, and everything between them would be fantastic—even better than fantastic. But then again, Tess could embrace her, and then Sophie would run screaming from the commitment, like she always did, and lose Tess forever.

She had to play it cool—ride it out to see if these feelings she was having were real or only temporary. If they *were* real, why hadn't she noticed them before now?

She killed the water and wrapped herself in a towel before she sat on the bed and read the text response from Tess.

Wasn't sure we were still going. Didn't know if you'd be up for it after a late night with Blair.

She quickly typed back. *No late night. She didn't call.*

She couldn't tell Tess she didn't want to talk to Blair last night, because then she'd have to explain why.

So, we're still on for brunch?

Of course.

She didn't plan to change her routine of having brunch with Tess, even if she was involved with Blair.

Okay. I'll be ready when you get here. Tess punctuated the end with a smiley face.

Tess was on her porch talking to her neighbor, Janet, when Sophie pulled up. Janet had retired from the military and kept an eye on the neighborhood. That was nice, but she could also be a bit of a busybody. On more than one occasion Janet had insinuated herself into Tess's life and gotten the wrong impression about things. Sophie couldn't complain, though. Janet was the one who had alerted her to Lindsay's horrible treatment of Tess. Too embarrassed to admit it, Tess hadn't told her anything other than she was okay.

Once Sophie dug deeper into the relationship it became clear that Tess was not okay. She wasn't going to stand for her best friend being treated badly in any way. Sophie had never thought Lindsay was the perfect match for Tess, and it seemed that the longer the relationship went on, the more toxic it became. By the time Tess left it, Lindsay had wrecked Tess emotionally. Sophie didn't know if Tess would ever be able to trust anyone except her again. She hadn't since the relationship ended. She'd vowed never to let that much space come between them again, even if one of them became involved with someone else.

Tess moved toward the car, and Janet kept talking. She moved farther…Janet followed. Soon Tess waved as she spun, sprinted to the car, and yanked open the door. "Oh my gosh. I'm so sorry."

"I thought maybe you were going to bring her with you."

"No. Absolutely not. She keeps trying to fix me up with her niece."

"What's wrong with that?"

"For one, she's not divorced yet." Tess whipped the seat belt from its reel and fastened it. "*And* she has three kids all under the age of seven."

"You'd be a great mom." Sophie laughed as she backed out of the driveway. "Think of all those kids helping you cook mac and cheese." She glanced at Tess. "Which was spectacular, by the way."

"No kids for me. You know that."

Tess had told her long ago that she didn't plan to have children, and Sophie hadn't heard anything different since then. "What if the love of your life has some?"

"Not going to happen." Tess raised her eyebrows "I already have one very large child to care for, and that's enough."

Sophie grinned. "And you do a hell of a job taking care of me."

"Guess I'll have to eat brunch alone next weekend while you're away."

"I'm not sure if that's still on. Blair said she might have to work."

"Well, then you can reschedule to the following weekend."

"I guess." She'd just find another excuse not to go. It just didn't feel right with Blair. Not like it did with Tess.

"So, what's the deal with Blair, anyway? She blew you off again last night?"

She nodded. "I guess she had something better to do."

"That's just weird. She's getting more and more unreliable."

"Seems to be." It was wrong to let Tess believe Blair was flaky, but that's the way she intended to play it for now. At least until she figured out her feelings.

"I'm sorry. That must be frustrating."

She drove slowly as they approached the cafe. "Not any more frustrating than waiting in that huge-ass line." She pointed to the string of people beginning to wrap around the building.

"Stop here. I'll get out and save us a spot." Tess reached for the door latch.

Sophie stopped the car, let Tess out, and then drove to the lot and parked. Judging by all the empty spaces, you'd never think the place was so busy. Everyone must've arrived in the same car. She hit the button on her key fob and set out to find Tess in line.

"You want to go somewhere else?" Sophie wiped the moisture from the back of her neck. They were next to be seated, and they'd only been waiting about thirty minutes, but it was hot and sticky outside the restaurant standing in the sunlight. There was only so much shade to be had, and Sophie let Tess stand in it.

"No. I'm good with waiting. We're almost up." Tess glanced at the menu she'd taken from the hostess stand. They'd arrived later than usual and seemed to have been caught in a much younger, hungover crowd. Sophie glanced around at the various people clad in random clothing and sunglasses. Her gaze landed on Tess, who looked beautiful in her short floral skirt and cap-sleeved white shirt. Sophie had thrown on a pair of white capri pants and a short-sleeved pink blouse. They were overdressed.

T-shirts, jeans, and sandals seemed to be everyone else's theme this morning.

"Was there a festival last night we missed?"

Tess laughed. "Probably." She leaned closer. "But I don't think it matters anyway. Remember our days of waking up craving carbs after a late night of drinking?"

Suddenly Sophie felt very old. "We still do that sometimes."

"And we always regret it." Tess glanced at the crowd. "Dry mouth, throbbing head, and a bolting stomach don't interest you anymore?"

Sophie laughed louder than usual. "I don't miss that feeling *at all*."

A preppy-dressed man pushed past Tess, knocking her into Sophie as he went to the hostess stand just outside the door. "I have a reservation."

"Sorry, sir. We don't take reservations for brunch."

"But my girlfriend said she made it last week when we were here." He held up a twenty-dollar bill. "Are you sure?"

That wasn't going to work. Sophie had tried it herself on occasion. Waiting was the only option at this point, and this guy was pissing her off. "Dude. You heard the woman. No reservations."

He glanced over his shoulder and waved at his girlfriend. She moved up the line to him.

No fucking way was this happening. "Absolutely not." She pointed to the back of the crowd. "The end of the line is back there."

"Thanks." The hostess smiled. "You wouldn't believe how many assholes try that."

She believed it, but when had she become her mother? She glanced at Tess. "Sorry. I didn't make a scene, did I?"

Tess shook her head. "No more than was necessary." Tess snaked her arm in Sophie's. "You were perfect."

Sophie focused on the hostess holding the menus as she motioned for them to follow her. A rush of heat hit her hard when Tess slid her fingers down her arm, clasped her hand, and led her into the restaurant. Sophie's head spun as she realized she and Tess were pretty much existing as a couple in all ways other than sex and cohabitation.

The hostess seated them near a window, where thankfully the line outside wasn't viewable, and then the waitress swung by to get their drink order. They ordered mimosas, as usual, that consisted of a half-bottle of champagne and a small pitcher of orange juice, spiked with a touch of Meyer lemon juice to give it the perfect balance.

She glanced over her menu at Tess. "You want the usual?" Neither of them deviated much, but she always like to check before ordering.

Tess nodded as she sipped her mimosa and stared out the

window. Set just above her petite nose, her eyes were a sparkling, pale blue in the sunlight.

The waitress appeared out of nowhere, it seemed. "Ready to order?"

"Yes. She'll have the mushroom frittata accompanied by a side of bacon and fruit. More strawberries than cantaloupe, please." Tess liked her fruit with a certain balance. "I'll have the chicken-fried steak, eggs, and home fries." Sophie closed the menu and handed them both back to the waitress. "We'll also have a side of pancakes to share." It was a ritual that rarely changed. Sophie was beginning to realize she liked it that way.

CHAPTER SEVENTEEN

Tess had been unsure of her current career path for quite some time. She'd remained at JB Marketing only because of Sophie. The week was almost over, and Sophie seemed to be doing just fine without her. Not a single phone call during work hours. She opened her laptop and scrolled through one of the job-listing sites she had bookmarked.

> Marketing Manager, Graphic Design. Location US-Remote (United States). The Graphic Design Marketing Manager will produce quality graphic designs across all global marketing channels. This position is responsible for creatively and proactively overseeing the planning, design, development, and management of corporate digital collateral. The GDM Manager is also responsible for the visual representation of the corporation and ensures that visually compelling and design elements are cohesive with brand strategy. This individual will work with stakeholders to help manage and implement the company's new corporate identity program.

Tess clicked out of the browser window at that point. She was good with stakeholders, but she didn't want to work in the corporate world. She'd tried it before Sophie had convinced her to come to JB and found it way too impersonal. The next one she came across was intriguing and might be right in her wheelhouse.

Orlando Museum of Art is currently seeking a Graphic Designer to conceptualize, design, and complete all internal and external communications and marketing collateral.

Duties and Responsibilities: Conceptualize and create all Museum advertising, both print and digital, including but not limited to magazine and newspaper ads, postcards, posters, web banners, and e-newsletters. This position works with the Director of Marketing & Communications to create all museum signage, brochures, invitations, and informational materials.

Nope. She exited out of that window as well. She wanted creative control, and working with any director meant she didn't have any—they had it all. She clicked past another similar one and a few others, including a graphic designer and social-media manager before she stopped on one for a freelance graphic designer and read through it. The company created clothing for men, and although she had a good eye for style, she wasn't interested in working in that line. It might bring too many unsolicited advances. Besides, freelance meant you worked when they needed you, and she couldn't afford not to have a steady paycheck. She closed her laptop and relaxed into the couch cushion. She was just going to have to wait it out at this point, unless something exceptional showed up.

She didn't want to jump from one hotbed of disagreement into another. As it was, she was being treated as though she had no expertise in marketing design, and that was simply untrue. She'd received her BA in marketing design at the University of Central Florida long ago and had kept up with marketing trends and design as they'd changed. It wasn't fair that someone with no design experience at all got to call the shots when it came to her creative ideas.

She checked her phone to see if she'd missed a message from Sophie. Nothing. She dropped it facedown onto the counter. It was probably better that she wasn't contacting her. Otherwise, Joy wouldn't miss her knowledge and experience.

Perhaps she could get work out of her mind if she wrote a few poems for Sophie to deliver to Blair. She sat down at her 1917 vintage, antique Underwood model #12 typewriter and rolled a piece of stationery into it. She also owned a #77 noiseless model, but she loved the way this one sounded when her thoughts went onto the paper. It was something from another time that no other device could replicate.

She sat staring at the paper. The words just weren't coming. How could she write romance verses when she didn't even like the person they were about? She hated the way Blair had been treating Sophie, and she hated that Sophie was okay with it. She shook her head. "Why her, Soph?"

She pressed her fingers hard against the keys, and the glorious sound of metal strikers battering the roller filled the room. She felt like she'd been magically catapulted back in time when she typed.

You came from nowhere, my love,
blazing into my life like a comet
shooting across the moonlit sky.
Scorching through my mind,
you landed directly in my heart,
burning a path to its very core.
My love for you knows no boundaries,
dearest. I am, and will always be,
right here for you.
Without question, I will love you,
comfort you, and keep you happy
and safe for all the days of my life.

She hit the carriage return several times, pulled the paper release forward, and took the delicate paper from the typewriter. The roller wheel whirred as she inserted a new blank page and advanced it forward to the top of the page.

My body warms
as thoughts of you trickle

through my mind.
Your loveliness, your beauty
fill all my senses.
With every breath,
I take in the soft,
sensuous tone of your voice,
and it sustains me.
For you have brought life
to a dying heart.
A heart left dormant for too long.
It blooms with radiance now,
a brilliance never to be lost again.
Simply because you care, my love.

One more was shoving to the front to escape her mind. She'd been holding back on these for far too long—wouldn't fight it any longer.

At night, as I slide into bed,
I long for the day when her warm, loving
body is there to greet me.
To hold me, comfort me,
and whisper sweet things in my ear.
To tell me,
no matter how hard life seems,
everything will be all right.
And I will believe her, trust her,
and have faith
because with her by my side,
I can do anything.

Oh, no. She shook her head as she pulled the last one from the typewriter and gathered them all together, searching through the words. This was a huge problem. She clasped the pages to her chest. How was she supposed to help her best friend woo another woman when she herself was in love with her?

She slapped the pages facedown onto the desk and went into the bedroom to change into a pair of yoga pants and a tank top. She needed to get her mind off Sophie, and the gym would be a good place for that. Physical exhaustion was the key. Sophie never went to the gym, so thoughts of her wouldn't haunt her there.

CHAPTER EIGHTEEN

Sophie's car jerked as she pulled into Tess's driveway and threw it into park. She glanced up at the sky as she walked up the pathway to the door. It was a beautiful night. The sky was clear, with the stars perfectly visible. It seemed like the first breath of fresh air she'd had all day.

Working without Sophie in the office was challenging and horribly boring, to say the least. Without Tess to protest her choices, Joy had adopted a queen complex even worse than before. It had taken everything Sophie had not to blast her more than once. She needed the job, or she would've said fuck it and quit on the spot today.

She hit the doorbell before she entered as usual and dropped her laptop on the floor by the couch on her way into the kitchen. "I hope you have bourbon. It's been a shitty day."

"You know where it is."

She went to the pantry, plucked the bottle from the top shelf, and poured herself a drink. She downed it. Poured another and downed it as well.

"Hey. Take it easy, or we're not going to get any work done tonight." Tess slid the bottle away.

"Fuck work." She tossed back another drink.

"Did you eat anything tonight?"

"Nope." She kneaded her forehead with her fingers. "Left work and came straight here."

"Okay." Tess went to the refrigerator, took out several hunks of cheese, and put them on a cutting board. "Can you grab the crackers from the pantry?"

She reached back inside and stared at the variety on the shelf. "Which ones?"

"Your choice." Tess was always so accommodating.

She glanced over her shoulder to catch a glimpse of Tess with her dark hair all mussed around her face. She was dressed in black yoga pants and a form-fitting hot-pink tank top. "Were you working out?" She grabbed the Triscuit crackers, opened the box, and let them spill out onto the board.

"I went to the gym. I needed to release some anxiety." Tess arranged the crackers next to the cheese. "I was just about to jump into the shower when you got here."

"Don't mind me. I'll just sit here and stuff my face." She popped a couple of crackers into her mouth, one after the other, and then finished with a piece of cheese. "Why is this always so good?"

Tess grinned. "I bought several different varieties of Triscuits last time I went to the store."

"Ohh." Her eyes widened like a child with a new toy. "I didn't see them." She twirled around to look at the others, then grabbed the box of cracked-pepper-and-olive-oil flavored and dumped a few of those onto the board as well. "These are really good too." She immediately ate one and enjoyed the zing from the pepper as it danced across her tongue.

"How did I know you'd pick those?" Tess fixed a plate of crackers with several different cheeses and fed her a slice before she took the plate to the coffee table. "If we're not going to work, do you want to hear what I wrote this afternoon for your communications with Blair?"

"Yes, please." She flopped onto the couch. Tess was always helping her.

"You mentioned that she's been working a lot. I thought she might be struggling with her job." Tess retrieved a piece of paper from her desk.

"Could be."

Tess sat next to her. "Okay, so I wrote something that might make her feel better."

You are not only who you are,
you are who you can be,
who you want to be,
who you are destined to be.
It may be a struggle,
and may be full of heartache and tears,
but it will take you one step closer
to whom you truly are.
That is who lives in your heart.
Make it happen,
please yourself, love yourself...
For that is all that matters.
You is all you can be.
You are beautiful.

Sophie listened and watched Tess as she read what she'd written. Something about the old-school typeface made it so much more special. Her stomach knotted as unfamiliar feelings swelled inside. She was seeing Tess in a totally different way. "Beautiful. Absolutely beautiful."

"Thank you. I hoped you'd like it."

"Not just the words, Tess—you. You're beautiful. Always have been." She couldn't believe she'd only begun to see it for the first time over the past few days—and even more tonight. Maybe the alcohol was bringing her feelings to the surface.

"Oh?" Tess stared at her with searching eyes.

Her stomach tingled. Everything Tess wrote was hitting her right in the heart—and the alcohol was hitting her brain quickly. She rushed closer to Tess, took her face in her hands, and kissed her long, slow, and deep. Tess's lips were soft and so much sweeter than she'd imagined. This was a total mistake, but in this moment it felt completely right.

She broke the kiss, and Tess seemed stunned before she hooked her hand behind Sophie's neck and pulled her into another scorching kiss.

Tongues mingled as hands roamed, and soon she was out of breath. She broke the kiss again. "I'm—"

Tess held her fingers to Sophie's lips before she took her hand and stood—led her across the living room to the bedroom and pushed her onto the bed. "Just give me a minute to clean up." She went into the bathroom and closed the door.

She heard the shower kick on and sniffed the collar of her shirt. Maybe she should shower too. She felt the cool sheet next to her—glanced at the wrought-iron headboard—imagined Tess holding the rails while Sophie buried herself between her legs. She was immediately wet—turned on to a degree she didn't quite understand. Were they really doing this? Could *she* do this without hurting Tess in the long run? No. This would ruin their friendship forever. What was she thinking?

Panic filled her, and she stood to leave. The room began to spin. *Nope. Not going anywhere tonight.* She'd have to find another way out of this. She kicked off her shoes and slacks before she crawled up into the bed, rolled to her side, and closed her eyes. After what seemed like only a few minutes, she heard the bathroom door click open.

"Sophie?" She felt the bed jiggle. "You awake?" Tess let out a soft sigh of what sounded like disappointment.

She heard something flop onto the hope chest at the bottom of the bed. A few minutes later she felt the covers lift as Tess slid into bed. Her stomach jumped when she felt Tess's arm around her waist, took in the scent of her freshly shampooed hair. She was definitely not getting any rest tonight, but sleeping with Tess in impulse mode while she was inebriated was a bad idea. Leaving this situation alone was the best decision tonight—maybe forever.

❖

Sophie felt like she'd just fallen to sleep when her eyes popped open. Since she'd turned forty, alcohol had become sleep's worst enemy, but she rarely remembered that when the bourbon was burning down her throat. She attempted to wet her lips, but her mouth felt like cotton. She reached for her phone and checked the time. Four a.m. Tess had left a bottle of water on the nightstand. *Sweet Tess.* She twisted off the cap and chugged before she turned over to face Tess, who was now lying on her back.

She watched Tess's chest rise and fall. She was so beautiful— not just on the outside—in every way. What had she done last night—what had they done? Had she destroyed their friendship? Would they be able to return to being only friends? Did she even want that? No. She thought about their multiple mind-blowing kisses, and her body reacted. She wanted so much more, but she was horrible at commitment. They both knew that. Tess shifted to her side, wrapped her arm around her, and Sophie felt safe, secure, loved.

Her anxiety kicked in as all the scenarios of how badly this could play out popped into her head. Why had she messed up the best thing in her life? She slipped from Tess's grasp, gathered her clothes, and tiptoed into the living room. Once she was dressed, she took one last look at Tess and knew that if she acknowledged what had happened between them, things would never be the same again. Her life as she knew it had just taken a disastrous turn.

CHAPTER NINETEEN

The kiss from Sophie last night had been totally unexpected—and Tess's response to it had been impulsive. The whole few minutes was scary and wonderful all in the same moment. What was she going to say to Sophie this morning? How was she going to explain it? She took in a deep breath. It was now or never. She closed her eyes and smiled as she rolled over, dragging her hand across the sheet. Cold cotton was all she felt. She widened her eyes as she bolted upright.

"Sophie." She scanned the bedroom. Her clothes were gone from the hope chest at the bottom of her bed. "Sophie." She said it louder as she bolted out of bed, yanked on her robe, and ran into the living room, and then the kitchen, hoping she was there. She rushed to the front door and pulled it open. No car in the driveway. She went into the living room, sank onto the couch, and wrapped her arms around herself. Sophie had left without a word. Was the whole thing a mistake brought on by frustration and alcohol?

She let her mind wander to the kisses they'd shared. Hot and urgent, with tongues battling for control as they swept into each other's mouths. She could almost taste the bourbon Sophie had been drinking. Breasts pressed against each other, creating a delicious friction that would lead to only one thing—she could feel it even now—but it didn't lead to anything. She let out a growl. She wanted Sophie back in her bed right now to finish what they'd started.

She picked up her phone and hit the button for Sophie. It went straight to voice mail. She quickly typed in a text. *Where are you?*

A text from Sophie came through soon after. *Went home to shower.*

Was that all she was thinking about after last night? *You could've showered here.*

I needed fresh clothes.

She didn't have a response to that—for any of it. Sophie had taken the clothes she'd left previously. All she could offer her was a T-shirt and leggings. Sophie would've still had to go home to change for work.

She typed a response. *We need to talk about last night.* Then she erased it and typed, *Bring me breakfast?* She wanted to talk to Sophie face-to-face.

Can't. Need to get to the office. Lots of work to do.

Sophie was blowing her off for some reason. She really wanted to discuss the kiss they'd shared last night, but it didn't look like Sophie was having the same thought. She stood and paced across the living room and back before she spotted Sophie's laptop next to the couch, where she'd dropped it last night. She was apparently in too much of a rush to get out of there this morning and had forgotten it. Had she talked to Blair this morning?

She took the laptop from the bag, opened it, and logged into Sophie's social-media account. She had to know if she'd been in touch with Blair this morning. She felt a little weird about it, but she wasn't really violating Sophie's trust. Maybe a little, in light of what had happened last night, but Sophie had given her the password so she could log in and see the messages Blair had sent.

"Let's just see what you've been up to, @blairsyrose." She clicked on the chat. Nothing from last night or this morning from either one of them. A surge of hope filled her. Maybe she wasn't wrong about what had happened between her and Sophie last night. She popped off the couch. If Sophie wouldn't come to her, she would go to Sophie. She heard the laptop chime from the bedroom and rushed out to see the message.

I missed you last night. A message from Blair.

She waited a minute or two to see if Sophie would reply using her phone. She must've realized by now that she'd left her laptop here. She'd just sat down when a message from Sophie popped up.

At work. Can we talk later?

Sure. We can plan our weekend rendezvous.

Might not be able to make it this weekend. Work is ridiculous. Sorry. I have to go. I'll get in touch later.

Was that really true? Had Sophie been hiding something at work from her? She clicked into her documents and found the newest folder created, Bahama Betty. She pulled up the proposal document, and the first line read leisure clothing for the woman over forty. What the hell? She still had a few more years to go before she turned forty, but that didn't mean she didn't know what appealed to women in that demographic. Why hadn't Sophie talked to her about this account?

She already felt like she was being squeezed out at work, and now Sophie seemed to be excluding her as well. That sealed it. She was going back to work, whether Joy liked it or not. It had only been a little under a week, but this new information made it clear that she'd been away long enough.

CHAPTER TWENTY

Sophie tossed her phone onto her desk. She didn't know where these feelings for Tess had come from, but she was totally enamored with her. She'd lost all interest in Blair and had probably been ruined for all other women. No way could she go on a weekend with any other woman now, or anytime in the near future. She'd just have to back out—tell Blair she had to work or some other big fat lie—and just get lost in her work until she got over these new feelings for Tess. If that was even possible.

"How's the new proposal going?" Joy raised her eyebrows. "Where's your laptop?"

"Forgot it."

"Not at Tess's house, I hope." Joy tilted her head. "You haven't been working with her on this, have you?"

"No, but I really need to be. She's much better at design than I am."

"If you need help, I'll pair you with someone else."

"Absolutely not. Unless you truly want Tess to leave." She thought that was Joy's goal in the long run, but making it happen now would leave them without the skills she required to get the current proposals done.

"I wouldn't be opposed to that."

"I told you. If she leaves, I leave." That might not make a difference in Joy's decision, but she still meant it. She wouldn't stay at JB Marketing if Joy chose to let Tess go. No matter what happened between them personally, Tess was still her partner at work. At least she hoped she would be.

"You win. For now." Joy crossed her arms. "You don't need her on this one. It's your demographic we're trying to reach. Not hers."

"Just because I'm in my forties *does not* make these clothes appealing to me." Pointing out the age factor to Joy wasn't making her reason for not involving Tess any stronger. She flipped through the catalog the client had provided. "I might wear one or two items in their line, but the majority of this clothing targets a much older, exclusive, wealthier market."

"Exactly. I want you to broaden their market to women your age by making it elegant and posh. Tess doesn't do elegant—she does antique." Joy turned and left the office.

That was so not true. It might not be elegant, but Tess had sophistication unmatched by anyone she knew. Her taste in clothing wasn't only vintage. It was girl-next-door and oh-so-feminine. Tess had a fabulous style all her own, and it fit her personality perfectly. She planned to ask Tess to consult with her anyway. She'd gone over there last night to do exactly that, but that scenario had gone way off the rails. She'd traveled to a delicious destination with Tess that she'd never imagined—was damn lucky she'd been sober enough to not complete the journey. She could still feel the force of Tess's lips pressed against hers, the sweetness of her tongue in her mouth, the soft curves of her hips pressed against her. Wetness pooled in her panties just as it had last night. She sucked in a deep breath to settle herself. This was going to be a long day, but she needed some space today—both of them did.

With her head down, concentrating, and working hard on the proposal for Betty Bahama, Sophie heard someone step into the office and glanced up from notes she was writing, hoping it wasn't Joy again. *Tess.* "What are you doing here? I thought you were off through the rest of the week."

"I was—I am." Tess set Sophie's laptop bag on her desk. "But you left this at my house last night." She stared at her. "You remember last night, don't you? You came over and we—"

"Ate cheese, and I drank way too much bourbon." She held her forehead with her palm. "I was in such a foul mood." That was the only excuse she could muster without giving her feelings away. "I must've passed out. I'm sorry about that."

"You did have quite a few drinks, and—" Tess raised her eyebrows and put her hand on her hip. "You don't remember anything besides the cheese?"

"Not really." She shook her head. "We were on the couch going over the poem you'd written." She glanced away. She couldn't look into Tess's eyes and lie. "Everything after that's a blur." She remembered every minute of their earth-shattering kisses and the feel of Tess's body against hers. It was a wonderfully awakening clarity that she'd ignored for too long—that she still hadn't quite settled from, but she couldn't tell her that.

"Oh my God. I didn't take advantage of you, did I? Cause you know I'm very irresponsible when I'm drunk." Total truth, but last night she knew exactly who she was with and what she was doing. She couldn't—wouldn't hurt Tess for her own gratification, and she wasn't entirely sure if it was more than that. Tess was a beautiful woman, she'd never denied that, but she seemed to be growing more beautiful with each day they spent together.

"No." Tess shook her head. "You didn't take advantage of me." She seemed relieved that the whole thing seemed to be forgotten. Perhaps she knew what it might do to their friendship as well. "What are you working on?"

She couldn't keep it from Tess now. "Joy gave me this new account." She flipped her pad so Tess could read it. "Betty Bahama."

"Is this what you have so far?" Tess picked up the pad and read several lines. "Clothes for the rich and famous. Gifts to buy your mother. Casual wear for life after forty…when you're almost dead." Tess raised her eyebrows. "Well, these will definitely bring in a certain type of woman." She laughed dropped the pad to the table. "I take it that you don't like the clothes?" She picked up the catalog and thumbed through it.

"Joy gave it to me because I'm over forty. Thinks I'm the market they're after."

"Well, you might be in that demographic, but I can't see you wearing any of these outfits—even when you're sixty." Tess knew her so well. "It would be the equivalent of buying me a tool kit for my house."

"Right?" She relaxed into her chair. "Just because I'm getting older doesn't mean I want to look that way."

"You want me to give it a shot? I can work on it this weekend while you're out of town." Tess continued looking through the catalog. "You're supposed to leave after work, right?"

"Yeah. About that." She took the catalog from Tess. "I'm not sure I'm going."

"But you have to. Blair will be crushed." Definitely getting mixed messages from Tess. She seemed to be okay with forgetting the kisses they'd shared last night as well.

"She'll get over it. I'll reschedule." Sophie stood and moved a few folders around on her desk.

"Why?"

The look of confusion in Tess's eyes made Sophie wonder if she should just spill all her feelings now.

"I have to work." She motioned to the Betty Bahama research on her desk.

"I can do this." Tess pointed to the catalog on the desk. "Seriously. Why aren't you going? You've been really excited about this woman since you found her. What's changed?"

"I don't know." She sank into her chair, then turned and stared out the window. "It doesn't feel right. Maybe it's too soon. If I go, we'll sleep together, and that will probably be the end of it." She spun around and stared at Tess looking for some sign of agreement—something that told her that Tess didn't want her to go any further with Blair. "Is that what you think I should do...sleep with Blair?"

Tess shook her head. "No. I don't think you should have sex and then be done with her." She looked away.

The back of her neck tingled as she waited for Tess to say more—to tell her to forget Blair, and that she was standing right in front of her feeling the heat burn between them—just as it had last night.

"You've put a lot of effort into this. Connecting with someone isn't easy. You can't just leave the woman hanging. That wouldn't be right. Especially at the last minute."

With her hopes completely dashed, Sophie couldn't go on with this conversation. "Don't push me on this, Tess. I just can't do a weekend with her right now." Afraid she might gut herself and let her feelings spill out all over the floor, she rushed out of the office and headed to the bathroom.

Tess followed her. "I know you've already had phone sex with her."

Heat filled her as she spun around to respond and realized that several people in the office were watching them. They were the unexpected free entertainment of the day.

"So you're done with her now?" Tess was no dummy. She'd seen the messages on the screen Blair had sent the other night.

She'd tried to respond discreetly, but Blair had been perfectly clear about what had happened between them. "I have, and maybe *I am* done with her. That's not your business."

"Are you serious? After all the communication you've had with her—all the communication I've written for you to send her?"

Sophie rushed into the bathroom. "Why are you doing this—in front of everyone we work with?"

"It's not like everyone here doesn't know your track record."

That one hurt. Her stomach lurched—felt like she was going to purge at any moment. Tess had never criticized her quite so harshly or publicly. She splashed her face with water, took in a breath, and narrowed her eyes at Tess in the mirror. "Not another word about this at work." She snatched a paper towel and dried her face as she bolted toward the door. "Go home, Tess. No one wants you here right now. Including me." She left Tess standing at the counter. That was it. Sophie refused to listen to another shitty word from Tess. She rushed into her office, grabbed her laptop bag, and headed to the door.

"Where are you going?" Joy's voice echoed through the office.

"I'm working offsite today." She left the office without giving

Joy a chance to respond. She didn't know where she was going, but she wasn't hanging around here to be insulted by Tess. Even though Tess was her best friend, she didn't have the right to talk to her that way.

CHAPTER TWENTY-ONE

Tess was angry at Sophie and herself for letting the argument escalate—for actually escalating it—for attacking Sophie that way. Who was she now? Gripping the counter, she stared at herself in the mirror. The door flew open, and a rush of relief hit her thinking Sophie might have come back. No such luck. It was Joy coming at her hot, angrier than Tess had ever seen her before.

"I don't know what the hell that was about, but you're on notice, Tess. The next issue you cause in this office with me, Sophie, or anyone else, you're out. I don't care if it's about staples, coffee, or noise. Understand?"

"Got it." She nodded and bit her words back. If she said them, she'd be out of a job with no way to support herself. She wished she had half the guts Sophie had. If she did, she'd have left JB Marketing years ago and taken the plunge to set up her own company. Her life was based on stability, and that would totally wreck it.

"Now go find Sophie and fix this. I need her focused."

Tess rushed out of the bathroom, didn't look at anyone, especially not Joy, and left the office with hyper-speed. She wasn't sure she could find her or fix any of it.

She hit the button on her phone to call Sophie, but it went directly to voice mail. She wasn't going to talk to her, and she couldn't blame her.

She typed in a text. *I'm sorry. I didn't mean what I said.*

Tess truly was sorry. She didn't know what had come over her. She had no idea why she'd been so cruel to Sophie. Admittedly, she was hurt that Sophie hadn't remembered any of what happened the night before. The rejection hit her harder than she ever could've imagined. Was she that forgettable—was she a horrible kisser? Sophie had started it, tugged her into the most spectacular of kisses. Inched her fingers up Tess's sides, pressed herself hard against her. A shiver struck her, and she let it overtake her for a moment.

Was Sophie just using her to channel her sexual frustration because she couldn't touch Blair? If that was the case, why was Sophie blowing off Blair now? It wasn't right to string Blair along like they had been and then just ghost her, which it seemed Sophie was planning to do—for *whatever* reason. Maybe it was because of what happened between them last night, but that was still thoughtless and mean, and she refused to be the reason for Sophie's bad behavior.

❖

As soon as Tess got home, she logged into Sophie's social media on her laptop and read through the new messages.

I'm not going to make it this weekend. Just got something more dropped on me.

I've put a lot of time and effort into setting up this weekend.

I'm sorry. It can't be helped. Sophie hadn't suggested changing it to another date. It seemed that her decision was final.

I'm already here. Let me know if something changes and you're able to get away after all. Blair punctuated the message with a sad face.

Blair was probably more upset than she'd let on in her message, and Tess couldn't blame her. She was going to have to make this right—go meet Blair and explain the whole situation. Her stomach churned. She'd helped Sophie mislead Blair into thinking Sophie was interested in something permanent, when clearly she wasn't as interested as she'd thought. Blair seemed to be another passing interest for Sophie. If Tess had known Sophie would eventually dump Blair cold without even meeting her face-to-face, she would've never agreed to help her.

She paced her living room before she raced into the bedroom and pulled her overnight bag from the top shelf of the closet and jammed it with clothes. She filled a small cosmetics bag with several items of makeup and hair fasteners that were scattered about the bathroom counter, then dropped it into her bag and zipped it up. Once she finished packing, she took the bag with her to the living room and dropped it on the floor next to the couch. She wasn't exactly sure how she was going to fix this, but she had to try. She plopped onto the couch and began plucking at the keyboard.

Hey there. Change of plans. I was able to get away after all. I'll see you soon.

That's great news. Let me know when you get here.

She grabbed her phone and sent Blair a quick text. *Switching to my phone.*

From here on out she would communicate with her by text rather than instant messaging to prevent Sophie from seeing the communication.

New number?

Tess had forgotten that she'd blocked her number when she and Sophie had used her phone to FaceTime Blair before. *This is my work phone. Personal phone is dead.* Hopefully, that explanation would do.

I feel like we've passed a milestone here. You're trusting me with your work number. Blair punctuated the sentence with a smiley face.

She let out a laugh as she responded. *Lol. I guess we have.*

Blair's optimism made her feel a little better about the whole situation. For now anyway.

But she needed to get on the road. It was just under a two-hour drive. She wanted to take the coastal route but also get there in time to freshen up before meeting Blair. She still hadn't figured out exactly how she was going to explain everything without Blair getting angry. The woman deserved more than to be ghosted due to no fault of her own. She would explain what had transpired among the three of them and hope Blair would understand, maybe even forgive her and Sophie for the ruse they'd instigated. That would depend on how invested Blair had become. She'd imagined all sorts of horrible scenarios, from Blair flipping out in public to being kicked out of the resort. Soon she'd settled on the worst-case scenario of having to pay for her own room, and she had plastic with enough unused credit on it to handle one night if that actually happened.

She couldn't get around the fact that Sophie was going to be pissed when she realized Tess was texting Blair on her own phone, but she really didn't have another way to communicate with her without spooking her.

When she reached the Florida A1A Scenic Coastal Byway, she glanced out the passenger window at the beach. She loved the ocean, the sight, the scent, and the sounds that came along with it. Someday she wanted to live in a house where her backyard would be the beach in all its glory. She saw the sign for Flagler Beach— more than halfway there. The tank almost empty, she pulled off at the nearest station to get gas. She'd been in such a hurry to leave Orlando, she'd forgotten to stop. When she finished gassing up, she ran inside the convenience store and got a cup of coffee. She was going to need it before the night was over. Before getting back on the road, she typed in a quick text to Blair.

Almost there.

A message came through immediately. *Can't wait to see you.*

Same here. She messaged back, even though she was dreading the confrontation.

Text me after you arrive and get settled in your room. I'll wait to see you in the bar.

She sent back a thumbs-up emoji. That was promising. Maybe Blair would have a drink or two in her by the time Tess got there and wouldn't be quite so upset when she came clean about everything.

CHAPTER TWENTY-TWO

Sophie changed into a hoodie and yoga pants before she curled up on her couch in the darkness. She'd left all the blinds closed—no sunshine for her this afternoon. Tess had called several times and texted an apology, but she couldn't bring herself to respond. She couldn't stop thinking about the awful things Tess had said to her today. Maybe she was right. Her life had turned out so much differently than she'd planned. She'd never intended to remain single into her forties. She'd dreamed of finding the perfect woman and settling down someday, but she hadn't done anything to actually make it happen or even move in that direction. Her heart broken early in her adult life by a much-older woman, she didn't know when *she'd* turned into *that* woman herself, but clearly she had.

Who knew it was going to be so difficult? She was living a sad, lonely life—didn't know exactly how alone she was until she'd started spending more time with Tess every night over the past couple of weeks. How could she find any happiness with Tess if Tess really thought she was such a terrible person? Could she show Tess she really wasn't selfish and inconsiderate? She closed her eyes and shook her head. Not likely, because Tess was right. Sophie was completely self-centered, thoughtless, and insensitive most of the time.

Except when it came to Tess. She was the only person who knew Sophie's faults and vulnerabilities. Trust was sacred between them—until now. She'd destroyed it by stepping over the line with Tess by kissing her and bringing her out of the friendship role she'd so meticulously placed Tess in over the years. Tears spilled out across her nose and onto her cheek.

It had been horrible to lie to Blair the way she had. She had no idea if Blair had responded to her last, very curt, message. Sophie had gone to the closest coffee shop, buried herself in work, and ignored social media all day. She pulled up the text messages from Tess and scrolled up to read through the poems Tess had written for Blair. It now seemed obvious that through all the help Tess had given her, Tess had developed feelings for Blair—all while Sophie was developing feelings for Tess.

What an idiot she'd been. Sophie had gotten caught up in the romance of it all and wanted to be the one Tess was writing the words for, but clearly it was Blair that Tess was enamored with. It made sense. Blair was much classier than herself. She needed to fix this with Blair if she was going to be able to fix anything with Tess. She sat up on the couch and clicked the button for her social-media messenger account. She scrolled down and read the most recent message at the bottom.

Hey there. Change of plans. I was able to get away after all. I'll see you soon.

That's great news. Let me know when you get here.

"What the hell?" She bolted up from the couch. It seemed Tess was corresponding with Blair, *and* she was going to the resort in her place.

She swiped down on the screen and refreshed the feed a couple of times to see if Tess had responded. Not another word. She read the response from Blair again and then paced the room, trying to decide which way to handle this. She could just let Tess go—let her be happy with Blair. Or she could message Blair, spill the whole truth, and blow the whole charade with Tess out of the water. Neither of these options would bring Tess back to her. She chose option three—follow Tess to the resort and fight for her. Tess was her ride or die, and she wanted that for life.

She raced into the bedroom, changed into a pair of jeans and a short-sleeved T-shirt, and began tossing clothes that she'd washed and folded earlier in the week into an overnight bag. She'd originally planned to go, so she was already semi-prepared. She rushed into the living room, dropped back onto the couch, opened her laptop, and went to one of the travel sites she regularly used.

The Palm Club Resort was expensive—four dollar-signs expensive. Her best bet for a semi-reasonable price would be to book online. She punched in the resort information and sighed. She'd been saving her travel miles for a nice vacation someday, but she would have to use most of them to pay for this weekend stay. She added them to the payment method and hit confirm. She didn't have to weigh the options—not losing the love of her life mattered most right now.

She left her laptop on the table. She didn't plan to do any work this weekend and would be able to monitor any communications Tess had with Blair via her social media on her phone. She quickly checked it again and found nothing. Tess was probably still driving.

❖

The drive had been a blur—Sophie was caught up in all the scenarios that could play out when she arrived. How Tess reacted was the key to everything. Tess was already pissed at her for planning to ghost Blair. She wondered if Tess would still be angry if she knew why she'd decided not to go. Yes. She'd still be angry because Tess was too sweet to hurt anyone, even for her own benefit.

Maybe Tess would be thrilled to see her—hoped Sophie would follow her to the resort and profess her love to her. The other night, Tess had kissed her with such passion and power, clearly ready to seal the deal. On the flip side, Tess could hate her forever, and she couldn't live with that. The knot in her stomach tightened. No matter how Tess reacted, she promised herself that she'd come clean with Blair, even tell her what her intent had been from the beginning.

She truly had started out with good intentions, but her heart had shanghaied her feelings—gathered all the scattered tendrils into a tight ball and planted them completely in Tess's garden. New shoots of life sprouted vibrant green from a friendship so deep that it was more than Sophie could deny. She was becoming a poet after all.

No one else besides Tess could provoke such beautiful words in her head and have them mean something so true.

She gripped the steering wheel and prepared herself for what was soon to come. If Tess had planned to tell Blair everything, this party was going to be a rager, and crashing it would only throw more dynamite into the mix. She gave absolutely zero fucks where this left her with Blair, but she had to handle it delicately. She had to show Tess she wasn't a complete shit.

CHAPTER TWENTY-THREE

When Tess walked into the lounge, she immediately spotted Blair sitting at the bar chatting with the bartender. She tried to remain out of view as she watched her interact. The catfish scenario was out the window now. This was definitely the same woman Tess had seen in the FaceTime call, only much more beautiful in person than she'd been on camera. She stopped for a moment to take in the full view. Blair was dressed in an oversized, faded, navy shirt that went perfectly with the long, tropical-patterned skirt she was wearing. She shifted to cross her legs and a beautiful, curvy calf appeared from a slit up the side that ended just above her knee. She quickly veered her eyes upward to make sure she hadn't been caught ogling. As she came closer, she realized Blair's conversation with the bartender seemed more friendly than the usual chitchat. Maybe she was her contact at the resort, the one who'd gotten them the rooms. She crossed the room to the bar.

"Is anyone sitting here?"

"Nope. As long as this one's free." She patted the spot to her right. "That one's all yours."

"Thank you." She set her phone on the bar and took the spot to Blair's left.

The bartender smiled. "What can I get you?"

"A glass of rosé, please." She glanced at the bartender's name tag. *Morgan.*

Morgan poured her a glass of wine and slid it in front of her.

"Thank you, Morgan." Chatting up the bartender would give her time to gain her courage to talk to Blair. "This is a nice place." She took a gulp of wine.

"Is this your first visit to the resort?"

"Yes." She glanced around, taking in the bar's breezy atmosphere. Decorated with wicker-style furniture and Panama fans, it felt like someplace you'd find in the Bahamas. "It's more tropical than the online pictures captured."

Morgan leaned closer. "It's all smoke and mirrors."

"Well, someone has done a great job of working the magic." Or maybe she hadn't been going to the right places. This was one she'd want to revisit in the future.

Morgan put a glass of ice on the bar, flipped around several different liquor bottles as liquid filled the glass before she slid a straw into it, and topped it with an umbrella. "Why don't you complete the fantasy with this?" She slid the glass across the bar to her.

Tess took a small sip from the glass, surprised by the burn that filled her throat. "What is this?"

"A mai tai." Blair smiled. "That was the one-fifty-one rum floater on top. Stir it up and drink it through the straw. It'll taste better, and you'll last longer." She glanced at Morgan. "You shouldn't do that to sweet, unsuspecting ladies."

"Just trying to round out the experience." Morgan raised an eyebrow. "Shouldn't your friend be here by now?"

Tess stirred her drink and then sucked in a gulp as Blair checked her phone and typed in a quick text.

Tess's phone buzzed on the bar, and she quickly flipped it over. The combination of the wine and mai tai were beginning to hit her.

Morgan glanced at the phone, then at Tess. "That was weird."

That was her cue. Her artificial courage took over. "I have something to confess." She glanced up at the bartender and then at Blair. "Sophie isn't coming."

Blairs eyebrows went up. "You know Sophie?"

She nodded, sucked in another swig of her drink, and swallowed. "I'm Tess. A friend of hers."

Blair's smile immediately faded. "She messaged a little while ago that she was on her way." She held up her phone and showed Tess the message.

"I messaged you." Tess held up her phone and showed Blair the same message. "I'm sorry."

"I don't understand." Blair didn't attempt to leave—didn't even move her foot from the rung on the barstool.

"She's some kind of catfish." Morgan tilted her head. "A really cute one, though."

"No." Tess held up her hand. "It's not like that at all."

"Is this some kind of joke?" Blair glanced around the room and then back at Tess.

"Absolutely not. I was helping Sophie." She sighed and took another gulp of courage from her drink. "It's a long story."

Blair rested one elbow on the bar and shifted to face her. "I'm listening."

Morgan grinned as she leaned closer. "Me too." The bar wasn't busy, and there was another bartender at the other end, so it seemed Morgan would be part of the audience.

"Sophie…my friend and I frequent The Speak Easy in Orlando fairly often."

"Yes. I know. She mentioned that."

"When we were there a couple of weeks ago, I found your social-media handle in the bill book. What you'd written intrigued me."

"What was it?" Morgan asked. Apparently, she was playing an active part in this discussion.

"You must dig deep within your soul to find the true happiness you deserve."

Morgan snorted. "Well, that's a bit—"

Blair held up her hand. "Let her finish." She focused on Tess.

"I always look at the writings in the book. It's a habit. Your words kind of rang true for my life right now."

"Then why didn't *you* contact me?" Blair seemed genuinely interested.

"I've met women in unique ways before in the past, and it

hasn't turned out well. So I ignored it." She took another sip of her drink. "But Sophie told me the next day that she'd contacted you later that night. She was anxious about messaging you because she's not the best at romance—in writing anyway. So I've been helping her."

"Let me get this straight. You've been messaging me?"

"We both have."

"We had—" Blair's eyes went wide. "Did you and I talk on the phone?"

"No." She fiddled with the straw in her almost-empty glass. "That was all her. I've never had phone sex with anyone." She sucked the last of her drink down.

Morgan grinned and slid another drink in front of Tess. "This is getting interesting."

Blair raised an eyebrow at Morgan and pushed the drink back to her. "But she told you about it?" She bit her bottom lip.

"Absolutely not." Tess shook her head. "I figured it out. She was with me when she received your message the next night."

"You were with her? She said she was working."

"Yes." *We weren't working, but that's beside the point.* "We work together in marketing. She writes the slogans, and I create the design."

"So *you* wrote all the messages?"

"Not all of them. Clearly, the two of you talked at times when I wasn't there."

"The flirting?"

"All Sophie. I'm not very good at that."

"The poetry?"

"That was me. We kind of balance each other in that way."

"Where is this other chick?" Morgan searched the bar. "Maybe all three of you should get together."

Blair stared up at Morgan, her expression blank. "Stop." She glanced back at Tess. "All that makes sense, except why are you here instead of her?"

"Sophie isn't good at relationships. I think she was afraid she'd ruin whatever was developing between the two of you."

"She said she had to work. That wasn't true?"

Tess shook her head. "I'm sorry. I feel badly about the whole thing." Tess put a foot on the floor and swayed toward the bar. She'd glanced at her empty glass. "What's in those things?"

"Rum. Lots of rum. Thanks to our amazing bartender." Blair flattened her lips at Morgan as she stood and steadied Tess. "Maybe we should get some air." Blair put her arm around her and led her outside to a table on the patio facing the water.

"I really am sorry."

"Not your fault...well, maybe a little, but Sophie put you in an impossible position." Blair stared at the water. "I appreciate you coming here to tell me."

"I'll find a hotel close by for the night."

"No. You're not driving anywhere. The room I booked for Sophie is yours for the weekend." Blair took in a deep breath. "Why don't we just make the best of it while we're both here?"

"Really?" She was taking this much better than Tess had imagined.

"Yeah." Blair shrugged. "I'm already familiar with the flirt I've been messaging. I think I'd like to get to know the poet."

"I'd like that too." She wasn't really sure if she should, considering her newly surfaced feelings for Sophie. Apparently, that seemed to be going nowhere, so what the hell?

Morgan appeared with a couple of glasses of water and set them on the table in front of them. "Everything okay out here?" She stared at Blair. "Can I get you some food or something?"

Tess's stomach felt like it was about to vault. "I don't think I can eat anything right now." Even though she probably should.

Blair glanced up at Morgan and then at Tess. "We're good."

CHAPTER TWENTY-FOUR

When Sophie pulled into the parking area, she'd gone back and forth about her plans to win Tess over several times. On one hand she wanted Tess to be happy with whomever she had the strongest feelings for. On the other hand, she wanted Tess to be happy with her. She didn't quite understand her feelings yet and didn't know if they were built on jealousy, love, or both. She'd finally worked herself up so much that she'd decided that this might end up being a war between her and Blair, if it unfolded that way—if she had to make it one.

She'd finally resolved to flirt mercilessly with both of them to gain Tess's interest—to see if she could light a spark in Tess. Make Tess jealous or at least reveal if she returned any of the feelings Sophie was experiencing. She had to find out if any of them were real, and waiting until Tess was living her happily-ever-after with Blair wasn't an option—she had to act *now*. Stealing her attention from Blair would be the key, especially if Tess truly was falling for Blair.

It was a little after eight when Sophie gained her courage and strolled into the resort. She glanced around the lobby as she entered to see if she could spot Tess or Blair. No luck. She headed to the registration desk, rolling her carry-on behind her.

"Good evening." The woman behind the counter smiled. "Checking in?"

"Yes. I have a reservation. Should be under Swanson."

The woman clicked a few keys on the keyboard and then a few more. It sounded like she was having trouble locating the reservation.

"I booked it online a little while ago." She'd found a last-minute deal.

The woman nodded and glanced up at her. "Sophie Swanson?" She nodded.

"Yes. I see it here." The woman clicked a few more keys. "I'll need to run your credit card. There is a standard fifty-dollar deposit for amenities, which will be refunded when you check out if you don't charge anything to your room."

"That's fine." The elevator chimed, and she glanced over her shoulder to see who was exiting. No Tess.

The woman took a keycard from the stack. "One keycard?"

"Yes. It's just me." She didn't know why she felt compelled to divulge that tidbit of information to a complete stranger.

The woman slid the keycard though the reader, wrote the number on the paper jacket, and slipped the card inside. "I found you a nice ocean-view room on the eighth floor." She pushed the card across the counter. "Take the east elevators just around the corner."

"Is there a bar in the hotel where I can grab a bite to eat?" She knew there was but had no idea where.

"There are actually three." The woman took out a small map of the resort complex and made three circles. "The best place for food this late is the Ocean Bar. It has a great view of the beach as well." She handed her the map. "Enjoy your stay. If you need anything else, just let us know. There's someone at this desk twenty-four seven."

"Thank you so much." She certainly hadn't expected an ocean-view room, but today must be her lucky day. She scanned the lobby one more time and headed to the elevators. Now, if she could just get that luck to run through the weekend.

She dropped off her bag in her room and went to the balcony to see the view. It was just as spectacular as she'd always imagined. The sun reflected off the blue-green ocean as the waves crashed into the shore. She opened the mini-fridge and checked out the amenities before she headed back down the elevator to find the bar. She didn't bother to change her clothes. Knowing Tess, she was probably already up in her room ready for bed by now. She always looked so cute in her pajamas. The elevator doors opened into the lobby, and she stepped out to find the Ocean Bar. She looked at the map before she folded it and tucked it into the pocket of her pants.

The bar was decorated in white paneling with square columns flanking each of the doors that led outside to the patio and then the beach. The breeze funneled through the room lightly, taking the edge off the summer humidity lingering in the air. She imagined herself sitting at a table outside having drinks with Tess. She shivered as Tess's smile flashed through her mind. She couldn't imagine being here with anyone else. Her stomach churned as she headed to the bar, which had only a few seats open.

She waited patiently for the busy bartender to notice her. Once she did, she immediately came her way. "What can I get you?"

"I'll have an old-fashioned."

"Coming right up." The bartender mixed the drink quickly and set it in front of her.

"Have you seen a dark-haired woman in here?"

"Can you be more specific? A lot of brunettes have come through here tonight."

"Not too tall—beautiful blue eyes? Possibly talking to another brunette?"

The bartender smiled widely. "You must be Sophie?"

She stared at the bartender. "Yes. Did someone mention me?" It wasn't like Tess to confide in strangers. Had she been drinking?

The bartender smiled. "I heard a little about you earlier tonight."

Fuck. "Not all bad, I hope." She glanced at her name tag, wanting to know the name of the person smiling back at her with familiarity. "Morgan."

"Nothing bad at all, but it sounds like you've certainly gotten yourself into a situation."

"Tell me about it." She glanced around the bar. "Where are they?"

"Beach, maybe? Or perhaps one of their rooms?" Seemed Morgan was into stirring the pot. "Went out onto the patio earlier, but then left about an hour ago." She wiped the bar down in front of Sophie. "Can I get you anything else?"

"No, thanks." She took her drink and crossed the bar to the patio doors. Where could they be? Tess would never go to Blair's room on first meet. She knew that much. Tess always gave her an earful when Sophie told her she'd slept with women immediately. The serial-killer and hygiene scenarios Tess recited flew through her head, and she smiled at the memory of Tess's furrowed brows and pinched lips. No one else had ever cared that much about her.

She took a seat at a table looking out onto the ocean and sipped her drink as she scanned the beach. There they were, sitting in the sand looking out onto the ocean. Blair's arm was draped around Tess as she leaned into her. They were nuzzled together watching the sunset like new lovers. Her stomach dropped. Was she too late? Had Tess sealed the deal with Blair already? All of a sudden Tess popped up, staggered to the shore, and dropped to her knees. Blair didn't follow. She leaned forward and squinted to see what was happening. Tess was puking.

Such a glorious sight to Sophie in a weird sort of way. She relaxed into her chair as the knot in her stomach loosened. They weren't nuzzling at all. Tess was leaning on Blair because she was drunk. She didn't like the idea that Blair had gotten Tess drunk right away. That was a sign she might be going to take advantage of her, and Sophie would never let that happen.

Tess wasn't moving now. She looked like a large piece of driftwood stuck on the shore. Sophie stood, went to the stairs, but stopped when Tess got up. Sophie went back to the table and forced herself to remain in her seat as she watched Tess walk slowly up the beach to where Blair was sitting. Tess seemed to be talking, she did a lot of that with her hands, probably embarrassed beyond reason. Blair patted the spot next to her, and Tess dropped into the sand a few feet away. Blair scooted closer and rubbed Tess's back. Apparently, she didn't like the distance Tess had put between them.

The heat on Sophie's neck rose. This whole scenario was meant for her, not Tess. Blair's attempts to get her drunk would never have worked on Sophie. She knew how to manage her drink intake, especially when she was with someone new. Tess, on the other hand, was an amateur when it came to alcohol. Blair seemed to be taking advantage of that fact.

Morgan appeared from nowhere. "You found them." She stared onto the beach.

She didn't take her eyes off them. "Seems that way."

"So why are you sitting up here?"

She glanced up and watched Morgan watching them. "She got her drunk."

"That was probably my fault." Morgan's tightened her lips. She tilted her head. "How so?"

"I gave her a mai tai after she finished her glass of wine. I think she was nervous. She sucked it down like it was juice."

That made sense and made Sophie feel a lot better about what was unfolding on the beach now.

Morgan turned her attention to Sophie. "So, why'd you send Tess to meet Blair first?"

Morgan obviously knew all the names of the players in this awkward game. "I didn't. I wasn't coming at all. Tess has a weird sense of obligation. Thought she should come and explain."

"She's not wrong about that. Blair seemed really excited to meet you."

Sophie scrunched her eyebrows together. "I'm confused. How do you fit in here?"

"Oh." Morgan seemed to fumble for words. "Sorry. Just an innocent bartender that got swept into the conversation earlier at the bar."

Apparently, Blair wasn't good at keeping her private life private. Seemed she'd dodged a bullet, but she still had Tess's heart to consider.

"Can I get you another drink?"

"No. This is it for me tonight." She was going to keep an eye on Tess and needed to stay sober. "Did Tess mention her room number, by any chance?"

"No room number, but she did say the ocean view on the ninth floor was perfect."

"Would you mind keeping my presence here to yourself?" She raised her eyebrows as she stared up at Morgan. "I'd like to surprise them."

Morgan smiled widely. "You bet. I can't wait to see that. Let me know if I can help in any way. Just leave a message at the bar, and it'll get to me."

"Thanks." She gave Morgan her sweetest smile. "I might take you up on that."

Morgan left her alone for now. She seemed to know more than the average bartender. Was it weird curiosity or intimate knowledge of the situation with Blair? Either way, Morgan might be useful in gaining more information about Blair.

❖

Sophie sat at the same table, nursing the same drink, for close to an hour before Tess and Blair got up and slogged through the sand to the lobby beach entrance. She raced through the bar to follow them and watched them get into the elevator. Once the doors had closed, she rushed to the elevators and pushed the button repeatedly until another one opened.

When she reached the ninth floor, she moved into the hallway and glanced both ways until she spotted them. She stayed out of sight in the small vending alcove as Blair helped Tess to her room. She was actually being very sweet to Tess.

"Are you sure you're all right?" Blair brushed the hair from Tess's face. "I can help you into bed. I don't mind."

"Absolutely not. I'm already embarrassed."

"Not your fault. Morgan's a little heavy-handed with her drinks. I should've warned you."

"It's okay. I'll be fine after I get some rest."

"Breakfast then?"

Tess nodded.

"Say about ten?"

"That sounds good."

"Okay. I'll swing by and get you." Blair rubbed Tess's

shoulders. "I'm just a couple of doors down across the hall in room nine-fifteen. Call me if you need something during the night."

The whole scene was sickeningly sweet, but she couldn't stop watching. She tore her eyes away to glance at the room-number arrows painted on the wall. Nine-fifteen was farther down the hallway. Blair wouldn't come her way. At least Blair hadn't booked connecting rooms.

Blair seemed to hold the door for a minute while Tess made her way into the room.

She heard a voice from behind. "Excuse me. I need to get to the ice machine."

She saw Blair look her way and quickly turned to the soda machine, then reached into her pocket for a couple of dollar bills and fed them into the machine.

She heard the door close and hoped to God Blair wasn't coming her way. She glanced around the corner, and Blair was nowhere in sight. Had she gone into Tess's room? *Fuck!* She rushed to the elevator and went down to her room on the eighth floor. She found it funny that her room was eight-twelve, directly under Tess's. She flopped onto the bed and read the last text Tess had sent her earlier today.

I'm sorry. I didn't mean what I said.

Tess's word still stung. She took in a deep breath as she typed a response. *I know, but you still said it.*

She saw the bubbles appear, which meant Tess hadn't passed out. *I was wrong to say it. I was angry. I really am sorry.*

Okay. I accept your apology. Now to see if she would come clean about where she was. *Can I come over?*

I'm already in bed. It's been a long day.

That wasn't a lie. It had been long for both of them. She wanted so badly to ask her if she was alone, but that would give her away. *Sweet dreams.*

You too.

A smiley face would've been nice, but she would be thankful for what she got. She hoped Blair wasn't with Tess, taking advantage of her in her drunken state. She wanted to race up there and stop whatever was going on, but she wouldn't. She would wait until tomorrow to talk to sober Tess. Drunk Tess might be too volatile tonight. She pushed the thought of them having sex from her mind. She had to, or the knot in her stomach would tighten, and then the tears would start. She refused to believe that Tess would have sex with Blair on the first night they met. She was probably going to have a raging headache in the morning, compliments of Morgan. She picked up her phone and began to type in a text.

Take some ibuprofen. She erased it—decided to let it happen.

She didn't want to give herself away yet. She hadn't figured out how to show herself tomorrow. She wouldn't interrupt their breakfast. She'd wait to see how Blair handled cranky Tess, which might be sort of amusing. She smiled. She'd always found hungover Tess enjoyable, if not completely entertaining, during Sunday brunch on the rare occasion she'd overindulged on a Saturday night.

Blair seemed to be considerate and caring. Well, as much as she could be for someone she'd just observed from a distance. It seemed Tess had seen more in her than Sophie had, and just maybe Blair was the right woman for Tess. Her stomach sank. Then that meant she'd probably lose Tess forever, especially after what had happened earlier today. She couldn't bear for that to happen.

CHAPTER TWENTY-FIVE

Sophie got up early, went down to the restaurant, and found a secluded table behind a column on the patio. Someone would have to be actually looking for her to find her there.

She ordered breakfast and was soaking in the sun while she sipped her coffee. She'd closed her eyes briefly when suddenly the warmth on her face vanished. She opened her eyes and felt a jolt because a shadowed figure stood in front of her. She tried to refocus. "Tess?"

"Nope. Just me." Morgan's voice was soft and light. "I saw you here alone. Thought you might like some company."

"I appreciate the offer, but I'm—"

"Watching your friend again." Morgan pulled out the chair across from her and sat. "Your cover might work better if you had company." She looked different this morning. Her platinum-blond hair wasn't spiked and hung loosely, blowing freely in the light ocean breeze. She wore peach shorts and a short-sleeved, white, patterned button-down shirt.

"Are you working?"

"Not now."

"Then why are you here?"

"Technically, today is my day off, but I'm covering for a friend for a few hours starting at noon."

"Oh. That's nice of you."

"I do what I can."

Sophie still didn't understand why she was here so early. "Do you live nearby?"

"Not too far, but I found an empty room and spent the night last night." She pointed at the water glass in front of Tess. "Do you mind?"

She shook her head and slid the glass across the table. "Go ahead."

Morgan took a drink of the water. "Might have had a couple of shots before I crashed." She winked.

"Perks?" Sophie raised an eyebrow. "Or perils of the job, I'm sure."

"Definitely perils." She took another gulp of water and swallowed. "I'm working here while I go to school."

Sophie really didn't want to have this conversation—to get engaged in Morgan's life—but, as Tess would say, ignoring her would be rude. "What are you studying?"

"Majoring in fashion with a minor in business management."

That information created a whole new aura around Morgan. She'd thought maybe psychology or philosophy, but fashion hadn't even entered her mind. "That sounds interesting."

"Not really. I've always liked fashion, and to succeed there you need business knowledge, or you could get screwed."

"I've never really thought about it that way. Do you go to school full time?"

"Yeah. I have some online classes this summer, but in the fall, I'll have to be on campus in Georgia for on-site classes. I can design online, but it's hard to make clothes remotely." Morgan waved at the waiter. "Working here comes in handy. I see a lot of ensembles that really pop and others that totally miss the mark."

"Seems you're a Morgan of all trades." Morgan was a real go-getter. "I'm impressed. You've got everything worked out."

"Just trying to get to where I need to be in life." The waiter appeared, and Morgan glanced up. "I'll have the steak and eggs, over easy, hash browns, and OJ to drink."

The waiter glanced at Sophie. "Shall I hold your meal and bring them out together?"

"Sure." She wasn't starving, and it would look better if Tess or Blair noticed her. "Can I get more coffee, please?"

"Oh, and bring a side of pancakes too. You know, the ones with the mouse ears." It seemed Morgan had a huge appetite.

"A little hungry this morning?"

Morgan leaned in closer. "I got the pancakes for you, but I'll have a bite or two." She grinned and relaxed back into her chair.

Sophie couldn't help but laugh. Apparently, Morgan was confident in herself and didn't put up any false fronts. She glanced around the dining area. Still no sign of Tess or Blair.

"So, why are you sitting here with me?"

"Why not? You're gorgeous and *alone.*"

A jolt went through her. She hadn't expected that response. "I'm flattered, but I'm not here to hook up." Especially with someone close to half her age. She didn't have the energy for that anymore.

"Then we'll just enjoy each other's company." The waiter dropped off Morgan's juice, and she immediately picked it up, took a drink, and let out a satisfying sound before she set her glass on the table and smiled widely. "Besides, I can help you. I know everything that happens around this place."

Sophie took in a deep breath. Morgan was gorgeous and interesting—the perfect entertainment for a resort weekend if she'd only met her a month ago. Now, oddly, even though Morgan hit all the marks, Sophie only had eyes for Tess. What was happening to her?

As their food arrived, a woman crossing the restaurant caught Sophie's eye. She was wearing flowing, wide-legged white pants along with a short-sleeved, unbuttoned shirt, with a tank underneath. All clothing items she'd seen in the Betty Bahama catalogue.

"Nice outfit, right?" Morgan noticed too.

"You think so?"

"Classy for sure." Morgan salted and peppered her food. "And the style fits her perfectly."

"Would you wear something like that?"

"Me?" Morgan shook her head as she ate a forkful of eggs.

"No. It's not really my thing." She cut her steak. "But you would look gorgeous in it." She chewed the steak and washed it down with her juice.

Sophie glanced at the woman again. It really did look good on her. "How old do you think she is?"

"Who cares? Everything about that outfit makes her ooze sophistication."

"Age doesn't matter to you?"

"Well, it does, but it doesn't." Morgan relaxed into her chair for a moment. "I only date women that are older than me."

"Why?"

"They're more interesting." Morgan reached across the table and touched her hand. "And have a little bit of life experience under their belt."

Sophie smiled widely as she slid her hand away. "We *are not* dating."

"Okay." Morgan focused on her food. "Then we'll just enjoy each other's company." She repeated the line.

"I *would* love to hear more of your thoughts on fashion. I work in marketing, and Betty Bahama clothing is a new client." She avoided the dating conversation, choosing to engage Morgan only in conversation about style while they ate.

"Nice." Morgan grinned. "Your client could get some great brand activation by selling in the resort boutique." She took another bite and chewed as she pointed her fork at another woman. "They're already wearing it, and the guests here usually buy more clothes while they're on vacation."

Sophie had to give Morgan credit. She was smart, engaging, and knew how to compliment a woman.

They'd long finished their breakfast and still no sign of Tess or Blair. It was almost eleven, and they'd analyzed every woman's ensemble in the restaurant. She'd actually learned quite a bit during the meal. It seemed the resort received many guests that would fit the Betty Bahama demographic, and Morgan took notice and had the eye to give an expert opinion.

Morgan looked at the time on her phone. "Looks like they're

not going to make breakfast." She stood. "Let me check with the kitchen to see if Tess ordered room service."

She nodded but hoped that wasn't the case. "Can you check to see if Blair ordered as well?" That would mean that Tess had become much more comfortable with Blair than Sophie had expected. She shook her head. She had no idea what Tess's comfort zone was with Blair at this point. Had Tess been talking to Blair outside of the social-media conversations? Had she planned to meet Blair all along? A whole new string of thoughts flew through her mind that she had to stifle. No. Tess would never do something intentionally to hurt her. Tess had come to clean up Sophie's mess, and that was all, right? That or she'd fallen for Blair. She had to stop this, or she wouldn't be able to put herself between them.

Morgan reappeared from the kitchen and crossed quickly to the table. "Blair ordered room service for both of them."

"Whose room?"

"Separate orders to each room. Tess probably has a rum hangover."

"Yeah. She probably didn't eat before she got here." Relief washed through her. Tess ate alone this morning, which meant nothing intimate had happened between her and Blair last night.

"So who are you here for?"

"What?"

"Is it Tess or Blair that you're here for?"

"Tess is my best friend—"

"And you're in love with her?"

She closed her eyes and took in a breath. "I don't want her to get hurt." Morgan was more perceptive than she thought. "I need to get back to my room to check on a few things at work." A total lie.

"And I have to get to the bar." Morgan picked up Sophie's phone and sent herself a text. "Now you have my number in case you need to get in touch. Will I see you later?"

"I'm sure you will. I'll be here through tomorrow."

Even though Sophie had made it clear that nothing was going on between them, Morgan's grin was ridiculous. It was clear she planned to push the boundaries.

❖

Sophie separated from Morgan, heading to the elevators as Morgan went to the bar. If Tess saw her with Morgan, that would cause a much larger problem than she already had. She hit the button repeatedly before it opened. She had to get out of the lobby. Tess was somewhere close by. She could feel it. The elevator doors opened, and she was face-to-face with Tess, the exact woman she wasn't prepared to see at this moment.

Tess stood frozen as the other guests exited the elevator. "What are you doing here?"

"I was invited." Sophie stepped into the elevator and pressed the button for the eighth floor. "The bigger question is, why are you here?"

"I felt bad about the situation and came here to tell Blair what we did."

"You told her everything?"

Tess nodded. "Yes. It was the right thing to do."

And now you're here romancing her yourself. "I can't believe this."

"What is wrong with you? You've been stringing Blair along for weeks, then you just drop her, and now you're here for what?" She shook her head. "To take advantage of her?" Tess had a way of making Sophie feel shitty even while being polite about it.

"You've been stringing her along as well, and you don't seem to be worried about it."

"What's that supposed to mean?" Tess pushed a finger into Sophie's chest. "I was helping you."

Sophie grasped Tess's hand and held it tightly. "You were a big help all right. So much so that you stole my weekend." She let her hand drop.

"What was I supposed to do? You weren't coming. Blair would've been devastated."

She doubted that. "Yeah, well, I'm here now. So you can go home." She gave her a backhanded wave.

"I will not. Once I told her the whole story we talked *a lot*, and she wants to have dinner with *me* tonight." Tess didn't mention all the alcohol she'd consumed.

"So, you're going to stay and romance Blair? The woman I had phone sex with…several times?"

Tess's mouth dropped open. "You did that more than once?"

She nodded. "I'm good at it." She didn't, but Blair was all in for more.

"You just never quit, do you?"

"Never had a reason to." *Before now.* Why was she provoking Tess? She'd come here to tell her how much she meant to her, how her feelings had changed. She raked her fingers through her hair. "Listen, why don't we both put an end to all this and go home? *Right now.*"

"I can't do that. I've already made plans with Blair. It would be hurtful and rude to just leave."

"So you'd give a stranger more consideration than you'd give me?"

"No. I mean yes. Blair is the innocent party here. Not you."

"You got that right. I haven't been innocent for a very long time." She blew out a breath. "I'll see you whenever you're done with this ridiculous charade."

The elevator doors opened, and she rushed out. She couldn't stay there talking to Tess any longer. If Tess wanted to date Blair, Sophie would put up a fight. Only she'd do it fairly by competing with Blair for Tess's affection.

CHAPTER TWENTY-SIX

Tess was still a bit shaken from her conversation with Sophie earlier. She wasn't sure how she'd expected Sophie to react to her coming to the resort in her place, but she certainly hadn't expected Sophie to follow her here.

The knock on the door came earlier than she expected. Blair had messaged her to let her know she'd pick her up, since their rooms were on the same floor. She'd also messaged her several times during the day asking if she was okay. By the last time she thought she'd worn out the hangover excuse. Even so, Blair had been disappointed but understanding. Tess hadn't mentioned her run-in with Sophie and thought perhaps by now she'd contacted Blair to let her know she was there as well. That didn't seem to be the case.

She checked her reflection in the mirror and straightened her vintage green floral Dior dress before she pulled open the door and let Blair into the room.

Blair smiled as she entered the room and made no attempt to hide her assessment of Tess's appearance. "You look lovely tonight."

"Thank you." She was skeptical about the compliment. Normally, she put quite a bit of effort into preparing for a date, but she'd been so rattled by her confrontation with Sophie that she'd walked for hours on the beach and hadn't given herself much time. She'd showered quickly and dried her hair, which was no help at all. The oceanside humidity always gave it a mind of its own. She'd tried to tame the dark, loose curls but gave up before she'd rifled through her suitcase and thrown on the least wrinkled dress she could find. Minimal makeup—only mascara, eyeliner, and blush—was all she'd been able to manage.

"You look very nice yourself." She'd noted that Blair was wearing a form-fitting black dress that hit just above the knee. It certainly fit her curves well.

"Are you feeling better?"

"Yes. Very much. Thank you."

"We'll be sure to stay away from the mai tais tonight." Blair pulled the door open and stepped into the hallway.

Tess followed her to the elevator. "I don't drink very often, and when I do, I usually stick to beer or wine."

"Noted." Blair smiled as the elevator doors opened, and they stepped inside.

They didn't talk much during the ride down or on the short walk to the Italian restaurant located in the hotel. The hostess appeared and led them to their table by the window, which provided a beautiful view of the ocean. She took her seat, but Blair remained standing, seeming to wait for someone—anyone to pull out her chair. The hostess was long gone, so she got up and helped her with it.

"Thank you." Blair gave her a smile as she slid into her chair and scooted closer to the table.

"My pleasure." It wasn't really. It was actually a bit awkward. She'd never been on the giving side of that particular nicety. Sophie had always done that *for her*.

Blair opened her menu. "Would you like to start with a charcuterie plate?"

"I'd love to, but that seems like so much food in addition to dinner." Charcuterie plates were one of her favorite foods in life, but pigging out on one wouldn't leave the lasting impression she hoped for tonight.

Blair peeked over the menu at her. "You're probably right. We should save room for dessert."

Tess looked at the specials menu. "Oh, they have olive-oil cake for the special dessert tonight." She glanced up at Blair. "Have you ever had it from Maialino in New York City?"

"I don't believe I've ever been there."

"To New York City or Maialino?" Sophie's voice startled Tess from behind her. "May I join you?" Without waiting for an answer, she pulled out the chair adjacent to Tess and sat.

Blair seemed startled as well. "The restaurant."

"That's too bad. Maialino is the perfect place for a late-night dinner. Topping it off by sharing a slice of their olive-oil cake makes it even better." Sophie glanced at her. "Right, Tess?"

"Yes. It absolutely is." This was awkward.

Sophie smiled at Blair. "I'm sorry I'm late. As I told you, I was hung up at work." She glanced at Tess. "It was so sweet of Tess to come in my place and keep you company until I arrived."

"Yes. It was." Blair smiled "It's been a pleasure getting to know her."

Tess wasn't quite sure how to deal with this situation. It seemed Sophie was going to compete with her for Blair's attention…in a weird sort of way. Sophie was looking hotter than hot in long, flowing, wide-legged black pants and a form-fitting floral tank that accentuated the definition in her arms. Tess almost couldn't drag her eyes away. With her bare arms and strong neck, she was sizzling.

Sophie flagged down the waiter. "Will you bring another place setting, please?" He nodded and swiftly retrieved the set-up and placed it in front of her. "Can we get a charcuterie plate to start?"

"That seems like so much food." Tess had already decided it was too much.

"But you love them." Sophie raised her eyebrows.

"Since there's three of us now, it'll be just enough." Blair seemed to be okay with the extra dinner guest. Either that or she was great at hiding her irritation.

Since she knew the whole story of their communications, maybe she was hoping for a twofer. She shook the thought from her mind. The weirdly rocky start of this weekend had her mind jumping all over the place.

Another woman appeared and rested her hand on Sophie's back. She vaguely remembered her as the bartender from last night. "There you are. Mind if I join you?"

Tess watched the two of them as they exchanged glances. She thought she was coming to take their drink order, but she was completely wrong. Another surprise. This night was becoming full of them.

Sophie glanced up, smiled widely, and motioned to the seat across from Tess. "Of course." She glanced back at Blair. "I'm glad you got a table for four."

"That worked out well indeed." Blair glanced at Morgan but didn't smile. Something else was going on here.

"We could've made do with something smaller." Morgan smiled at Sophie and then leaned toward her. Was she reaching under the table—touching her leg?

"This is Morgan."

"We've met." Blair tilted her head, and smiled after a minute. "You work here, right?"

"Yes. It's nice to see you again." Morgan took a sip of Sophie's water.

This was going to get ugly. Tess just knew it. "You and Sophie know each other?" Tess had to ask—had to know what was going on here.

Morgan nodded as the waiter slid a set-up in front of her and poured her a glass of water. "We had breakfast together."

She snapped her gaze to Sophie. "When did you get here?"

"Last night."

"Last night? Seriously?" Why hadn't Sophie shown herself then? Why hadn't she told her that earlier today?

"I sent you a text. Remember?"

Tess's stomach tightened. She'd lied, said she was tired—they'd lied to each other. When did they start doing that? "Last night is still a little foggy, thanks to Morgan's potent mixology."

"My bad." Morgan shrugged. "I didn't realize you might not have eaten yet."

"Thank God you won't be mixing my drinks tonight." Tess picked up her menu. "I think I'll try the spaghetti and meatballs." She glanced at Blair. "It's one of my favorites, but there's always too much. We can share if you'd like."

Blair shook her head. "Spaghetti is too messy for me." She quivered like there was something more behind her reasoning. "I believe I'll try the grouper piccata."

Tess thought that was an interesting reason not to order it. She imagined Blair with sauce all over her face. A simple *no, thank you* would've sufficed. "Then I'll get the chicken parmigiana." A little less messy, but still delicious, and it came with pasta.

"No matter the mess, I'm going to try the spaghetti and meatballs, and a Caesar salad." Sophie looked up from her menu and smiled. "I'll be happy to share." Not Sophie's usual dish of choice at any Italian restaurant.

"I'll share with you." Morgan closed her menu and set it on the corner of the table. "The meatballs are delicious."

Tess had been totally aced out of sharing the spaghetti with anyone.

"Sounds good." Sophie continued scanning the menu. "Caesar salads for everyone?"

"I'll have the house salad. It's perfection. You should try it." Blair's eyes rolled back as she described it. "Greens, sunflower seeds, goat cheese, dried cranberries, poached pears, and champagne vinaigrette."

"That sounds wonderful, but Tess isn't a fan of goat cheese," Sophie said.

This was getting annoying. Tess couldn't seem to get the words out fast enough before Sophie spoke for her. "That's true, but maybe they can make it without the goat cheese."

Sophie stared over her menu at her. "We'll find out." She closed her menu and slid it to the side of the table before she took a drink of water.

She watched the beads of sweat crawl down the glass as Sophie raised it to her lips. She was struck by her beauty as she drank. She hadn't noticed earlier, but Sophie was wearing lipstick—and mascara. She had no idea why. Sophie was one of the rare light blondes gifted with darker eyebrows and lashes.

The waiter approached, snapping her out of her daze. "Are you ready to order?"

Sophie set down her glass. "We are." She motioned toward Tess, who was sitting next to her. "This lovely lady will have the chicken parmigiana with a house salad." She motioned toward Blair. "This one will have the grouper piccata, as well as house salad." She grinned at Morgan. "And this handsome young stag will be sharing the spaghetti and meatballs with me."

"Salads?" He waited for her to continue.

"Caesars for both of us." Sophie smiled widely at the waiter. Such a gorgeous smile. "Would it be too much to ask the chef to leave off the goat cheese on one of the house salads?"

He smiled back at her. "I'm sure the chef will be happy to accommodate your wishes."

"We'll also have a bottle of California pinot noir."

"Might I suggest a sauvignon blanc to pair with the grouper?" The waiter glanced around the table.

"Two bottles of wine might be a bit much." Tess didn't intend to get drunk tonight.

"That sounds lovely." Sophie smiled up at him. "I think it will pair nicely with the cheese as well."

"Very nicely indeed." The waiter turned and left the table.

Sophie had ordered for all of them, and Blair hadn't seemed to be irritated at all. In fact she seemed to be impressed by Sophie — interested even. Maybe she was used to being pampered. Tess had absolutely no skills in pampering of that sort. And when had Sophie ever been interested in someone as butch as Morgan? Soft butch maybe, but Morgan didn't appear to be soft in any manner. Sophie liked to take the lead on everything.

Another waiter came to the table and removed the extra wineglasses. Fancy restaurants always seemed to have so many. A lovely show to begin with at dinner. Soon after, their waiter brought the bottle of white wine and presented it to Sophie. He seemed to know who was in charge at this table. Sophie nodded and then, surprisingly, she deferred to Morgan and waited for him to pour a taste. Morgan picked up the glass and let the bouquet waft into her nose. She probably wasn't a wine connoisseur, but any bartender would know when one was bad. She set the glass on the table, nodded again, and the waiter poured them each a glass. Tess was always amazed at how cool Sophie acted when they dined out. She was never able to pull that off herself.

The charcuterie plate was delivered soon after. It was a beautifully presented selection of cured meats and cheeses, accompanied by honey, mustard, and maple syrup. Olives and dried figs were scattered between the cheeses. Tess wanted to try each and every item immediately, but she held back and swiped only a piece of Gouda cheese. She could survive on it alone for dinner. She took a sip of wine and enjoyed the mix bouncing on her tongue. Sophie was right again. Sauvignon blanc was a perfect pair.

"This is so good." Tess popped another piece of cheese into her mouth.

"Shall I bring the bottle of pinot noir now to let it breathe for a bit?" The waiter was completely on top of the timing of the meal.

"That would be wonderful." Sophie leaned forward. "This waiter really knows his wines."

Blair grinned. "As, it seems, do you."

"Not really. I've made plenty of bad wine choices in the past. Hopefully this won't be one of them." Sophie put her wineglass to her lips and glanced over it at Blair.

Here it comes. The self-deprecating flirtiness. Tess knew it was just a matter of time before Sophie started showing Blair exactly how fabulous she was.

"I trust you completely to develop my palate." Blair lifted an eyebrow. "For wine or anything else you might want me to taste."

What the hell is happening here? Her date was being hijacked. If Sophie wanted a battle, Tess would give her one. "I'm sure I can introduce you to a new taste or two. I mean food-wise. I'm an excellent cook." She cringed at herself. That sounded more like a sales pitch than flirty banter. Maybe more wine would help. She picked up her glass and took a gulp.

A woman stumbling as she crossed the room caught Tess's eye. An opportunity to get the spotlight off herself. "Think she's had too much to drink?" She slyly glanced at the woman.

Sophie watched the woman for a moment. "She does look a bit unsteady, but I think it's the heels. She's probably just not used to walking in them." Sophie grinned. "Kinda reminds me of you."

The spotlight, front and center, focused on her again. She blew out a breath. "That's not a very nice thing to say."

"I'm sorry." Sophie's eyebrows pulled together. "I didn't mean to upset you." She seemed genuinely concerned. "I think it's adorable when you strap on a pair of three-inch stilettos and take the plunge into the walking perils of modern fashion." She gave her a soft smile. "Don't you?" She glanced at Morgan.

"Absolutely. There's nothing more impressive than a woman who can recover from a stumble."

Tess flattened her lips. So, it was meant as a compliment—a backhanded one—but a compliment, nonetheless. "Oh. I see. You like klutzy women."

Sophie let out a hearty laugh. "I never thought about it that way. I guess I do."

Tess couldn't help but laugh along with Sophie. Her laughter had always been a contagious happy spot in Tess's life.

"You two are so cute together. Have you ever dated each other?" Morgan popped a piece of cheese into her mouth.

"No," they said in unison, then looked at each other and laughed again.

"We would never want to ruin our friendship." Tess said it before Sophie could. She wondered if Blair was going to ruin it for them.

Sophie glanced up from her plate at Blair. "Do you golf? Perhaps we can get in a round while we're here."

Blair swallowed the fig she'd just eaten, set her fork on the side of her plate, and picked up her glass of wine. "No. I'm not a golfer." She glanced at Tess and raised her eyebrows. "I thought we'd just take advantage of the beach and enjoy the ocean."

Tess smiled. "That sounds lovely."

"I play golf. Took it up a few years ago." Morgan stared over her glass at Sophie. It seemed she was fascinated with her.

"Okay. Me and you tomorrow for an early round of golf and then to the beach." She glanced back at Blair. "I hope you're a good swimmer. The undertow can be mighty strong here."

"Oh. Have you stayed here before?" Blair plucked a piece of cheese from the plate with her fork.

"Not since I was a child, but I've visited Flagler Beach plenty, and I'm sure they're similar. Same ocean and all."

Tess scrunched her eyebrows at Sophie. "Then we won't plan to do more than dip our feet in the water. Just enjoy the beauty and the sound it brings."

"Will you excuse me for a moment?" Blair set her napkin on the table. "I need to go to the ladies' room." She stared at Morgan. "Anyone want to accompany me?"

Morgan stood. "I'll be right back."

Tess watched them walk across the restaurant. How had she gotten herself into this mess?

CHAPTER TWENTY-SEVEN

Sophie watched Blair and Morgan walk across the restaurant and disappear through the door. They both seemed a bit tense, and more familiar with each other than she'd anticipated. "Do you think they know each other?"

"You should know. You invited Morgan to join us."

Sophie raised an eyebrow. "Technically, she invited herself." Sophie chuckled. "It's turned out to be quite an interesting party."

Tess leaned closer. "What are you doing? One minute you're flirting with...everyone, and the next you're being ridiculously antagonistic."

"I'm only trying to get my date back."

"Well, this is a peculiar way of doing it. Are you staying here again tonight?"

"All weekend." Sophie took a sip of wine.

Tess scrunched her eyebrows together. "How are you going to pay for it?"

"I'll manage." She'd maxed out her card with the balance left after using her frequent-flyer miles. "Why are you interrogating me like I've committed the crime of the century?"

"Sophie, I don't understand why you're here. You said you weren't interested in Blair."

"I thought about it a little more, and I've changed my mind."

"Because I'm interested?"

"Are you?" She softened her voice. She would remove herself from this awkward mix if Tess truly wanted to date her.

Tess hesitated as she stared into her eyes. Maybe she wasn't sure how to answer. "This is ridiculous." She dropped her napkin onto the table and started to get up. "I'll just go."

Did that mean she wasn't interested in Blair? Sophie put her hand on Tess's. "No. You will not. We've already ordered, and we're going to enjoy our meals—all four of us. Besides, there's nothing wrong with a little bit of friendly rivalry, is there?"

Tess blew out a breath. "I don't like it."

She caught sight of Blair and Morgan as they appeared at the entrance to the room, then went to the bar. This was going to make an interesting foursome, for sure.

The salads arrived before Blair and Morgan crossed the restaurant to the table and took their seats.

"Do you know her?" Sophie asked. Blair seemed to be friendly with all the bartenders.

"Who?"

Sophie raised an eyebrow. "The bartender. It looked like you were having an in-depth conversation with her."

"No. Not at all. Morgan and I were discussing cordials as we walked, and we stopped by so she could show me what they have at the bar. I thought we might have a small glass of sambuca after dinner. It symbolizes health, wealth, and good luck." She slid her napkin onto her lap and picked up her fork. "This looks delicious."

"I'm not sure I'll be able to drink anything after several glasses of wine. Especially after what happened last night." Tess picked up her fork and speared a few of the greens. "Are you Italian?"

"No. I'm actually Irish and Scottish, but I have several friends who follow the tradition religiously."

Sophie laughed. "Sounds like an excuse to get drunk."

Morgan took a drink of wine and then held up her glass. "Cheers to the abundance of alcohol."

"Sophie." Tess pulled her eyebrows together. "That was rude."

"Oh." Sophie glanced at Tess, then at Blair. "That was totally not intended as an insult. I drink my fair share of alcohol. Tess can attest to that."

"No offense taken." Blair methodically gathered a variety of vegetables from her salad onto her fork and slid it into her mouth.

Tess did the same with her salad and took a bite before she set down her fork and chewed for an exceptionally long period of time. Sophie noticed that she didn't seem to be thrilled with the salad after all. The mixture of fruits and greens had probably sounded good at the time they'd ordered, but it wasn't Tess's usual with Italian food, and her tastebuds seemed to know it. Tess, in her usual polite way, would eat an acceptable amount, then push it aside and wait for her meal.

"That salad looks really good." Sophie picked up her salad. "Would you mind trading?"

"Of course." Tess seemed relieved as she passed the plate to Sophie and took the Caesar salad from her.

Sophie took a bite. It was actually better than she'd expected. The goat cheese would've been a nice addition.

Time to get this party started. She glanced up at Blair. "I read through some of our messages last night."

"Oh?"

"And then you made an appearance in my dreams." She forked another bunch of greens.

Morgan reached for Sophie's free hand. "How can I make an appearance in your dreams?"

Sophie pulled her lip up and gave Morgan a one-sided grin. "We'll have to discuss that later. Won't we?" She was sure Morgan had already appeared in plenty of women's dreams.

"I'll be happy to make that happen." Tess continued eating her salad while everyone stared at her.

Sophie lifted an eyebrow, and Tess's cheeks reddened.

Tess looked at Blair. "I mean, appear in your dreams. Do wild erotic things…to make you never want to wake up." Her cheeks were beet red now.

"Tess," Sophie said under her breath as she grinned. "I had no idea you had such provocative thoughts. Didn't know you had it in you." Tess wasn't good at witty banter like Sophie was. No matter how she said it, everything always sounded awkward coming out of her mouth. Sophie thought it was adorable. Sophie glanced back at Morgan and smirked. "Maybe you should leave that to the professionals."

"Are you sure you want to broadcast that fact about yourself." The words flew out of Tess's mouth.

Sophie was shocked. Tess had never been so critical of her—not until whatever this was had started with Blair. "Touché." Sophie focused on her food, forked the last few bites of salad, and bit the fork as she dragged it off into her mouth.

"I'm sorry. I didn't mean that." Tess spoke softly as she pushed the romaine lettuce around on her plate.

Sophie didn't quite believe that after what had happened yesterday. Only the arrival of their main courses interrupted the awkward silence. Once the salad plates had been collected, Sophie twirled a bite of pasta and put it in her mouth. It tasted divine. It was rare event when she indulged in such a meal these days, and she intended to enjoy every bite. She let out a soft moan, which made Tess glance her way and smile. Its calming effect on her was unexpected, even after the insults Tess had spewed at her. Maybe she should just go home and let Tess alone. She didn't look up for several minutes, and then not toward Tess at all. She couldn't. Her stomach churned as she swallowed a bite of meatball. She couldn't even enjoy it now. They all spent most of the meal eating in silence, except for Blair's or Morgan's occasional comment on the food.

Tess stabbed her chicken parmigiana with her knife, cut off a piece of chicken, and speared it her fork. "Unfortunately, this is the last bite I can eat." It seemed Tess was having the same problem Sophie was.

Sophie pushed her plate away and finished the wine in her glass, and Morgan immediately picked up the bottle and refilled it. She didn't stop her. A little buzz would do her good tonight. This little game wasn't turning out to be as much fun as she'd thought it would be.

After the busboy removed their dishes, the waiter brought the dessert menus.

"I think I'm going to have the limoncello cake." Blair glanced up at Tess. "Would you like to share it?"

Had Blair not been listening to Tess at all earlier? "The olive-oil cake is really not something you want to pass up."

"Neither is the limoncello." Blair raised her eyebrows as she set the menu on the table. "I'd rather have it."

It seemed Blair didn't care what Tess liked. Sophie was going to make sure Tess got the dessert she wanted. "I'll order it, and Tess can share with me."

"And I'll share the limoncello cake with Blair." Morgan smiled.

Blair didn't seem at all thrilled about that arrangement.

When their desserts were delivered, Tess immediately took a bite of the cake and moaned. Sophie's stomach dipped, and just like that she knew she couldn't let Tess go that easily. Whether it was an unexpected infatuation or the love between them had suddenly become clear, she wouldn't let it go without a fight—even if the fight was with Tess.

The waiter delivered the small decanter of sambuca and four delicate glasses. Tess put her hand over her glass. Sophie guessed she'd decided to skip the cordial to avoid another hangover.

Sophie was kind of sad about that. Tipsy Tess was fun. She'd been intrigued by her flirty banter earlier and would love to hear more. But considering some of the nasty comments that came along with it, maybe it was best not to press that no-filter button any harder tonight.

CHAPTER TWENTY-EIGHT

Tess didn't quite know how to escape for the rest of the evening. After a good two plus hours of food and wine, dinner was finally over. Everyone seemed to be at a loss for more conversation, except Morgan. She'd been whispering things to Sophie all night, which was annoying as fuck. She didn't like being replaced that easily. Among the four of them, she wasn't sure who wanted to get out of the restaurant and who wanted to stay. Tess's intuition was off tonight, and she couldn't really tell which one Sophie wanted. In any case, Tess was ready to hightail it back to her room away from this awkward party. Right now, she wanted nothing more than to get out of the confines of her dress and into her comfy yoga pants. She'd eaten so much it was threatening to cut off her air supply.

The whole dinner show and assorted players had confused her. Sophie had flirted with both Blair and Morgan, yet she'd looked out for Tess's wants throughout the evening, even after Tess had been nasty to her. Blair seemed to enjoy the attention but clearly didn't take note of anything Tess said during dinner—proved by her choice of dessert. Blair had convinced Tess to try the house salad, but that was a mistake. Sophie had known that from the beginning. She should've just gone with her first choice of the Caesar, or nothing at all. Her first thought had been there was no way was she going to be breathing garlic dragon fire tonight when she was alone with Blair—and she would be alone with her at some point, whether she wanted to or not. But now she didn't care.

Morgan clasped Sophie's hand and squeezed it softly. "When do I get to see you again?"

"Is the night over already?" Sophie's gorgeous copper eyes focused on Morgan. They were light and glassy, just as they always were when Sophie had a bit of alcohol in her.

Morgan smiled. "That's exactly what I wanted to hear." She moved closer and kissed Sophie on the cheek.

That sight hit Tess hard. Her stomach knotted, and she thought she might lose everything right there, including her dignity. That was it. This night was completely over for her. She couldn't sit here and watch Sophie flirt any longer.

"I'm a bit tired. I'm going to head up to my room." She stood and maneuvered her chair from behind her. It was clear Blair wouldn't do that for her.

"Not too tired, I hope." Blair stood as well and took her hand. "I'll walk you up."

Sophie glanced up at her, expressionless. Her mouth opened, and Tess thought maybe she was going to say something—object in some way—but then Morgan whispered something in her ear and caught her attention again.

She turned immediately, tugged her hand out of Blair's grasp, and sped to the exit. How could Tess expect Sophie to want her more than a gorgeous twenty-something-year-old with a perfect smile and a perfect body? Tess would never be perfect in either way.

Blair trailed her closely. "Hey. Hold on a sec." She took Tess's hand again. "They're holding a bottle of champagne for us at the moonlight bar on the roof. I thought we could go up and have a glass."

She glanced back to the table where Sophie seemed to be captured by Morgan. "I need to use the ladies' room. I'll meet you by the elevators."

"Okay. I'm going to drop back into the bar down here and make sure everything is set. Don't go up without me."

Tess rushed to the bathroom. She really didn't have to go, but she needed to get out of the restaurant. She couldn't stand watching

Sophie romance Morgan or vice versa. It seemed she'd done everything wrong by coming here. Instead of letting Blair down easy, she'd made her think she was interested—and let Sophie know that as well.

When Sophie had asked her why she'd come, she had to admit to herself that she really wasn't sure anymore. At first, she'd felt bad about the way Sophie was planning to ghost Blair, and now that she'd gotten to know Blair a little, she liked her. Not that she saw any future with her other than friendship. She still had a big space in her heart for Sophie that Blair couldn't fill. She was certainly screwing up her friendship with Sophie royally. When she'd sniped at Sophie, she'd seen the sparkle in her eyes dim, and she'd felt horrible. She obviously didn't know how to flirt around Sophie without her jealousy showing through. She was so confused by her feelings, and her actions plainly revealed it. She'd made a complete mess of everything and wasn't sure how to get herself out of it. She was going to have to be honest with Blair.

She checked her makeup, straightened her dress, and went to the elevators. No Blair. She went back into the restaurant. Sophie and Morgan were gone. She really didn't want to go anywhere but her room right now. Definitely not to the rooftop bar with Blair to drink champagne. She was already tipsy enough. She had to find Sophie and put an end to this madness.

She went back to the elevator and hit the button, and the elevator chimed, the doors opening immediately. When the elevator stopped on the eighth floor, Tess shot out of it and around the corner.

Tess's timing was horrible, as always. She rounded the corner only to find herself faced with the vision of Sophie backed up against the door with her hand on Morgan's chest about to be kissed. Then it happened—Morgan leaned in and kissed Sophie. The move looked sweet, tentative, and unplanned, at least on Sophie's part. Now came the stare, and the move closer. It seemed Morgan wanted more. Tess's stomach lurched. She quickly spun and headed back to the elevator. Getting drunk with Blair might just be the answer tonight.

CHAPTER TWENTY-NINE

Sophie shoved Morgan away. Morgan had kissed her—totally unsolicited and unwanted. Had she really let that happen? Here she was pining away for her best friend, but also willing to let Morgan satisfy her sexual desires. With the feelings in her heart for Tess, how could she separate the two? She was a total shit. "No. I can't do this." She paced the hallway. "I won't—I don't want to." She certainly hadn't expected her feelings to change this way, but they had, and she couldn't do anything about it.

"Maybe you should just go after her." Morgan chuckled as she leaned against the wall watching her. "I'm more than willing to fill in for Tess, but we both know you're in love with her."

"Is it that obvious?" Sophie held her hand to her forehead.

"I didn't know for sure until now." Morgan pushed off the wall. "I could see it in your eyes earlier, and do you know your heart beats faster when you think about her?" She took Sophie's hand and pressed it to her chest. "That thumping isn't for me."

"*It does?*" She felt the pounding in her chest. "It does."

"It was pretty apparent at dinner. When you two look at each other, you have an aura about you that says it all." Morgan smiled. "I've seen plenty of people in that state before, and you two are definitely in love."

"I'm not sure if it's love, but it's something." She squeezed Morgan's hand and released it. "You're very understanding for someone who's been led on all night." Morgan's maturity was surprising. Sophie wasn't so sure she'd have reacted so calmly if the situation were reversed.

"It was a nice meal with good company." Morgan smiled and shrugged. "Why don't you tell her?"

"We've been friends for a long time. I don't want to mess that up." She took in a deep breath. "With all that's happened this weekend, we're already on shaky ground."

"If that happens, you'll deal with it, but if it doesn't…then you'll have something really special between you. Isn't that worth the risk?"

"I'm not sure she feels the same way. I think she might truly be interested in Blair."

"I don't think Blair is a good fit for Tess, even if she's interested. Blair is kinda high maintenance."

"How do you know that?" She still suspected some connection between them.

"Just from seeing her here this weekend and watching her interactions. The way she waits and lets people do things for her. You know, the things you do automatically for Tess."

She did know and had noticed that herself. She'd watched as they were seated earlier, and Blair had clearly waited for Tess to pull out her chair.

Morgan took out her phone and checked a text message. "Looks like I'm needed at the rooftop bar." She hit the button for the elevator. "Want to come along?"

"No. I need to talk to Tess." She had no idea where she stood with Tess and needed to find out.

"Okay." Morgan raised her eyebrows. "Are we still on for golf in the morning?" The elevator opened, and they both stepped in.

"I don't think so. You'll be a great catch for the right woman, but—"

"That woman's not you."

"I'm sorry." She felt bad about the ways she'd used Morgan to make Tess jealous.

"No worries. I'm not ready to be caught yet." Morgan winked

as the elevator doors opened on the ninth floor. "Go get that girl." She exited with Sophie.

She took in a deep breath and stood a moment to gain her courage. She'd never had a problem with any woman, but Tess was different. A lot was at stake here. She'd been telling herself for years that there could never be anything between her and Tess. She'd never trusted herself not to hurt her. At times she'd thought she'd found the one, and after the initial infatuation she'd always gotten bored and moved on. She'd never moved on from Tess.

Hearing Tess's words over the past couple of weeks had changed her somehow. It was as if she was truly seeing only her now There could never be someone who knew her better or loved her more. Could she possibly make a lifetime commitment with Tess? Would Tess want a lifetime commitment with her? A chill ran through her, and the fear took over again. Everything was moving too quickly— maybe faster than she was ready for. *Here goes nothing…*

Sophie headed down the hallway and took in a deep breath before she knocked on Tess's door. No answer. She knocked again. Still no answer. Her worst nightmare was coming true. Tess was already in Blair's room. She moved down a few doors and knocked on room nine-fifteen. She remembered overhearing Blair tell Tess the number last night. She waited a few minutes and knocked again. She was just about to give up when the door opened.

Blair appeared. "Oh. I thought you were room service."

"Is Tess here?"

"I'm here." Tess's voice floated softly throughout the room before she appeared behind Blair.

Timing was everything. She had to break this up somehow. "I'm sorry to interrupt, but I need a minute with Tess."

"Now? Can it wait?" Blair seemed annoyed. "We were just going to have a drink."

"Sorry. Can't wait. It's work." No fucking way was she letting Blair ply Tess with more alcohol, and have her way with her. Not tonight—not ever. Tess had already had enough to drink at dinner. Had Blair not learned anything from the night before?

Tess seemed to flounder a bit at first, then maneuvered herself from behind Blair and out the door. "I'll be back soon." She moved down the hall to her room, swiped the key, and opened her door.

Morgan appeared and passed them in the hallway. "I can help you with this bottle of champagne you ordered." She held it up as she continued to Blair's room. "We'll see you two in a bit." She glanced over her shoulder and winked at Sophie.

Sophie nodded. Morgan had turned into the best wingman ever. She'd been disappointed again, when Sophie had made it clear she wasn't interested in anything sexual with her, but Morgan seemed to get it.

She turned back to Tess and followed her into her room. Tess looked spectacular tonight, just as she had the night before when Sophie had glimpsed her on the beach from the bar. Even after puking, she was beautiful. Maybe, just maybe, she could make everything right between them.

CHAPTER THIRTY

W hat was all that about?" Tess rushed farther into her room. "I can't believe the way you're acting. I've never seen you be so rude."

"You're going to fuck her, aren't you?" Heat burned the back of Sophie's neck.

"Why do you have to be so crass about something so wonderful?" Tess spun and paced to the other side of the room. She unzipped her dress, pushed it to the floor, and kicked it aside.

Sophie tried to ignore the beautiful sight in front of her as she picked up Tess's dress and slung it over the chair. "Because that's what it will be with her. You don't love her."

Tess pulled a T-shirt over her head. "When has love ever had anything to do with sex for you? Not ten minutes ago, you were kissing Morgan."

A rush of panic hit her. She hadn't seen Tess earlier. "We're not talking about me, but I *did not* kiss her. She kissed me." She hadn't—she couldn't.

"Oh." Tess tilted her head, her blank expression completely innocent. Was she getting the picture now? "So, you don't want to fuck her?" The words crossed her lips softly.

"God, you're beautiful. Even when you're angry." Sophie shook her head slowly as she took in a deep breath and tried to calm herself. "But you're so dense sometimes." She rushed forward. "I don't want her or anyone else. I want you." She took Tess's face in her hands and kissed her.

Heat rushed through her and she exploded with chills at the same time. This, right here, was something she'd hoped for but hadn't expected—ever—and it was lighting her on fire.

Tess wrapped her arms around her, and Sophie felt the softness of her hips before she gripped her ass and pulled her closer. Tess deepened the kiss, and Sophie had to break for air. Tess stumbled backward to the bed with her arms still wrapped around her, pulling Sophie along with her. Paper crackled as she landed on top of her poetry. Tess began shoving the pages aside.

Sophie stopped her. "Wait. Stop. Don't ruin your pages." She began putting them all into a pile and stopped to read one.

Not to be moved,
my heart beat slow and steady.
Drained of all emotion,
dormancy came, and my heart froze.
Like a flower, pressed between the
pages of a book, it was crushed,
never to be whole again
until you opened the book
and nurtured the petals,
bringing them back to life,
just as you did my heart.

"I wrote that for you." Tess glanced at the rest of them. "I wrote all of these for you."

Sophie picked up another and read it.

You've taken me to places
deep inside your soul.
Places you've kept hidden away
for far too long.
Beautiful, echoing emotions within you
that show me who you truly are.
Yes, you are beautiful.
You, my love, are like an unfinished canvas,

every day like a freshly made brushstroke,
adding another vibrant layer of color,
to you,
an incredibly remarkable work of art.

"Is this really how you feel?" It was clear that Tess saw things about her—in her heart—that no one else did.

Tess nodded. "I can't explain it, but over these last few weeks you've done something to me, Soph. I don't know exactly when or how, but you've changed me."

Sophie felt the warmth as a tear fell from her cheek onto the page. "Oh my God. I've ruined it."

Tess scrambled to get a tissue from the bathroom and blotted it dry. "No. You haven't." She held up the page. "See? It's fine."

Sophie kissed her but then broke the kiss. So many emotions were bursting inside her—and so many questions. "I don't think I can do this." She rushed to the door, grasped the handle, and glanced back at Tess. "I don't want to hurt you."

"I want this—even if it's just for tonight." Tess's beautiful, pleading blue eyes stared back at her.

Sophie let the handle go and pressed her hand against the door before she turned around. "You know I'm not good at relationships, Tess." She walked slowly toward her.

Tess met her halfway. "I know." She cupped her hand behind Sophie's neck and brought her mouth to hers—explored it with her tongue.

A jolt coursed through Sophie's system that dispatched an immediate wake-up call between her legs, as did the hand down her pants roaming between her legs—fingers searching for the edge of her panties—the moan coming from Tess's mouth when she realized Sophie wasn't wearing any. The light stroke to her clit pushed the tingle in her groin to an off-the-charts throb. She couldn't turn back now. She wanted this—she wanted Tess.

Tess led her to the bed, and they fell onto it, tearing at each other's clothing as they landed. Sophie made swift time in pulling Tess's T-shirt over her head and taking her breasts into her hands, just a little over a handful, perfect for her hungry mouth. She took a nipple into her lips and swirled it with her tongue, let it go with a loud suck and then attacked the other. Tess moaned, tangled her fingers in her hair, as Sophie played with her hard peaks. Still fully dressed, she stood and began quickly removing her clothes as Tess stared up at her with the most beautiful, dazed expression. She was sure she would never forget it. It was like they'd just launched into the most spectacular ride at Disney World.

Once Sophie was undressed, Tess sat upright and took in a deep breath as though she were inhaling her very essence. She pressed her mouth amid her curly locks and dipped her tongue inside. A wave of arousal pulsed through Sophie, and she bucked against her, forcing Tess's tongue in harder—deeper. Tess wrapped her arms around her thighs and held tightly as Sophie grabbed hold of her shoulders— then tangling her fingers in her hair as she quaked—letting out a breathy scream as the orgasm ripped through her. Tess slipped a finger inside as she pressed harder with her tongue, pushing Sophie into another earth-shattering orgasm.

Tess slowly released her, letting her hands roam across her thighs as she stared up at her. "Come here and kiss me."

This certainly wasn't going as Sophie had thought. Pleasing Tess, making her scream, was on the top of her list, and instead Tess had done that exact thing to her. She was completely in *her* control. Tess's wish was her command.

Sophie took in a slow, deep breath to get her bearings before dropping down to kiss Tess, then crawling on top of her, as Tess maneuvered farther onto the bed. She left her mouth, trailed her lips across the small of her neck to her collarbone, then to the soft, creamy white skin of her chest. As she kissed her way down Tess, she reveled in the sweetness of her—the softness of her. Until recently, she'd never imagined anything like this could ever happen between them, never allowed herself to even go there. Tess was too special to let go—ever.

She wanted to take her time, enjoy the taste of her from head to toe, but Tess let out a moan, and her desire surged. She wanted all of her—now. She quickly reached her goal, let the soft curls tease her lips before she dragged her tongue lightly across her, then through her folds. She enjoyed the zap coursing through her as Tess moaned, then ventured deeper into the treasure she sought. The taste was like the finest Bordeaux bouncing off her tongue, a taste so exquisite she hadn't realized she'd been longing for it. When she slipped her finger inside, she felt an ocean of wetness, and it was all for her. She dove in completely. This was definitely love.

CHAPTER THIRTY-ONE

Sophie's eyes were the deepest copper Tess had ever seen them, focused and filled with desire as she came down on top of her. Mouth to mouth, chest to chest, hips to hips. The feeling rising within her was nothing short of primal as she grabbed Sophie's ass and pulled her hard against her, enjoying the delicious friction between them.

The hot tongue that danced over her neck made its way across her, stopping to pivot several times on her nipples and then the sensitive spot just above her hip. She jerked as the quiver shot through her.

She tried to hold off and enjoy the dazzling intro a moment longer. The low moans escaping Sophie's lips made her tingle all over, and at the moment her tongue swept across her clit, she simply let go—spiraled into pure pleasure—something she'd never experienced to this measure before. Sophie shoved her hands beneath her ass and lifted Tess's hips as her mouth latched onto her—sucking, licking, consuming her completely. Tess pressed into her as though Sophie was a magician and levitation was only the first of her magic. She cried out as Sophie swirled her tongue and took her racing to the peak, then crashing into orgasm again.

She quivered again as Sophie kissed every inch of bare skin on her way back up to her mouth and then covered her like a blanket of pure satisfaction. She'd never been with a woman more interested in pleasing her than anything else—and sweet Lord, Sophie knew all the right spots to make Tess crawl out of her skin and still beg for more.

When Sophie rolled off to her side, Tess immediately missed her warmth and the weight of her body on top of her, the caress of her fingers rushing over her. She curled up next to her to reclaim the heat of the fire she'd been immersed in just a few moments ago.

"You okay?" Sophie sought out her eyes, focused on them.

"I'm perfect." Tess wanted to say so much more, but it might ruin everything if she did.

"Me too." Sophie kissed her softly, reached down, and pulled the sheet over them before she nudged Tess into the crook of her arm.

She hoped so, because she wanted her more now than ever. She'd told her she wanted it even if it was just for tonight, but that wasn't true. Tess wanted much more than a night with Sophie, but she wouldn't press her. Not tonight. She would enjoy what Sophie was giving and hope for a lifetime of it.

CHAPTER THIRTY-TWO

Sophie hit the button for room service, and the voice came through the phone louder than she'd expected. "Room service, can I help you?"

She leaned to the side of the bed and whispered into the phone, "Yes. I'd like coffee and continental breakfast for two this morning, please."

"The wait is one hour and thirty minutes."

Seriously? She couldn't wait that long. "Never mind. I'll get something downstairs." She set the phone lightly into the cradle before she kissed Tess on the forehead and whispered in her ear, "I'll be back in a little while."

Tess didn't move. She was out—totally exhausted from so many screaming orgasms that Sophie had lost count. Tess knew ways to please her that she hadn't known herself, and she'd made her experience them fully. She lifted the sheet, let her gaze sweep over Tess's perfectly curvy nakedness. It took every bit of her willpower to cover her again and slide out of bed ninja style. She needed coffee—lots of it—if she was going to continue this marathon.

She threw on a pair of Tess's yoga pants and a T-shirt, then took the key card from the dresser before she stepped quietly out of the room and slipped into the elevator. Thankfully, it was still early, and no one else was on the floor. She stared at herself in the mirrors. Her cheeks were flushed, and her hair was all over the place—the look of someone who'd been thoroughly fucked. She smiled as she finger-combed her hair and rubbed at her eyes.

She wasn't the kind of girl who fell asleep after sex. She was usually up and out before sunrise. But she'd turned her normal sprint into a marathon last night and had indeed fallen asleep in Tess's arms, slept until she saw the wee bits of sunlight peeking through the curtains. Tess made her want to rethink everything in her life. Warmth spread throughout her chest as she realized she wanted Tess again and again. She thought now that she probably would forever. How could she have missed what could've been between them for so long? So many moments lost in the past. She smiled as she thought about their lives to this point. They weren't actually lost moments. They were only different.

The line at the coffee bar was much longer than Sophie had expected. She saw the sign in the lobby for the early morning fishing excursion that started in just under an hour. This was the reason for all the people in Magellan shirts and quick-dry pants.

As she took her place in line, she glanced around the lobby. Was there nowhere else to get coffee in this hotel? She should've just gone ahead and ordered room service. She was about to bolt out of line and back to the elevator when she heard Blair's familiar voice behind her.

"Mind if I slip in line with you?" Blair smiled and waited for her to agree.

She sighed. Just who she wanted to see this morning. "Sure."

"You're up early for someone who apparently had to work late."

"I'm an early riser." She could hear the hoarseness in her own voice, remembered briefly how Tess had made her scream during the night. She cleared her throat. She wouldn't discuss what happened with Blair. It was private. "Sorry I ruined your plans with Tess last night." She wasn't sorry *at all*, but she was trying to play nice.

"Are you?" Blair raised her eyebrows.

She pulled her eyebrows together. "Absolutely, but work doesn't wait." And Tess's work on her last night had been impressive. Even thinking about it made her heart race. The ache in her legs brought Tess's impassioned voice front and center. *Yes...right there... harder...don't stop...I'm going to come...now.*

"You okay?" Blair stared at her. "You seemed to go somewhere."

She had indeed gone somewhere magnificent and couldn't wait to get back there again. "I'm fine." She stepped forward as the line moved. "Did you have a nice time with Morgan?" Sophie was sure Morgan had kept her occupied. They knew each other somehow, perhaps from a previous visit. It was obvious there was some familiarity between them. She'd seen the glances between them at dinner, and Blair hadn't looked very happy when Morgan had shown up at the start.

"She stayed only until I realized Tess wasn't coming back." Blair glanced around the lobby. "We were supposed to meet for breakfast." She glanced at her phone as though waiting for a text.

She glanced at her own phone. She'd been gone for close to an hour. "*What is* going on with this coffee bar?"

"It's always like this in the morning with the fishing excursions and all." Blair was still scanning the area. She was going to be disappointed.

Sophie finally got to the counter and ordered a large vanilla latte and a large mocha, along with two buttery croissants.

"Ordering for two?" Blair raised an eyebrow.

Sophie shook her head. "This line is ridiculous. I don't want to have to stand in it again." She dropped her cash onto the counter and motioned for the cashier to put the change into the tip jar.

"I'll take your advice on that." Blair ordered the exact same drinks and charged them to her room.

Was that her usual order? Oddly enough, Sophie had never cared to ask what specialty coffee Blair liked or, for that fact, how she liked her coffee in general. Was the second cup for Morgan? Sophie scrutinized her. Blair looked well put together for so early in the morning. They both moved to the end of the counter to wait for the drinks to be prepared and delivered.

Once her drinks were delivered, Sophie picked them up. "Guess I'll see you around." She had no plans to do that at all. She was going to spend the whole day with Tess—possibly in bed. She had a lot of time to make up for.

"I'll be soaking up the morning sun." Blair picked up her coffees and headed toward the beach.

She watched Blair saunter to the door and wait as someone rushed to open it for her. The woman had a ridiculous amount of confidence.

She turned and ran right into Morgan, sending the croissants flying and spilling the drinks she'd just purchased. "Oh my God. I'm so sorry."

"No worries." Morgan grabbed a handful of napkins and blotted the front of her shirt with them. "You're all smiles this morning. How'd it go with Tess?"

"It went great. I only came down to get coffee and spent close to an hour in line."

"I'll get you a couple of new ones. What were they?"

"No. I can't wait." She started to the elevators. "I'll order room service when I get back to the room." Hopefully Tess was still asleep.

Morgan raised her eyebrows and followed her to the elevator. "So, it was a good night?"

Sophie smiled, unable to hold her happiness in any longer. "A very good night." She pressed the button for the elevator. "How about you and Blair?"

"That's not happening."

"Sounds like you have experience with Blair."

"Let's just say, we've met before."

There was some connection between them, just as Sophie had thought. "Well, then we'll just have to find you another eligible woman."

"Not here. It gets too messy."

"I understand. Mixing work with pleasure could get complicated." Sophie hadn't even thought about how she and Tess were going to work that out.

The elevator doors opened, and she waited for a couple more would-be fisherman and women to exit before stepping in. "I'm going to get back upstairs before Tess misses me."

"I'm glad everything worked out." Morgan smiled.

"Me too." She waved as the elevator doors closed.

When Sophie got back to the room, Tess wasn't in bed. She excitedly rushed to the bathroom. A shower with Tess would be a fantastic addition to last night. She had no idea why she hadn't pushed this scenario before. Tess was the perfect everything—they complemented each other in so many ways, and if last night was any indication, they fit perfectly together sexually as well.

Not there. Hmm. She didn't remember Tess telling her she had any activity scheduled this morning. Blair had mentioned breakfast, but she hoped Tess wouldn't have left for that. She opened the door and looked in the hallway—no Tess. Where the hell had she gone? She pulled open the sliding door to the balcony and stepped out onto it. The sunrise was spectacular, and she wanted to share it with Tess. She caught movement on the pathway to the beach. *Tess.* She warmed as she watched her hips sway gracefully. She spun and rushed out the door to the elevator. She didn't want to miss another moment with her. She'd already done enough of that.

CHAPTER THIRTY-THREE

Tess sat on the beach completely alone, watching the sunrise. Last night had been everything she'd dreamed of—everything she'd wanted for so long. She'd given Sophie every piece of her heart—revealed her deepest feelings. What had she done? She'd just ruined any chance of remaining friends with Sophie—made love to her with the type of passion she'd never shown anyone before—and Sophie had left her lying alone in bed like she had done so many times to other women. She'd been a fool to think it would be any different with her. She tugged her knees to her chest, pressed her face against them, and sobbed. For once in her life she had no idea what to do—and no one to talk to.

She heard soft footsteps pushing through the sand, and her heart raced. She quickly wiped away the tears, hoping with every last drop of her optimism that it was Sophie and she'd been wrong about her this time.

"Good morning." Blair's low, sexy voice told her it wasn't. "I missed you last night."

She slipped her sunglasses over her bloodshot eyes and contemplated her next words. "Sorry. It was late after we finished working, and I thought you were probably asleep." A total lie. Why did she say that? She'd been completely honest with Blair since she'd told her everything she and Sophie had done. She didn't know whether it was guilt or embarrassment, but she couldn't be straight with her about her feelings for Sophie.

"I saw you stroll out here from the cafe. I didn't know if we were still on for breakfast, but I got coffee." Blair held up the cups. "I got two different kinds. A vanilla latte and a mocha. You choose." Blair grinned as Tess chose the mocha. "When I realized you weren't coming back last night, I booted Morgan out." She laughed that amazingly attractive laugh. Why couldn't she just fall in love with Blair? It would be a whole lot easier on her heart for sure. "I know you weren't working. I'm not an idiot."

She closed her eyes briefly. "I'm sorry. I really am. I didn't expect anything to happen with Sophie." *And now I wish it hadn't.*

"I think she did."

"Yeah. Me too." *I've probably been on her "to do" list for a long time.*

"Where *is* she?"

"Beats me." She shrugged. "I woke up this morning, and she was gone."

"Oh." Blair's voice rose, and she pulled her eyebrows together. "Really?"

She nodded. "I guess I set my expectations too high."

"I didn't get that vibe from her about you. The way she's been competing with me since she arrived gave me the impression she has feelings for you."

"If she does, sex seems to have gotten in the way." The same as it had with so many others.

Blair put her arm around her, tugged her close, and kissed her on the temple. "Maybe you should wait and see. I mean, instead of assuming the worst."

"She was *gone* this morning. I know what that means." She shook her head. "I've seen her do it too many times to too many women."

"What do you want from Sophie?"

"I want her to hurt. She needs to know how it feels."

Blair squeezed her shoulder. "That's not really what you want. Is it?"

She shook her head. "No. I want her to love me back with all her heart." She wiped a tear from beneath her sunglasses. "I don't think that will ever happen."

"If I were your best *friend*, I'd be jealous of you giving attention to anyone else."

"I'm not sure I'm the one she's jealous of."

"Are you sure? She canceled on me—wasn't going to come until you came in her place. People in love want to be with each other all my time…It seems like Sophie was doing that by coming here this weekend."

"I wish that were the case. But no. I think she's done with me now."

"How can you say that?"

"She left me—in bed—alone. After we…" The tears started again.

"Maybe she was just scared? Needs a little confirmation that you're not going anywhere."

"That's a funny way to ask for it." Tess wiped her cheeks dry.

"She's not as secure as you might think. I see a lot of vulnerability in her."

Tess scoffed. "Sophie, vulnerable? She's the strongest woman I know."

"Maybe at business or even with other women, but when it comes to you, I don't think she has any walls." She tugged her closer. "Who knows her better than anyone else?"

"I do. That's why I feel so used. What happened last night—this morning is her MO. She sleeps with women and then leaves them. No strings is what she prefers."

"You're not just any woman."

"That's why it hurts so much."

"I feel like I'm talking to a brick wall here."

"I guess I just don't see what you see."

"Yet."

She glanced over her shoulder and spotted Sophie trudging through the sand. "I don't know what to do. Please don't tell her about our conversation."

"Treat last night the way she does."

Tess pulled her eyebrows together. "I don't know what you mean."

"Like it was only casual sex. Like it didn't change anything between you." She sipped her coffee. "Follow my lead. I'll get you out of this."

Sophie appeared and dropped into the sand next to her. "How long have you been sitting here?"

"Long enough to catch a beautiful sunrise together." Blair smiled.

"Blair got us coffee." Tess held up her cup.

Sophie glared at Blair. "I did the same."

"Oh?" Tess raised her eyebrows. "Where is it?"

"I spilled them in the lobby. After that fiasco, I went back to your room—thought we'd just order room service. Then I saw you on the beach from the balcony. I went up to change before coming back down."

Sophie *had* changed her clothes, but almost two hours for getting coffee and changing seemed excessive. Sophie had had second thoughts.

Blair touched her shoulder. "We have to go. We've got a yoga class scheduled this morning."

"We don't want to miss that." Tess stood and brushed the sand from her shorts.

Sophie pulled her eyebrows together and stared up at her. "I thought we were going to spend the day together."

"I'm sorry." Tess raised her eyebrows. "I didn't get that impression when I woke up alone this morning." She couldn't suppress the tinge of anger in her voice.

Sophie grabbed her hand, forced her to look at her. "Tess." She blew her name out in a sigh. "Can we just talk for a minute?" The confused look on Sophie's face hit Tess hard. Was she really upset or just jealous that she was spending time with Blair?

"No worries. We're good." Lowering the importance of what happened between them last night was difficult, but it was the only way Tess was going to get through this and still remain friends with Sophie. If that was even possible now.

Blair glanced at Sophie and then at Tess. "I can do yoga alone if you want to stay here with Sophie."

"No." Tess pulled her hand loose from Sophie's. "I need to relieve some of this stress." She rolled her shoulders. "Perhaps we'll see you later." She turned quickly and trudged through the sand. She needed to get away from Sophie now.

When they made it back to the resort pathway, she turned and looked at the beach. Sophie had leaned back onto the heels of her hands and seemed to be staring out at the beach. She grabbed a handful of sand and threw it into the wind, then stood and walked down the beach. Had she really gone to get them coffee, or had she just used that as an excuse for leaving and not coming back? Wouldn't she come after her if she really wanted to talk about what happened?

"You should really go talk to her. She did get you coffee this morning." Blair stood beside her and watched Sophie walk farther down the beach. "Sophie loves you. She might be having a hard time realizing the implications of it, but I think she really does love you."

"Don't try to cover for her. You don't leave someone alone in bed after the first time you've had sex if you love them." She turned and headed inside. "I need time to absorb it all, including Sophie's reaction, and figure out how I feel. I can't do that if I'm with her. She'll explain it away, and we'll go back to the way things were. Either she wants to be with me or she doesn't. It can't be that hard a decision for her."

"What if it did mean something to her, and she doesn't know how to handle it?"

"I don't know. I can't tell her how to fix her insecurities." Tess didn't intend to try to convince Sophie that they were meant to be together—in an actual relationship other than friendship. She had to come to that realization herself.

CHAPTER THIRTY-FOUR

Sophie had no idea what had just happened—why Tess was acting the way she was—why she'd left the beach without talking to her—without believing her. She'd been so excited to get back to the room this morning to talk to her, but she was gone. When she'd seen Tess walking to the beach, she'd gone straight to her room to change out of her coffee-soaked clothes and rushed down to tell her all of her hopes and dreams for their future. But when she'd gotten to the beach and plowed across the sand, she'd stopped hard. The sight of Tess sitting in the sand enjoying the sunrise with Blair made her stomach drop.

How could Tess do that—be wrapped up with Blair—after what they'd shared last night? Bile had risen in her throat as the crash of the waves filled her ears. She'd watched them interact—Blair's arm around Tess's shoulder, nuzzling and whispering in Tess's ear. Her stomach had churned as heat raged through her. She was filled with jealousy and then despair.

Tess's words echoed in her mind. *I want this—even if it's just for tonight.* Had Tess done to her last night exactly what Sophie had done to so many other women in the past? Enjoyed the moment without thinking about the consequences—the impact on their lives? Tears welled in her eyes and sprang onto her cheeks. She stopped and stared out onto the ocean. *No. You will not do this.* She took in a deep breath, wiped the tears from her cheeks, and made her feet move forward. She would walk until she had no salt left in her to cry. Tess would not see how much this hurt.

❖

It seemed like Sophie had been walking the beach for hours. Her legs felt like jelly as she slogged out of the sand and onto the concrete pathway. She glanced around as she approached the Ocean Bar. Tess and Blair were nowhere in sight, which was probably a good thing right now, because Sophie had no idea what she was going to say to her. Walking hadn't done anything to help her unscramble her thoughts—or figure out why Tess had reacted the way she had this morning. She was going to ignore the whole thing until she could talk to her alone.

When she realized Morgan was behind the bar, she debated whether to stay. Morgan would be curious about this morning, and she didn't want to talk about it.

As soon as Morgan spotted her, she came her way. "What can I get you?"

"Bourbon, neat, and a water."

Morgan filled a glass with ice and water, then slid it in front of Sophie.

"Thanks." She took a huge gulp and felt the coolness spread throughout her.

"You okay?"

She guessed she looked a little ragged from crying. "I'm fine. Allergies."

"Where's Tess?"

"I don't know."

Blair appeared beside her. The woman seemed to be everywhere she wasn't wanted. "Is Tess going to be another conquest on your list?" Her voice screeched through Sophie, like fingernails on a chalkboard. How things had changed from a week ago.

Sophie shifted on the stool to face her. "What are you talking about?"

"Your track record with women isn't the best, is it?"

Heat burned her neck. "Did she tell you that?"

"Is it true?"

"That's none of your business. I would never hurt Tess."

"I hope you mean that. It looks to me like you treated her like you treat every other woman you've slept with." Blair's tone was quick and angry.

"Did Tess say that?" Had Tess really confided in Blair about her dating habits?

"She didn't have to." Blair narrowed her eyes. "I've seen you in action. I was there that night at The Speak Easy, the night you contacted me." She blew out a breath. "I purposely sent the book with the quote inside, hoping Tess would see it."

"What? How?"

"I'm the day-shift bartender there." She tilted her head. "I've seen you go home with plenty of women."

"Oh, wow. That makes sense." Morgan chimed in as she slid the highball glass of bourbon in front of Sophie.

"When you contacted me, I thought I'd just roll with it. I was honestly happy when Tess showed up here instead of you. But then you arrived after her and were so persistent and competitive, I thought, what the hell. I'd wait and see how the whole thing shook out. After all, you're both beautiful women." She shook her head. "But the two of you getting together...I didn't see that one coming *at all*."

"Oh my God. Tess was right about you." She got up to leave.

Blair caught her by the arm. "Not entirely. I'm not exactly who I've led you to believe, but I am fairly well read, and I'm taking college classes to better my life and start my own business."

"Then you're just who Tess is looking for."

"Tess is perfect. Believe me. I'd jump on that train in an instant, but I'm not a complete shit, either. She's in love with you, and I'm not going to get in the middle of that."

"You're the reason we're at this point. You've completely messed everything up between us."

"Or maybe she's brought everything between you to light." Morgan seemed to see through all the bullshit.

"You're a fake, trying to be someone you are absolutely not. I should've seen through you from the start."

Blair stood. "That's my cue."

Morgan interrupted. "Will I see you again later?"

Blair glanced at her and scrunched her eyebrows together. "You promised to show me how to make that drink."

"Sure." Blair turned back to Sophie and touched her hand. "I really do wish you the best of luck with Tess."

Sophie watched her walk away, ambivalence hitting her square in the chest. "And now I'm alone again, as usual." She took a gulp of her drink and winced as the alcohol burned her throat.

"If you ask me, she just did you a huge favor."

"I'm not asking." Unsolicited advice had gotten her into the mess in the first place. Everything would've been fine if she'd just left Tess alone last night. Once she found her in Blair's room, she couldn't do that.

"Got it." Morgan stared at her for a moment. "Blair just told you that your best friend is in love with you, and from what I've seen while you've been here, you seem pretty captivated by her too." She stood tall and motioned to herself. "I mean, you passed up this."

She smiled. Morgan's humor made her feel a little lighter. "I think I've lost her." She shrugged.

"So, go find her. Tell her how you feel."

"It's not that simple."

"Why not?"

"I slept with her last night, and now, apparently, she thinks I'm a cad."

"Are you?"

"Yes, absolutely, with all women." She took in a deep breath. Her heart hurt. "But not with Tess."

"Then prove her wrong."

"I think I'll give her some time to calm down." She pushed her glass to the Morgan. "I think we both need that." Plus, it would give her time to figure out exactly what she wanted from Tess and how to tell her. A new drink appeared in front of her, and she drank it down before she headed back to her room.

CHAPTER THIRTY-FIVE

Tess had cried—sobbed, even—as she drove home, ignoring traffic as she thought through everything that had happened over the weekend and the past couple of weeks. June had been the month of all things bad. She'd been perfectly happy with her life at the beginning of it, and somehow everything in it had gone completely to shit. Her career, her friendship, and her love life were all in total turmoil now. No way would everything return to the way it was. And even if it could, she wasn't going to let it. She was so tired of being second-guessed at work that she just couldn't do it anymore—especially now. Sophie would still stand up for her, but working closely with Sophie would be difficult at best. Besides, she didn't want to work for someone who didn't value her ideas or at least consider them. Joy had never done either one of those things.

She pulled to the side of the road, searched for Joy's number in her phone, and hit the call button. Ringing blared through the speakers of her car, and then Joy's voice-mail message sounded.

"Hey, this is Joy. Please leave your name and number, and I'll get back to you as soon as possible." How could such an evil woman sound so sweet on the phone?

"Joy, this is Tess." She didn't know why she'd identified herself. Joy should recognize her voice. "I've had a lot of time to think during my forced time off this past week." Having second thoughts, she sucked in a breath. *You can do this.* "This is my notice that I will not be returning to work at JB Marketing. We can talk later this week about what you need from me for the transition."

She was nicer than she should be to Joy, but she felt bad about not giving her two weeks' notice. Either way, Joy was probably going to be thrilled to be rid of her. She hung up and relaxed into the driver's seat. She suddenly felt unbelievably relieved—good, in fact—about her decision. It had been weighing heavily on her for months, and now the weight was completely gone. It was clear she'd made the right move.

As soon as she arrived home, she tugged her bag from the back seat and dropped it. The contents spilled out onto the driveway. Just another fucked-up consequence from her weekend. She screamed into the air and then sobbed as she gathered her toiletries one by one and shoved them into the bag. She saw Janet step onto her porch and wave as she rushed to get inside. Tess avoided looking her way—swiping at her face and trying to stop crying for the few moments it took her to get her key in the lock and open the door.

She'd ignored the doorbell after she'd gone inside, knowing it was Janet. She'd been unsuccessful at hiding her anguish, or Janet wouldn't have been at her door. She was a sweet neighbor, but Tess couldn't talk about what had happened now—to anyone. Everything was too raw. She'd done it all to herself—set herself up for rejection—but that didn't make it any easier to accept.

Tess ached all over as she rolled off the couch and headed into the kitchen to make coffee. She turned her phone on and listened to it beep as a string of text messages came through. She'd ignored all Joy's calls last night. She guessed Joy wasn't as thrilled with her resignation as she'd thought. She'd ignored Sophie's attempts to reach her as well and had finally turned off her phone when they both continued. Sophie had stopped calling later in the evening and begun texting instead. She scrolled through the texts Sophie had sent before she got into the shower.

I need to talk to you and explain some things.
What happened today was ridiculous.
Blair made everything I did look bad on purpose.

Please answer your phone.
At least let me know you're all right.

Tess wasn't ready to let Sophie explain anything—or blame it on Blair. She didn't think she could even see her without bursting into tears. Last night, lying alone in bed, she'd gone into the living room and clicked on the TV, the silence too much for her. She'd fallen asleep watching every sappy movie she'd recorded that had ever made her cry—which was a lot. She'd tried to keep her mind off the night before, but everything she watched made her think of Sophie because she'd watched them all with her. Even when she'd been in a relationship with Lindsay, Sophie was the one she could always count on—the one who'd kept her sane and made her happy. But Tess had made a vow to herself last night. It was the final night she would want for anything that she couldn't have. She was going to move forward from now on—with or without Sophie.

The scalding-hot water eased the stress in her shoulders. She rolled them forward and then back again as she let it run over her head and onto her face. She shouldn't have looked at the text messages from Sophie. Now she couldn't get them out of her head. Blair had said nothing to make her look bad. To the contrary, she'd been really understanding about the whole situation, which was more than she would've been. What was there for Sophie to explain other than what Tess already knew? She'd told Sophie it was only for one night, and now she had to live with it. Sophie didn't do relationships.

She flipped off the shower, got out, and wrapped herself in a towel. The woman she saw in the mirror had begun to make some huge changes in her life and was going to have to continue on the new road of uncertainty she'd paved for herself. Today she would make a plan to build her own business. She headed into the bedroom and slid on a pair of blue jeans and a long-sleeved V-neck shirt before she went into the kitchen and poured herself a cup of coffee.

She logged onto her computer and pulled up the business plan she'd been working on. It was always there, but she'd never found the right time when she was financially able to bring it into play. Little had she known that choice would be forced upon her before she was ready. She'd planned to show it to Sophie in hopes of going into business with her, but that didn't seem likely now. So, ready or not, she was going to make it happen.

She finished the last of the coffee in her cup before she headed out next door to Janet's house. She'd felt bad about ignoring her the day before. She just couldn't talk to anyone until she got her feelings in check. She wasn't sure she was calm enough yet, but possibly she could handle small talk. Maybe that would get her mind off the disaster that had just decimated her friendship with Sophie.

She strolled across the yard to Janet's porch and took in a deep breath before she knocked lightly on the door. It swung open almost immediately.

"What's going on with you? I could see from my porch how upset you were yesterday."

"I'm fine." She said it but didn't mean it. "No. I'm not." Tears welled in her eyes. "I had my life all together—wasn't going to worry about being with anyone. She's messed all that up. I definitely wasn't looking for this, and now I don't want it to end." She paced to the end of the porch and back.

"Who messed it up?" Janet opened the door wider and motioned her inside. "Would you like some coffee?"

"No. Thank you." She continued inside and followed Janet to the kitchen to refill her cup. "Sophie—me—both of us."

Janet led her back to the living room. "I thought you said you were going to meet with someone named Blair?"

"I was—I did, but then Sophie showed up." She swiped at her tears. "I thought she came because of Blair." She sat in the corner of the cream-colored, Lawson-style sofa and stared out the huge picture window that spanned the living room. It provided a perfect view of the neighborhood.

"She didn't?" Janet sat next to her in the adjacent, matching chair.

"No." Tess shook her head. "Maybe that was her plan to begin with, but she met another woman—a bartender—Morgan, and I was left with Blair."

"You don't like Blair?"

"It's not that I don't like her. I only went there because Sophie wasn't going. I wanted to explain why, and apologize. It's complicated."

"Sure sounds like it." Janet's forehead crinkled.

"The thing is I never really clicked with her. Not like I do with Sophie."

"You finally saw Sophie." Janet grinned.

She flopped back against the sofa cushion. "I never took the time to realize what was right in front of my face until I thought I might lose her. Then I slept with her, and that changed everything. When I woke up the next morning, she was gone."

"You don't think she feels the same?" Janet shifted in her chair.

"Isn't that obvious? This weekend was a complete disaster, and now I think it might be too late."

"I don't know. Is it? Have you talked to her?"

"No." She shook her head. "I blew it off like it meant nothing. I can't talk to her until I get my feelings under control, or she might run away again."

Janet pulled her eyebrows together. "Seems like you're the one who ran away."

"She ran first. I just got the hell out of there before the situation got worse. Sophie can't know how I feel about her, or our friendship is done."

"You've been friends for an awfully long time. Can't you work through it together, somehow?" She patted her hand. "You should talk to her. Get it all out in the open. Who knows? She might surprise you—have feelings for you too."

"If she doesn't, I'll never be able to face her again."

CHAPTER THIRTY-SIX

Sophie sat at her desk staring at the other side of the room where Tess's desk was impeccably clean. The woman was perfect. Why had it taken her so long to realize it—to realize she was the one woman in her life who had never let her down? Never left her alone when she needed someone—never hurt her in any way—ever.

She glanced at her phone, checked the time, and set it back onto the desk. It was almost ten, an hour and a half past when Tess usually arrived. It wasn't like her to be late. When she'd left the bar at the resort, she'd gone to Tess's room to see her and found housekeeping changing the sheets. Tess had left without even letting her know—the first clue that they might not recover from this fiasco. She'd called and sent her several texts to see if she was all right, but Tess hadn't responded—the second clue. She should've gone straight to Tess's house when she got back to town, but Sophie was too chicken—afraid the truth would destroy her world—and their friendship.

She picked up her cell phone and scrolled through her messages. Nothing from Tess. She started typing a message, then erased it as she headed into Joy's office.

"Any idea where Tess might be?" She picked up the coffee decanter on the table. "You send her out for coffee or something before I got here?"

Joy glanced up from her desk. "Really? You're going to play it that way?"

"I'm not playing, Joy. Where is she? We've got a lot of work to do."

"Then you'd better get on it." Joy remained focused didn't look up. "It's going to take time to find a replacement."

Replacement? "What the hell are you talking about?"

Joy slapped her hands to the table. "Listen. I don't have the time or energy for your games." She stared at her for a moment before she tossed her pen on to the desk and relaxed into her chair. "She really didn't tell you?"

"What, Joy? What didn't she tell me?"

"She called me yesterday and quit."

"Why?"

Joy shrugged. "Didn't give me a reason. Not a real one anyway. Just said she didn't want to do it anymore."

Her stomach knotted. She braced herself on the doorjamb. There it was—the third clue that nothing would ever be the same again. Tess had left because of her. She never thought Tess would leave her job—especially without a word to her.

Joy leaned forward, picked up a few papers, and dropped them back onto the desk. "She's not getting a reference from me. I can tell you that right now."

"You better give her a sparkling reference." She pushed off the doorjamb and rushed toward Joy's desk. "She left because you sucked all the creativity out of her." She waved her finger in the air in front of Joy. "Tess has a beautiful imagination, but you had to mess with everything she created. Not for the better." How was Tess going to make a living now—how was *she* going to live without Tess?

"I have to go." She spun and rushed out of the office. Sophie had always thought she was strong for being able to leave relationships when she wanted. Now she realized she was weak for not sticking around when things got tough. She had to fix this rift between them somehow—even if Tess *didn't* love her.

CHAPTER THIRTY-SEVEN

Tess glanced through Janet's window and saw Sophie screech into the driveway, jump out of her car, and rush to her front door and ring the doorbell. Now she was banging on the door—loudly. What the hell? She popped up off the sofa, went to the door, yanked it open, and rushed across the yard to her porch.

"What the hell are you doing? Trying to make me a spectacle with my neighbors?" She glanced around to see who was watching. No one but Janet, who had followed her out and was now standing at the end of her porch.

"You quit without telling me?" Sophie's eyes were wide and filled with hurt—or maybe it was anger. She couldn't seem to tell anymore.

"I did." She glanced away. She couldn't stand to look into Sophie's eyes. "I knew you'd try to talk me out of it again." She glanced at her. "And I just can't stay there with all that's happened now...between us." She shook her head and looked away again. "Was anything you ever said to me real? Did you mean any of it?"

Sophie let out a breath, and her shoulders sank like she was going to deliver bad news. "Remember that night when I passed out in your bed after we kissed?"

She nodded. How could she forget?

"I wasn't asleep. I didn't know what to do, so I faked it. I was afraid it would ruin our friendship."

She took in a breath. "Seems you've done that anyway." She walked around Sophie to the mailbox at the curb and retrieved the letters inside—several bills she would now have to pay out of her savings and a letter from Sophie. She must've dropped it off yesterday. She ripped it open and read the words Sophie had written.

Like the leaves of winter,
dark and wilted—
my love has dried, turned to dust.

It was a beautiful haiku. She glanced up to see Sophie rushing toward her. "Don't read that."

She held the note up in the air above her head and then behind her back to keep it from Sophie. "You wrote this?"

Sophie nodded. "That's personal." She reached around her, snatched it out of her hand, and folded it, kneading the crease between her fingers.

"Then why did you leave it for me?" She could see the sadness in Sophie's eyes, tears welling in the bottom, the copper color so vibrant now. Something must have happened between Sophie and Morgan after she left. "I'm sorry I haven't been there for you." She pointed to the paper. "To help you with whatever you're dealing with." She felt the words stick in her throat and couldn't keep eye contact. "I got caught up in the romance of it all. I thought your feelings were about me, but clearly they weren't. Or you wouldn't have run away."

"I ran away? You're the one who left me alone at the resort."

"You weren't alone. You were with Morgan. I'm sure you made good use of your time—got her into bed too."

"Is that really what you think of me?" Tears crested over onto Sophie's face. She swiped them away just as she had Tess's feelings.

"I don't know what to think anymore. I woke up in bed *alone*. Do you know how that made me feel?" Tess blew out a breath. "Used and abandoned. That's how."

"I felt exactly the same. For your information, I did come back, just like I told you. I only left because I tried room service and they were backed up. So, I went to the lobby to get coffee, and just my luck, every person in the resort needed a cup before they went fishing. By the time I got some, the whole spill thing happened. I said, screw the coffee. I just wanted to get back to you, but when I got to the room, you were gone. Then I found you on the beach all snuggled up next to Blair. Who, by the way, had been in line with me getting coffee."

Blair had told her that, but she hadn't believed her. "I was upset."

"Well, so was I." Sophie poked a finger into her own chest. "It isn't every day you realize you've been searching for a love that doesn't exist. A love that sweeps you off your feet in a single moment and you know it immediately." She paced the walkway. "That it actually takes time—sometimes a lifetime—and plenty of nurturing." She kneaded her forehead with her fingers. "And when you find that love and figure it all out…"

Tess stared at Sophie, realizing she might have been wrong about what had happened. "You figured it out?"

Sophie nodded and moved closer. "It's scary as fuck wondering if that person loves you back." She moved swiftly, took Tess's face in her hands. "It's you, Tess—it's always been you."

She could see the heartbreaking emotion in Sophie's eyes, wanted to save her from it all, put her mind at ease and tell her it would all be okay. She pressed her lips against Sophie's and floated to where she'd always dreamed of being—surrounded by strong, soft arms. This kiss was different than before somehow. It was long, slow, and searching, a kiss that happens only once in a lifetime when you realize you're with the person you're destined to be with for the rest of your days.

She broke the kiss and took in a deep breath. "You love me?"

Sophie nodded. "I do. I think I always have. I never expected love would be like this. I was dreaming about a life I already had. You're the one I want to spend the rest of it with."

"I thought I'd lost you." She kissed her slowly, passionately, the subtle taste of salt from their tears drifting between them. Every doubt she'd had over the past few days melted away.

"You two should take that inside before someone calls the police." Janet's voice brought her out of the dream she seemed to be living.

They stared at each other and laughed.

Sophie touched her cheek, wiped the moisture from it with her thumb. "Can I stay…with you…today—tonight?"

Tess took her hand and led her up the walkway and inside the house. "I'd be happy if you spent every day and night with me for the rest of my life."

"I'd like that too."

"You won't have any space. We'll be around each other all the time." She shut the door and kissed Sophie softly. "I wake up happy every morning. You'll have to put up with that."

Sophie grinned. "You make me laugh even when I don't want to—I know I'm not perfect. I'm pretty much a fuck-up that shouldn't be with anyone. Especially someone as sweet and beautiful as you." She took her hands and held them tightly. "But I promise to kiss you like it's the first time forever and make sure you're in love with me until the day I die."

"I haven't stopped being in love with you yet." She pulled Sophie into her arms and kissed her again. "It'll make life interesting, for sure."

"Yeah, it will." Sophie took her hand and tugged her into the bedroom. "Now, since you're unemployed, let's make use of some of your free time."

"I hated that job."

Epilogue

It was the first vacation Tess and Sophie had taken since starting their own firm—So Tess Marketing. The last six months had definitely been a struggle. It had taken everything each of them had in savings and a small-business loan to get up and running, but it was totally worth it. No one was killing their creativity now. They were in charge of the show and running it their way.

They'd been able to take few accounts with them, including Squisito as well as Boho Clothes, because they'd brought them in to JB. They hadn't come to the agency on their own. If Joy hadn't been sorry to see them go at first, she certainly was by now.

Tess sat on the beach and took her camera from her bag. She'd been dabbling in photography lately, along with painting. Sunrises on the Palm Coast were so vivid she couldn't possibly capture their beauty. She'd tried every morning since they'd arrived at the beach house they'd rented, but the camera just didn't do them justice.

She heard Sophie approaching and glanced over her shoulder When she got closer, she had to stop and take a breath to calm herself. Her smile never failed to set off a tingle in her belly. She thanked the stars every night for aligning to bring them together. Sophie plopped down next to her and nestled their coffees in the sand—Sophie's with a touch of cream and hers with a spoonful of chocolate powder.

Sophie took the camera from her and set it on the beach.

"Forget about the pictures this morning. Just watch. Enjoy the beauty." She clasped her arm, held it gently with her fingers, and heat rushed through Tess like a flash fire that had just been released behind a closed door. That response hadn't faded since their first time together. She suppressed the urge to tug her back inside and make love to her again this morning.

Instead, she leaned closer to Sophie and watched the hues of reds, purples, and oranges come up over the ocean and splay into the clouds. "It's gorgeous." So much better than through the lens of a camera, just like their new relationship. They'd spent so much time worrying about the aesthetics of it, they'd never stopped to enjoy each other in the best ways possible. She glanced at Sophie and saw the happiness in her face as the sun glowed upon her. She'd never seen her quite the way she had over the past few months. It had been a rocky start, but once they'd set their fears aside, life had never been better.

Sophie snaked her fingers between Tess's and held her hand gently. "Describe it to me."

Tess honestly didn't know if she could capture the beauty of it. "You do it."

Sophie took in a deep breath. "I'm not sure I can do it justice, but here goes.

As the day rises over the ocean,
the water is lined with
silver strands of foam.
Still and slick, it glows
as the sunlight caresses it.
Radiant beads of light dance across the
mirrored surface with graceful elegance.
As dawn finally breaks, the sun rises,
letting threads of light glide
over the sheet of glass.
Its warmth melts the froth from its edges,
giving way for the life beneath the sea

to take in a long-overdue breath.
A mind awakens, and life begins again.

Just as mine has with you." Sophie kissed her softly.
And just like that, Tess was in love all over again.

About the Author

Dena Blake grew up in a small town just north of San Francisco where she learned to play softball, ride motorcycles, and grow vegetables. She eventually moved with her family to the Southwest, where she began creating vivid characters in her mind and bringing them to life on paper.

Dena currently lives in the Southwest with her partner and is constantly amazed at what she learns from her two children. She is a would-be chef, tech nerd, and occasional auto mechanic who has a weakness for dark chocolate and a good cup of coffee.

Books Available From Bold Strokes Books

A Convenient Arrangement by Aurora Rey and Jaime Clevenger. Cuffing season has come for lesbians, and for Jess Archer and Cody Dawson, their convenient arrangement becomes anything but. (978-1-63555-818-0)

An Alaskan Wedding by Nance Sparks. The last thing either Andrea or Riley expects is to bump into the one who broke her heart fifteen years ago, but when they meet at the welcome party, their feelings come rushing back. (978-1-63679-053-4)

Beulah Lodge by Cathy Dunnell. It's 1874, and newly betrothed Ruth Mallowes is set on marriage and life as a missionary...until she falls in love with the housemaid at Beulah Lodge. (978-1-63679-007-7)

Gia's Gems by Toni Logan. When Lindsey Speyer discovers that popular travel columnist Gia Williams is a complete fake and threatens to expose her, blackmail has never been so sexy. (978-1-63555-917-0)

Holiday Wishes & Mistletoe Kisses by M. Ullrich. Four holidays, four couples, four chances to make their wishes come true. (978-1-63555-760-2)

Love By Proxy by Dena Blake. Tess has a secret crush on her best friend, Sophie, so the last thing she wants is to help Sophie fall in love with someone else, but how can she stand in the way of her happiness? (978-1-63555-973-6)

Marry Me by Melissa Brayden. Allison Hale attempts to plan the wedding of the century to a man who could save her family's business, if only she wasn't falling for her wedding planner, Megan Kinkaid. (978-1-63555-932-3)

Pathway to Love by Radclyffe. Courtney Valentine is looking for a woman exactly like Ben—smart, sexy, and not in the market for anything serious. All she has to do is convince Ben that sex-without-strings is the perfect pathway to pleasure. (978-1-63679-110-4)

Sweet Surprise by Jenny Frame. Flora and Mac never thought they'd ever see each other again, but when Mac opens up her barber shop right next to Flora's sweet shop, their connection comes roaring back. (978-1-63679-001-5)

The Edge of Yesterday by CJ Birch. Easton Gray is sent from the future to save humanity from technological disaster. When she's forced to target the woman she's falling in love with, can Easton do what's needed to save humanity? (978-1-63679-025-1)

The Scout and the Scoundrel by Barbara Ann Wright. With unexpected danger surrounding them, Zara and Roni are stuck between duty and survival, with little room for exploring their feelings, especially love. (978-1-63555-978-1)

Can't Leave Love by Kimberly Cooper Griffin. Sophia and Pru have no intention of falling in love, but sometimes love happens when and where you least expect it. (978-1-636790041-1)

Free Fall at Angel Creek by Julie Tizard. Detective Dee Rawlings and aircraft accident investigator Dr. River Dawson use conflicting methods to find answers when a plane goes missing, while overcoming surprising threats and discovering an unlikely chance at love. (978-1-63555-884-5)

Love's Compromise by Cass Sellars. For Piper Holthaus and Brook Myers, will professional dreams and past baggage stop two hearts from realizing they are meant for each other? (978-1-63555-942-2)

Not All a Dream by Sophia Kell Hagin. Hester has lost the woman she loved, and the world has descended into relentless dark and cold. But giving up will have to wait when she stumbles upon people who help her survive. (978-1-63679-067-1)

The Secrets of Willowra by Kadyan. A family saga of three women, their homestead called Willowra in the Australian outback, and the secrets that link them all. (978-1-63679-064-0)

Turbulent Waves by Ali Vali. Kai Merlin and Vivien Palmer plan their future together as hostile forces make their own plans to destroy what they have, as well as all those they love. (978-1-63679-011-4)

Protecting the Lady by Amanda Radley. If Eve Webb had known she'd be protecting royalty, she'd never have taken the job as bodyguard, but as the threat to Lady Katherine's life draws closer, she'll do whatever it takes to save her, and may just lose her heart in the process. (978-1-63679-003-9)

Trial by Fire by Carsen Taite. When prosecutor Lennox Roy and public defender Wren Bishop become fierce adversaries in a headline-grabbing arson case, their attraction ignites a passion that leads them both to question their assumptions about the law, the truth, and each other. (978-1-63555-860-9)

Unbreakable by Cari Hunter. When Dr. Grace Kendal is forced at gunpoint to help an injured woman, she is dragged into a nightmare where nothing is quite as it seems, and their lives aren't the only ones on the line. (978-1-63555-961-3)

Veterinary Surgeon by Nancy Wheelton. When dangerous drugs are stolen from the veterinary clinic, Mitch investigates and Kay becomes a suspect. As pride and professions clash, love seems impossible. (978-1-63679-043-5)(978-1-63679-051-0)

All That Remains by Sheri Lewis Wohl. Johnnie and Shantel might have to risk their lives—and their love—to stop a werewolf intent on killing. (978-1-63555-949-1)

Beginner's Bet by Fiona Riley. Phenom luxury Realtor Ellison Gamble has everything, except a family to share it with, so when a mix-up brings youthful Katie Crawford into her life, she bets the house on love. (978-1-63555-733-6)

Dangerous Without You by Lexus Grey. Throughout their senior year in high school, Aspen, Remington, Denna, and Raleigh face challenges in life and romance that they never expect. (978-1-63555-947-7)

Desiring More by Raven Sky. In this collection of steamy stories, a rich variety of lovers find themselves desiring more: more from a lover, more from themselves, and more from life. (978-1-63679-037-4)